IRON HORSEMEN

A NOVEL

BRAD R. COOK

www.bradrcook.com
@bradrcook

Cover design by Kristina Blank Makansi
Illustration background: Shutterstock
Steampunk frame: Illustrator Georgie Retzer
https://www.facebook.com/Illustrator.Georgie
Rearing horse: Celtic Cat Photos
https://www.etsy.com/shop/Celticcatphotos

Interior layout by Kristina Blank Makansi
Interior art by Jennifer Stolzer
http://www.jenniferstolzer.com/

ISBN: 9780989207959

For Amber

IRON HORSEMEN

CHAPTER 1

KIDNAPPED
London 1881

I'd always wanted to be like the heroes in my favorite stories—George Washington, or Sir Galahad, maybe King Arthur, Robin Hood, or Robinson Crusoe—but I knew those lives belonged to great men, not young boys trapped in stuffy old offices in pretentious British preparatory schools. If I wanted adventure, I'd have to make my own. I could not live vicariously through someone else's. Unfortunately, my opportunities for adventure were not only limited, they were non-existent.

I spent much of my time in a dark, wood-paneled prison cell lined with cabinets stuffed with odd objects and ancient artifacts and surrounded by floor-to-ceiling shelves jammed with leather-bound books in every language imaginable. What my cell didn't have was a single painting or photograph of me. That might not have been surprising if it really was a prison cell, but it wasn't. It just felt like it.

My father peered down at me as I picked at the corner of the ancient Greek text I was supposed to find fascinating. His brow lowered into harsh lines as he rebuked me once again.

"Young man, those words are priceless! How many times do I have to tell you?"

"I didn't do anything." To prove my point, I moved my hand away from the torn corner to the nearest bit of text. "Look, you can still read the words."

Professor Armitage, my father, removed thin wire-framed glasses from the end of his nose and rubbed his eyes. He waved his hand over the old manuscript he'd been studying, one of several scattered around his knotted oak desk. The leather chair creaked as he leaned back and gazed out the window.

"Alexander, I'm almost done with these translations."

I said nothing as the professor returned to the page, but I saw it—the expression of satisfaction and pride one might expect to see light up a father's face on his only son's birthday. But the expression wasn't for me.

"If my theory is right, this is the lost account of a Stone Age civilization's destruction on the island of Malta."

"Exciting," I groaned. "I'm hungry and it's almost eight o'clock." The lines on his forehead deepened to crevasses. After a moment's pause, when I was certain the thick vein in his neck would pop, I mumbled, "Get out of your dreams and into your Greek. Yes, sir. I will, sir." But it was lie, a bold-faced one, too. I'd been dreaming of flying, of bursting through a dense cloud bank to surprise my enemy, retrieve a stolen treasure after a terrifying swordfight at dizzying heights, and rescue a damsel in distress. There were no clouds in my book.

"As punishment for the damage, I want you to read aloud—in the original."

Dreams had to wait, as usual. I tossed back two locks of hair and began to read aloud. After a few moments, he tapped the thin metal pointer he'd been using to read, and I looked up.

"The correct way to say it is *xi-fos*. Now, what does *xifos* mean?"

"Sword." I quickly replied. One of my favorite words in

any language.

"Once again, but this time in Latin."

I repeated the sentence in Latin, and he nodded his approval.

"Now in Aramaic."

"But no one even speaks...." My voice trailed off. The stern look on my father's face meant a whipping was imminent if I continued. Under my breath I mumbled, "If Mom were alive, she wouldn't make me."

"I will not listen to that kind of talk."

Since my mother's passing, each new school brought more and tougher studies. Maybe my father thought the languages would ground me, or all the studying would keep me out of trouble, but it only filled me with useless information—and endless frustration. Now, we'd landed in Eton, and I wondered when I'd ever go home to America again. A small sigh escaped, but I did what I was told and repeated the sentence in Aramaic.

"Good. Now continue your homework. I must finish this translation tonight."

Relieved, I returned to my silent reading—and to my daydreaming. After a while, when I was sure he lost in his own world, I slid open one of the cabinet drawers and peered at the small leather pouch sitting alone on a folder. I flipped it open to reveal two lenses trimmed with polished brass.

"Can I use your telescope?"

"No, put it back."

That word, always that word. *No.* No sweets. No, you're wrong. No, you can't stay in America. My jaw clenched, and I watched my father's eyes glaze over again as he reentered his world of ancient letters. I reached back in the drawer, plucked out the pouch, dropped the telescope into my bag, and slowly shut the drawer. My father would never miss it, and I thought it made a fine birthday present.

The moments crept by, and I wondered what the boys in the dormitories were doing. What my friends back home were doing? What normal boys with normal fathers were doing?

"Alexander." A single shaft of light clung to my father's face as he snapped up from his work. "There's something I should tell you."

I half listened, ready for another lecture on something old and uninteresting. "Huh."

After a moment of silence, I glanced up and saw my father watching me, studying me like one of his yellowing codices. He shook his head sadly. "Never mind, you're not ready."

Ready for what? Whatever it was, it didn't matter. Even if I was ready, he'd never see it. To calm myself, I refocused on the book. I certainly didn't want to transcribe the sentence into hieroglyphics.

My stomach roiled—we never ate dinner until our work was done for the evening—and I suddenly had the feeling that I might be getting sick. My pulse quickened and I sat up. Something nagged at me, but I could not say what, just that everything felt off kilter somehow.

A loud bang rang out from the hallway and we both jumped.

"Probably just the janitor," the professor said. "Nothing to worry about."

Nothing to worry about. Right. I shook my head in disbelief. Eton College might be the most exclusive school in the British Empire, but I had plenty to worry about. The heirs of British aristocracy, my classmates, had treated me like a second-class citizen since I set foot in the place, and because of my father's position, I couldn't fight back when they tormented me. There were probably some snooty upper-crust dandies lurking out in the hall, just waiting to pummel me again. If only I was back home in America. I imagined whipping out a saber and showing them what a real sword fight was like—not that I was ever allowed to practice.

"Don't worry," my father said again, as if to reassure himself more than me. "There'll be no intruders at Eton. They promised we'd be well-protected here."

"Well-protected? Who promised—" I started to ask just as the door blew off its hinges and slammed into the far wall, a long crack seamed down its center. I screamed and scrambled to my feet as four stocky brutes marched in wearing long, dark overcoats and derby hats with rounded goggles. Wielding menacing, short black clubs, they looked like they'd just come from London's Whitechapel district with murder on their minds.

My father was on his feet in an instant. He grabbed one of the ponderous tomes from the pile on his desk and slammed it down on the nearest derby. A dusty cloud enveloped the intruder's head like a halo as he staggered back.

My father just clocked a nefarious henchman! I'd never even seen him make a fist.

"Get back!" my father yelled, shoving me toward the windows.

The dusty bruiser regained his footing, grunted in annoyance, and snorted from his nose like a raging bull. He raised a fist the size of my head.

My father held the book in front of his face. "Why did I have to grab *this* one?" he moaned.

The book took the punch, and my father fell against his desk, but quickly scrambled away as a second blow whooshed past.

The men surrounded him with raised clubs.

I wanted to scream, but found my voice trapped in my throat like it was stuck behind a locked door. These were not annoying classmates. They were not from Eton at all.

The biggest brute, with a mask of bronze plates fastened over the right half of his face and an eye that sparked with electricity, stepped forward. "Ya'll gonna be comin' with us, Professor." His deep southern American drawl had a harsh, guttural tone.

They weren't even from England!

"Who are you?" My father demanded.

"Nevermind 'bout that." A whirring sound buzzed past my ear as a grappling hook connected by a thin wire shot out from the leader's sleeve. I barely uttered, "Watch out!" before it had snagged my father's shoulder.

My dad pushed me aside. "Run!"

But I was frozen in place.

The grappling hook yanked my father off his feet and dragged him across the floor. The leader of the group pressed his heavy booted foot down on my father's chest as the grappling hook retracted into his sleeve. The lamplight reflected off the man's belt buckle. It was unmistakable: engraved in silver, the crossed bands of stars from the Confederate flag flickered like they were waving in the wind.

The henchman looked down at my father and gave him a crooked one-sided smile. "Now, what you gonna do? Speak Greek to us?" The other men laughed as if that was the funniest joke they'd ever heard, but their laughter was cut short when the room exploded in glass.

CHAPTER 2

SAVED BY THE BARON

The window beside my head shattered, and I ducked as wood and glass rained down around me. The whir of wings whizzing past, the whipping of a cloak in the wind, and the solid thud of feet landing on stone made me look up to peer through the protective shield of my arms.

"That's not how you treat an Etonian." The same aristocratic British accent of my classmates cut through the night air. The glint off polished steel flashed in front of me and the closest bruiser grunted in protest as the blade sliced through him. Blood poured from his chest, his eyes rolled up under the brim of his hat, and he slumped to the floor. My heart burned and lurched against my ribcage as I realized his had stopped. I trembled in shock.

The Englishman, a tall, broad shouldered man in a blue cloak, wrenched his sword free, and spun on the heel of a well-polished boot. His thin double-edged sword struck the Confederate, slid upward, and flung the black derby right past my head. The bronze clad man's right eye sparked even brighter at the affront, and a thick serrated blade just over a foot long slid out of his right sleeve and clicked into place.

"Yeow!" My father yelped as his foot struck a metal

plate on the man's chest. "What are you?"

I retreated further into the corner, pulled my knees tight against my chest, and buried my face as the two men circled my father.

But when the man my father had pounded with the book began screaming, "Get this thing off me!" my head snapped up and saw him, face splattered with blood, flailing against a small bronze dragon slashing and biting, all talons and teeth.

"You'll not eat me!" The last bruiser covered his head and bolted for the hall.

The little creature locked eyes on the fleeing long coat and screeched. Bronze wings stretched out and flapped as it launched and soared out of the room, spitting a fusillade of fireballs toward its prey as it exited.

I squeezed my eyes and shook my head as if to clear the vision from my head. *Was that a real dragon?* Couldn't be. There are no such things as real dragons. Besides, that creature was made of metal.

When I opened my eyes again, a different room lay before me. Gone was my quiet prison. With one henchman dead, the dusty one blinded by blood, and the third running in terror, only the bronze-clad Confederate remained.

"Yer one of *them*, ain't yah?" he asked the Englishman.

"Doesn't matter who I am, what matters is that you're not leaving with the professor." He whipped his cloak back and kicked the serrated blade into the desk with the heel of his polished boot. The thick blade stuck in the oak, and with a quick flip of his wrist he brought his sword down upon the Confederate's right arm. The blade sliced off the man's sleeve clean and neat, and the fabric slid to the floor in a heap. What remained behind, attached to the man's upper arm, were the gears and wires of a complex animatronic arm.

My eyes bulged out in surprise.

"Colonel Hendrix!" The bloodied henchman cried out in a thick cockney accent. "A Bobbie's whistle!"

I locked on to the rapid high pitched sound. Was help coming?

The colonel snarled. "Get out of here and see where that yellow-belly went!"

Wrenching his blade free from the old oak, Hendrix retracted it back into his arm. With the claw that replaced it, he snatched the desk and threw it at the Englishman.

I screamed and tucked back into a ball. The desk tumbled and slammed into the wall and settled in front of me. The shelf collapsed, pottery smashed all around, and a Bronze Age dagger tumbled blade-down and stuck in the floorboard between my legs with a sharp *snick*.

I yelped and struggled to get to my feet, but the desk was in my way. I could only watch as Col. Hendrix snatched the ancient manuscript with one hand and my father with his mechanical arm. I opened my mouth to cry out but my voice failed, choked by tears.

"Alexander!" my father screamed as the colonel dragged him out the door.

Kicking the desk away, the blue-cloaked Englishman scanned me for injuries, and then ran into the hall. Alone, I climbed over the desk. There, on the floor at my feet, my father's eyeglasses lay atop scattered papers. I picked them up and stared at the warped office through the lenses.

After a few moments, the man in the blue suit returned and reached out his hand. "Professor Armitage's son, I presume. Baron Kensington, pleasure to meet you."

"Thank you, I'm Alexander." My chest seized, and I could hardly breathe. Red-stained parchment lay beneath the dead henchman. I'd never seen so much blood, but the baron didn't even notice. I slumped back onto the floor.

"Are you injured?" the baron asked, his hand still extended. I grasped it and he helped me to my feet as papers still drifted through the air.

"What? No, just confused. Where's my father?"

"They've fled for now." The baron sheathed his sword in a cane scabbard. "I'm afraid you can't help him at the moment."

"Who was that, and why did he take my father?" Pain wrenched my gut, worse than any bully's punch. I was alone.

"They won't hurt him, they need him." The baron kept an eye on the opening where the shattered door used to hang. "Her Royal Highness sent me to retrieve you and your father."

"The Queen?" *The Queen?* What would she want with my father?

"Yes, gather your possessions, you'll come with me for now."

I placed my father's glasses in their case, put them in my leather bag, and slung it over my shoulder. The dead man's baton lay at my feet, and I scooped it up and dropped it in the bag, too. Then I grabbed my leather coat from the overturned rack.

The nobleman motioned toward the door. "My carriage is waiting outside."

As the small bronze dragon flew through the doorway, I clutched my bag to my chest, in some strange sort of defense. I probably should have covered my face, but it was instinct. The dragon landed on the baron's shoulder. The nobleman rubbed the horned nubs on its head and fed the creature a bit of dried meat from a suit coat pocket. I could see now that it was the size of an eagle or a hawk, and watched in wonderment as it wrapped a long tapering tail around the baron's shoulders.

I wondered if it could be a machine, but the eyes held the glimmer of intelligence. "Is that a dragon?"

"His name is Rodin," he said, ignoring my question and striding forward. I rushed to catch up with the baron. After a pause, he said, "There'll be plenty of time for questions later."

A steam-powered carriage waited outside with a squat man atop the driver's perch. He jumped off, opened the door, and the baron climbed inside. I nodded and stepped into the carriage. The driver lifted his cap, revealing long scattered locks of bright orange hair.

I had so many questions to ask, but I fell silent when I caught the shattered window of my father's office out of the corner of my eye. I heard the driver climb atop his perch and release a lever. A loud *chug chug chug* from the back of the carriage made me turn just as the steam engine belched a puff of white smoke, and we lurched forward and started down the cobblestone road.

CHAPTER 3

AGENTS OF THE QUEEN

"Ow." My shoulder banged into the plush, burgundy-velvet interior and I clung to the carriage's brass handle as we tore around a cobblestone corner on the outskirts of London. The chugging engine behind me roared like a trumpeting elephant. "Does he always drive like this?"

"Finn was thrilled when I converted the carriage. He never liked horses."

"Oh." I stared at the baron who sat perfectly centered, with the small dragon perched on his shoulder as though it was a pleasant Sunday drive. The delighted cheers of the mad driver made me wonder if I would lose my dinner before I met the queen.

As we rumbled round a corner, I muscled to remain upright. "What about my father?"

The baron said nothing. He pulled a braided cord which rang a bell beside the driver.

Adults never listened.

The carriage stopped in front of a row house with a large red door carved with a rose motif and inlaid with gold. But this wasn't Buckingham Palace. The Irishman leapt from his perch and opened the carriage, holding his hat to the side as he bowed.

The baron stepped out of the carriage, and I shouldered my bag, jumped out, and ran after him, not wanting to be locked in this death trap any longer. I once saw a steam car in New York, but with Finn as the driver, the baron's steamcarriage was like a train in desperate need of a track.

I followed the baron to a bookcase in the basement. The nobleman twisted the spearhead on the statue of a knight locked in a desperate struggle with a dragon. A click was all I heard, and the shelf slid back to reveal a hidden hallway. "A secret passage," I gasped.

The damp, musty air drifting in offended my nose. I rushed forward through the narrow tunnel stretching into darkness and saw a sleek, streamlined metal bullet with windows along the side. Metal wires reached to the ceiling like an insect's antenna.

"Why only one train car?" I asked.

"It's an electric trolley, invented last year by your countryman, Thomas Edison."

My shoulders shrugged up against my cheeks. "Never heard of him."

"Her majesty has, she wanted a private transport for the royal family and her agents."

Even though the underground trolley sat still, it looked liked it was moving. I wondered where the train engine connected, and couldn't even see latches for the other cars.

I stepped onto the trolley. Trimmed with gold and decorated with elaborate curled detailing, it was certainly outfitted for royalty. The seats, arranged in two semi-circles, faced either direction and had been covered in plush blue fabric. Now *this* was how someone should arrive at a palace. We sat and the trolley car sped through the circular brick tunnel snaking underneath London.

I scooted back against the velvet cushions. "Where's the driver?"

"A central operator controls them all."

"Oh." I wanted to ask more, but then I saw the dust on my uniform. I tried to brush it off, but the dirt was caught in the wool fibers and wasn't coming out anytime soon. "I really wish I could have changed. I'm not dressed to meet Queen Victoria."

The baron smiled. "You won't be meeting her Highness; she has more important matters that require her attention."

My gaze shifted to the windows. "Of course." I tried not to sound disappointed, but I had really wanted to meet the queen. She probably only ever saw aristocrats.

"She did send me to save you, and you should be grateful she did."

"I am, but my dad wishes you'd gotten there sooner." *I wish you'd gotten there sooner.* My face pressed against the window as the wall rushed by in a reddish blur. "Where are we going?"

"To my place in London. You'll be safe there."

The trolley car stopped beside a brick platform. The royal coat of arms–a quartered shield flanked by a crowned lion and a chained unicorn–marked a lone wooden door. I followed the baron through a long hallway lined with non-descript doors. Finally, we stopped in front of one labeled three twenty-one.

Removing a key from an inner vest pocket, the baron unlocked the door. We climbed several flights of dark, cavernous stairs that echoed with every step. The door at the top led to a small cupboard. The nobleman pressed a button on the floor with his boot. The door opened into a kitchen and a false wall slid over the passage.

"Wait for me in the dining room." The baron pointed across the hall as Rodin flew off his shoulder.

I walked into a lavish room decorated with curled, gilded detailing. An elaborate microscope projector sat on one end of the table and a folding screen on the other. I had only seen this type of equipment in class, and now I wanted one of my own. The urge to reach out and fiddle with it overtook me, but I hesitated; everything looked expensive and rare. I never liked rooms you weren't supposed to touch.

A man in a fine suit entered carrying a briefcase. His sunken eyes were shadowed by dark circles. He didn't look well, but carried himself like so many in this country—with stern resolve.

The baron said, "Alexander Armitage, may I present Lord Marbury, another agent of Her Royal Highness. We're both Old Etonians."

That didn't surprise me; it seemed like every nobleman had attended Eton College.

"Thank you, Maximilian." Lord Marbury set his brown leather briefcase down on the table. He turned to me. "May I say, I am sorry to hear about your father."

The nobleman leaned over and shook my hand. His weak grip was one my father would have railed him for; he thought a handshake should say something.

"Thank you, but where was he taken and what are you doing to save him?"

Lord Marbury's haunting expression made me wiggle in my skin. The lord turned to the baron. "Were there any issues?"

I dropped onto one of the straight-backed wooden chairs. "I'll say…"

The baron silenced me with a stern gaze. "There were four members of the Knight of the Golden Circle; one of them had an animatronic arm and a bronze-covered face. I believe he was American. They addressed him as Colonel Hendrix."

"He had a southern accent," I said.

"That fits the rumors of a former Confederate soldier recently brought over from the states," Lord Marbury said.

I fell back into the chair and gripped my shoulders. A metal monster and an American. Did my father know him from before? Is that why we're in England instead of back home?

Lord Marbury unsnapped the brass fittings on his briefcase. He removed old parchment held loose in a thick wooden cover bound by braided leather cords. A heavily worn insignia etched on a bronze plaque sat in the center of the cover. "Do you know what your father was working on?"

"He taught languages, all the dead ones that no one speaks anymore."

"He also translated for her majesty. That's why he was given the post at Eton." The baron's stern tone reminded me I was among superiors.

Lord Marbury turned on the microscope projector and adjusted the brass lens housing to its broadest setting. A bright light cast its glow on the unfolded screen. He removed the bronze plaque and braided leather cord, then placed a page under the projector. "Is this what your father was translating?"

Rodin flew in and perched on the table. Bathed in bright light, his dramatic shadow arced across the screen until shooed away by the baron.

I studied the image and the ache in my heart returned. "Yes, he was reading it when I found him after Quiet Hour."

The baron's tone lowered. "Alexander, your father was kidnapped because there are people who want him to translate those ancient languages. They will keep him safe, which gives us the opportunity to rescue him." He walked over to the Waterford decanter and poured the amber liquid into a glass. "I assure you, retrieving him is our highest priority."

I sprang up. "I want to help!"

Lord Marbury snapped his briefcase shut and looked at me with an air of dismissal. "You will return to Eton and continue your studies."

"So why is this destruction on Malta so important to

you? What was my father doing? What are you involved in?"

The baron choked on his surprise. "You can read that?"

"My father's been teaching me dead languages since I was five."

Lord Marbury and the baron looked at each other, and I lifted my chin, the pain in my heart subsiding. Maybe they'd let me come along after all.

"This is a copy of the one they stole. It was made in 1581 by an agent of Queen Elizabeth." Lord Marbury's gaze burned right through me. "Can you finish the translation?"

"Sure." I walked toward the screen and ran my hand over the image. "This line is about an expedition to colonize the Island of Malta. That's in the Mediterranean Sea, right?"

The baron smiled. "Yes it is, very good Alexander. Can you read more?"

I ran my finger back and forth to keep track of the sentence. "They wanted a new city...for trade...no, to conquer North Africa. They found... cities in ruin...that people had lived in before but were wiped out." I stepped back and cocked my head. "I'm not sure about this next part. The people stopped a great evil ... four ... four horsemen and hid their secret ... the rest is missing."

Lord Marbury asked with a twinge of fear, "Did you just say four horsemen?"

I leaned back and nodded. "It's probably just imagery. It's two thousand years too soon to be the Bible."

The baron nodded. "Her Majesty was right to put her faith in the Armitages. So Malta is where they are heading." He walked up and placed his hand upon my shoulder. "You'll stay here this night; it will be safer than Eton."

I didn't know what else to do, but maybe I'd wake up in the morning and this would all be over.

The baron turned toward the hall. "My dear do come in, it's rude to lurk outside rooms where gentlemen are conversing."

A young woman stepped into the doorway. Auburn hair fell past her shoulders, but was pulled back from her face with a ribbon I could see trailing over her shoulder. A locket hung around her neck on a silver chain. She wore the high collar and long skirt popular with the noble women of London, but lacked their usual docile expression. She nodded to Lord Marbury but her eyes widened when she spotted me. She was so beautiful. I couldn't stop staring. I turned away before anyone could note my fascination.

Her soft voice carried an accent like a sweet melody. "Father, I was not lurking, mere curiosity drew me."

"Genevieve, Master Alexander shall be staying the night. Mrs. Hinderman has already prepared the Blue Room, please escort our guest there."

Genevieve bowed and I followed her out of the room. She led me to the second floor. Trailing her, the smell of rose petals caused my mind to slip. I studied the way her hair brushed against her back as I fidgeted with the strap of my bag.

Once on the second floor her demeanor changed. No longer did she float, there was hardness in her steps and she appeared annoyed. "Did you hear him? I was not lurking. How dare he say such a thing in front of—" She stopped and turned to face me. "I am sorry about your father."

The words stuttered out of my mouth. "T-thank you." Smooth, real smooth, why don't I just spill something and fall down while I'm making impressions.

"It's Alexander, isn't it?"

"Yes, my father is sort of obsessed with the Greeks. He has high aspirations. I'm surprised my middle name isn't 'The Great.'"

She laughed and I smiled. Maybe she wasn't like the other nobles.

We reached the end of the hall and entered the Blue

Room. It was indeed a blue room. Dark blue paper with gold accents covered the walls. The ceiling had been painted a lighter blue and the four-post wooden bed was covered in a blue spread; even the paintings depicted great ships or seaside landscapes. I couldn't escape the blue. The only thing not blue was me.

She motioned to a braided cord hanging by the bed. "Ring the bell for Ms. Hinderman if you need anything."

I nodded.

Genevieve paused by the door. "I'm certain he'll find your father. We won't get to know the details, but my father has never failed her majesty."

I tried to smile, but the ache in my heart returned with a vengeance.

CHAPTER 4

LIFE AT ETON

A shrill voice jarred me awake as Mrs. Hinderman said, "Good morning, Master Armitage."

Light stung my eyes as she threw open the curtains. I rubbed the sleep away and Mrs. Hinderman stood at the end of the blue bedspread.

What could she want? I grumbled, but her smile grew.

"I've cleaned your school uniform, and breakfast will be served momentarily."

"I'll be down in a moment."

The hem of her long skirt brushed the floor as Mrs. Hinderman swept out of the room. "Don't be long."

I struggled to get my school uniform on, as I did every day. It was stiff, it was tight, and once bound in all the layers I could hardly move.

Genevieve opened the door and I snapped up. "Mrs. Hinderman asked me to bring you to breakfast."

I pulled at the white bow-tie and starched collar. "Thanks, I'll be there as soon as I can breathe."

She waved my hand away. "Stop tugging. You'll tear off your buttons and wrinkle it."

"My father said it was like a suit of armor, but it's not, feels more like a strait jacket."

Her cute little chuckle, like a cooing bird, drew all my

insides up into my throat, choking my words.

I cleared my throat, forcing everything back into place. "Do you think the baron will find my father today?"

"I hope so. Maybe by the time you return from Eton, he'll have news."

I wanted to believe her, but my thoughts shifted to the teasing that was certain to come from the aristocratic bullies at school. I heard their annoying voices already. "I'm not looking forward to my classes."

Genevieve stepped back. "Why not?" her eyes grew and held a glimmer of surprise.

Had I said something wrong? My foot hit the floor. How could I not admit that the noble kids would tease me? "Umm…"

Her hand glided over the window sill. "I would be ecstatic if I could go to Eton."

"Where do you go to school?" I asked. Hopefully we wouldn't go back to subjects I'd rather not explain.

"I don't go to school. I have a tutor."

"That is so much better than school."

Her hands clenched in fists and she stomped her foot. "I only get to study what my father decides, and he's deemed certain subjects inappropriate for a lady. It's frustrating."

My shoulders slumped. I'd upset her. "Sorry, I didn't know you couldn't go."

Of course there were no girls at Eton, just the future aristocratic leaders of Britain, and me.

We didn't say a word on the way down to breakfast. Genevieve held her lip between her teeth and her gaze fell far beyond the walls. My thoughts drifted to my father, my joints stiffened with every step, and my heart slipped deeper in my chest. *Where was he? Was he alright?*

The juice, eggs, fruits, pastries, and bread overwhelmed me with choices, delicious smells, and the tastiest treats I'd had since arriving in London.

I devoured the pastries and fruit like I'd forgotten how to use a fork.

Mrs. Hinderman took away my plate and said, "You look very dapper, Master Armitage. Let's keep it that way."

Heat rushed to my cheeks, but I managed a smile. "Where is the baron?"

The elderly lady supported her back with her hand. "Oh, he left with the rising sun. Didn't say where he was traveling, but I'm certain he's doing all he can to find your father."

I nodded and my smile stretched across my cheeks as I wiped my face. I could suffer through the day if my father would be waiting when I returned. Even with his strict manner and emphasis on my studies, he was my father. I wanted him back safe and sound.

I stepped toward the front door. Mrs. Hinderman held my leather bag. She placed it over my shoulder and kissed my head. "Now you have a good day at Eton, pay attention, and put this business out of your head for a while."

How could I forget? My head shrank into my shoulders to avoid her, but no one had been so tender since my mother's passing. Mrs. Hinderman's bright smile reminded me of a grandmother. "I'll try."

"Finn will take you to school and bring you home." She gripped my shoulders. "The baron was very clear that you should not go with anyone but Finn. It's for your safety, do you understand?"

I said, "Yes," but that was before I'd thought about the question: Was I in danger? Would the men in long black coats come back? My legs twitched as if electricity pulsed through my veins. The baron wouldn't let me go to Eton if it weren't safe. *If I keep repeating that, maybe it'll be true.*

Finn sat on the driver's perch of the steamcarriage. I nodded and stepped inside. Soon the carriage belched white smoke and cruised down the cobblestone streets.

The world raced by and I tried to remain upright as the baron had the day before. I finally had what I wanted, to be on my own, free from my father's stern looks. Now, though, all I wanted was to be forced to read some ancient Greek text.

The carriage stopped before a red brick building. Lighter colored stones formed patterns while black segmented rainspouts climbed the walls. The old building had an eerie look, brightly colored by a morning rain. I opened the door and joined the stream of boys in black coats and white ties that filed into through the main door.

Finn called from the carriage, "Try and have a good day, kid."

With a nod I turned and walked into Eton, lost in a world blurred by tears.

As I passed through the colonnade of one building, I saw the shattered window of my father's office across the courtyard. Its jagged edges mirrored my world, and just like that window, I couldn't put the pieces back together. Two days ago, my biggest concern was homework, but now fear for my father crushed my shoulders and weighted down my back. With hunched shoulders, I found my way to class, without even knowing how I'd gotten there. I stepped into my school and all eyes turned toward me, their questioning gazes like arrows piercing my heart.

"Glad you could join us Master Armitage. Please have a seat," the professor said.

Obviously the professor knew what had happened. Otherwise, I'd have been reported for being late. I wanted to rip off my wool armor and run, but I sat down.

Eton's desks were connected in long rows unlike my classes in America. I took a seat on a bench in the back of the class, but had to slide past some other boys. I slumped down and tried to disappear.

The professor pointed to the black board. "Well

gentlemen, I hope you're ready for the exam. Remember this will focus exclusively on the Tesla experiments we ran last week."

A loud groan erupted from my classmates, and I slipped further into my chair. *Could this day get any worse?*

The white parts of the test, the part I was supposed to fill in, stared back like a vast arctic expanse. I dipped my quill pen in the inkwell at the top of my section of the bench desk. I wrote my name—that was easy—but as I tried to read the first question my mind spun and tears blurred my vision. *Why was I taking a test when my father could be in danger?*

The other students stood to leave and beyond a couple of ink dribbles from the end of my quill, the page was empty. I flipped it over hoping the answers would be on the back: blank.

I'd spent the class worried about my dad, not the answers. I hadn't taken the test. My classmates handed over their exams and filed out the room.

I quickly scribbled 'Sorry' at the bottom of the page, ran up and slipped the paper into the middle of the stack. I ran from the room, the long tails of my coat flapping behind him.

I ran until my arm was snatched by Count Blackthorne's son. "So what happened to your father, colonist?"

"Let me go!"

"I saw his office. Did the cowboy trash it like some western saloon?"

"Thadeus, leave me alone."

The young nobleman with the good looking hair turned to his friends and laughed. "Ah, poor baby, do you need a wet nurse?"

Anger swelled within me until I was nearly blind with it. I wasn't a baby. I was tired of being bullied, and my fists clenched until my knuckles hurt. I couldn't punch him. I wanted to, but my father and the headmasters of Eton had made it clear. If I fight, I get shipped back to America.

Thadeus pressed both palms against my chest. I stumbled over his feet and slammed into the wall. Pain rippled across my body as he and his friends laughed wildly.

I whipped around and locked eyes with the nobleman's son. "Don't push me!" The strap's rough edge of my leather bag dug into my tightening palms. I swung the bag loaded with books into Thadeus' side.

"Stop, you crazed colonial." Thadeus and his friends tried to run, but I kept swinging in a wild rage. Tears streamed down my face as I continued to pummel the nobleman's son.

Thadeus and his friends charged through the nearest door yelling for a master.

I struggled to catch my breath and calm my nerves as I leaned against the bricks. I punched the wall, hoping to force these hateful feelings out, but all I did was scrape my knuckles which started to ache.

Beside me an engraved plaque had been mounted in the wall. It had been engraved with several names and above them was written: Waterloo 1815. These memorials scattered throughout Eton held the names of those students who made the ultimate sacrifice in war.

I knew I shouldn't have lashed out at my classmate. Seeing these names reminded me of what really mattered in life. Would my father be the next name added to one of these plaques? My fingers traced each name and the fire tearing through me eased as my breathing slowed. Life was never easy.

Just when I thought the Headmaster would come and kick me out of Eton for good, Finn walked up.

"Come on, kid." Finn wrung his hat through his hand. "The baron sent me to fetch you."

"Did he find my father?"

"The baron's in the carriage."

I cautiously approached the steamcarriage. Finn opened the door and I climbed in. The baron and his daughter sat on one side, so I dropped onto the other seat with my back to the driver's perch.

"Did you find my father?"

The baron shook his head. "Not yet. I'm about to arrange passage to pursue him."

I didn't understand what that meant, but the baron's expression didn't look like he wanted to talk. Then the carriage sped off.

I gripped the seat and tried not to slide as the steamcarriage tore through the streets. Genevieve and her father both sat perfectly. How did they do it? Was there some secret technique that I'd be taught at Eton in the coming years?

CHAPTER 5

THE SKY RAIDERS

The legendary London docks stretched for miles downriver. The bound masts looked like a forest of trees in winter. I stared with awe through the window of the steamcarriage at the four masts of a large Windjammer.

When my father and I crossed the Atlantic, we traveled in a wooden-hulled vessel that felt ancient compared to the steel-hulled Windjammer and like a dinosaur when I saw the airships nestled in a web of iron at the end of the pier.

I pulled myself closer to the window. "Are we going to the airdocks?"

The baron nodded. "I have to meet an airship."

"Can I get on?"

Genevieve blurted out, "I want to get on, too."

"No, that is not why you both are here. This was supposed to be finished this afternoon, but the airship was late."

I pressed against the window to get a better view of the airdocks. Metal planking formed a gantry around the ships while large iron moorings clamped and secured the airships. People milled about as towering cranes hoisted cargo into their holds.

The steamcarriage stopped in front of an aero-dirigible. *An actual aero-dirigible!*

I gasped. I had read about the cross between an airplane and a Zeppelin in the newspaper, but never imagined I'd see one up close.

Its outstretched wings—canvas pulled taut with yardarms running through them like the sail of a Chinese Junk—billowed with the wind. The gun-metal gray underside contrasted with the darkened blue top. A small set of fixed winglets stuck out of the nose. Its smooth, curved lines gave the vessel the look of a giant bird.

I saw three gun ports running along the side and other mysterious hatches on the hull. What could they be hiding? I wanted to burst from the carriage and study every part of the majestic vessel but a firm hand on my shoulder kept me still.

"I want both of you to stay put." The baron stepped out of the carriage. "Finn, keep them here. I'll be fine."

"Of course, Baron."

I watched the baron approach the aero-dirigible's gangplank. Genevieve slid over to peer out the window, too. I wondered what she thought of all this—the airdocks, the aero-dirigible, and this quest her father would undertake to find my father.

I turned to her. "I've read about the aero-dirigibles in the newspaper."

"It is impressive." Her attention returned to her father.

She didn't look interested. How could that be? There was an aero-dirigible just sitting in front of us and she was more focused on the people walking around. She stared at her father and the man who walked down the gangplank to join him.

He had a swish in his step like he owned the dock—a pirate's swagger. A long burgundy leather jacket whipped about and revealed a hand cannon strapped to his hip. "Who do you think he's meeting?" I asked.

She shrugged her shoulders. "The captain, I would

imagine."

"He doesn't look military."

"Maybe he's just a merchant captain."

"That's a big pistol for a simple merchant."

"What else could he be?"

I pulled back from the window. "A Sky Raider! The scourge of the four winds. My father says they're like Caribbean pirates only they prowl through the air."

"He does look like rough stock."

I wondered what that meant, rough stock. Sure this guy's scraggly moustache connected to his sideburns and his hair was pulled back in a short ponytail, but that didn't mean he was a bad person. To prove my point I pointed to the man. "He's smiling."

"That could just be from knowing he's double crossing a baron."

All I saw was a jovial man with a cautious demeanor. "The baron is smiling, too. I think it's going well."

The two men grabbed each other's forearms and their hands went to each other's shoulders.

I smiled. "Yep, definitely a success. Think he'd let me go, too?"

"No."

She was right. The baron would never let me go, but it was *my* father. I wanted to help. I had to help. Maybe it would lessen the pain building in the empty cavity of my chest.

The baron walked back to the carriage and I noticed the Sky Raider watched his every step. The baron seemed to know. He kept his focus on Finn, whose eyes never left the Sky Raider.

Finn opened the door and the baron climbed inside.

Genevieve asked. "Who was that?"

"The captain of the Sparrowhawk." He turned to me. "I'll be heading after your father soon."

"Thank you, Baron Kensington. I want to go, I can help."

The baron smiled. "No, you'll return to Eton." He pointed at Genevieve. "Don't you get any ideas, either."

Genevieve slumped back against the carriage.

I crossed my arms over my chest. I knew they'd never let me help. I was just a kid, I wasn't even a noble, but Genevieve's lineage didn't seem to be helping her. Apparently being a teenager meant no one got to do anything fun—no matter their station.

The steamcarriage stopped outside the baron's house. Finn hopped down, opened the door and we all filed out. As I followed Genevieve into the house, the baron paused to speak with Finn.

Slowing my steps, I couldn't hear their whispered voices. Finn climbed back atop his perch and the baron waved him off with his cane.

Finn adjusted his floppy cap, and said, "No worries, Baron. See you before the witchin' hour."

"Just drive carefully, and Finn, no rides for strange ladies."

With a large smile and short laugh Finn grabbed the reins. "Only on me off days."

The baron chuckled as the steamcarriage chugged down the street. I waited by the front door, but rushed inside before the baron turned around. I ran into Mrs. Hinderman.

Startled, she shooed me along. "Up to your room, young man. I want you washed and changed for dinner."

I ran up the stairs but as I reached the top, I felt a gaze upon my back. I turned and saw the baron watching me with a keen eye. I didn't know why, but I quickly ran into the Blue Room to get ready for dinner.

CHAPTER 6

THE TEMPLAR & THE SERPENT

After dinner, I plopped in a blue chair, and stared out the window. A light knock on the door, made me sit up straight. "Come in."

The door opened and a cautious Genevieve slipped inside. "Can I ask you about America?"

"Yes, of course."

"I want to know everything about your country."

The steamcarriage belched and chugged just outside. I leapt up, looked out the window and saw Finn open the door. A figure tightly bound in a black cloak quickly slipped into the house.

"Who could that be?" Genevieve asked as she crossed the room to the door.

"Wait, you're not going to lurk without me!"

Genevieve and I tiptoed to the top of the stairs. Lord Marbury and the baron stood in the foyer. The figure dropped his black cloak to the floor and flung his top hat, revealing thick gray hair and matching beard.

"His cane, I've seen something like that before," I whispered, staring at the elaborately decorated gold handle.

Genevieve put her finger to her lips and gave me a stern look.

As the three men stepped into the dining room,

Genevieve and I crept along the wall to the doorway.

The ease of her movement surprised me; she was well practiced at parental defiance. I'd slipped past my father many times. It had been easy at the universities, but at Eton, not only would my father find out, but there was the House Master, the House Captain, and the Praepostors who logged every infraction. After my first caning, I stopped, worried that Eton might not keep a professor's son who was labeled a troublemaker.

I heard the baron's voice. "I depart soon. I have contacted a group of Sky Raiders. Their aero-dirigible will get me into the Med."

A trembling voice said, "Sky Raiders, but they're the cutthroats of the four winds."

I smiled and nodded at Genevieve, delighted that I was right about the Sky Raiders. I leaned closer and cupped my ear, not wanting to miss a word.

The baron's voice was calm. "No need for alarm; I know one of the crew. I saved his life in India."

"We need to be careful," Lord Marbury said. "Look what's already happened."

A Scottish accent from within the dining room joked, "I think I'm insulted they went after the professor, but it makes the most sense."

How could they not be serious about this tragedy? An angry fire ignited deep within me. I shrugged off Genevieve and stormed into the dining room. "He took my father and had a mechanical arsenal for an arm."

The three men narrowed their gaze at my interruption.

Baron Kensington walked over to me. "No one is making light of your father, but this is bigger than him and he knew that. We will find him, but charging in is foolhardy."

The gray-haired man had a large belly that matched his frame. "The lad has fire, I like that. But he's an insolent pup."

I eyed the older man who spoke with a Scottish accent.

"Genevieve." Baron Kensington sounded annoyed.

She stepped into the room.

The gray-haired man stopped the baron. "There are a few things both of them should know." He placed his large hand over my entire shoulder, pulling me closer. "I came here, lad, to talk about your father. He was doing good work for the cause."

I noticed a medieval signet ring on his hand. The emblem, a large red cross on a plain gold background, was familiar. The shape. The Templar Cross.

The baron wore the same symbol on his cufflinks, and it adorned the cover of Lord Marbury's pocket watch. Tension seized my spine. These men were more than they appeared, and I kicked myself for not seeing it sooner.

"You've noticed our crosses." The gray-haired man removed his hand and walked over to the table. "It's good to have a keen eye. It'll keep you alive."

"Alexander, we are Templars." The baron motioned toward the gray-haired man. "This is Sir Archibald Sinclair, Grand Master of the Order. He's brought something we all should see."

Excitement sparked my imagination. I'd read tales of the Templars, the poor knights who had ridden two to a horse. Did my father belong to their order?

Finn carried a wood and bronze chest decorated with elaborate symbols that I couldn't decipher. Setting it down on the table, he nodded and returned to his carriage.

Grand Master Sinclair made a fist, and pushed his signet ring into the chest's lock. "Alexander, your father is the latest in a line of scholars stretching centuries who've studied these Horsemen."

He turned his hand a quarter to the right and then a half turn to the left. Instead of popping open like the treasure chests of my favorite adventure novels, the lid folded backward as the front and sides opened. Inside, nestled in velvet, were various artifacts and scrolls arranged on shelves.

The gray-haired Grand Master pulled a few items from the chest: a charred parchment, a tattered piece of tapestry, an etching with the lines carved deeply into the block of wood, and a salt-encrusted clay seal. I noticed the old man's gaze never left the artifacts, as if guarding them even from the people in this room.

Baron Kensington looked at Genevieve and me. "You may examine them, but if I ever catch you speaking about them, you'll be locked away in the Tower of London."

I wondered if my father had seen them. He'd be lost in their history for weeks. Feeling the pain of his loss shudder inside, I swallowed the lump in my throat.

I found a common thread, as my father had taught me to look for. The woodcut, the tapestry, and the clay seal all depicted a comet crossing the sun with four Horsemen below it. I looked up. "What do they mean?"

The baron replied, "A month ago, Lord Marbury investigated some rebels who turned out to be members of a secret society searching for the four Horsemen."

I asked, "What secret society?"

Grand Master Sinclair's knuckles turned white around his cane. "The Knights of the Golden Circle are determined to re-forge the chains of slavery and oppression."

A haunted look overtook Lord Marbury, who remained silent. The chill between them told me he had seen something that deeply disturbed him.

"What is this comet?" Genevieve asked.

"The Sungrazer Comet," Grand Master Sinclair said. "Aristotle named it in 372 B.C. when he prevented the Horsemen from appearing by stopping it from passing over the sun."

I couldn't believe my ears. Aristotle had taught Alexander

the Great. My father had made me read the philosopher's writings in their original Greek, and he was smashing comets. I forced myself to listen so I wouldn't miss a word.

The gray-haired man continued. "Aristotle's teacher, Plato, had gone to the Pillars of Hercules seeking the wisdom of an ancient civilization."

I tensed thinking the legend might be true. My father had spent countless sleepless nights over the last semester poring over old manuscripts, and now I understood why.

Genevieve stepped forward. "How old is the legend?"

Grand Master Sinclair removed a small stone seal decorated with hieroglyphs. "The first account we have is from the reign of Pharaoh Hatshepsut in 1581 B.C. Her army fought and defeated them." He leaned on his cane. "But the account the professor discovered is even older. More than five thousand years.

Lord Marbury quivered. "So they're going after the oldest known source of the Horsemen's power."

I glanced at Genevieve. Her brows knitted together in worry.

Baron Kensington tugged at the cross on his cuff. "And they want Plato's and Aristotle's papers on the comet, but we don't know why." He walked up to his daughter and me. "That's enough mystery for one night. You two should get some rest."

"Yes," the Grand Master said as he picked up his top hat. "You have all you need from me, Baron. You know what to do. Start on Gibraltar, they'll take him there first. Maybe we can get him before they arrive on Malta. Don't worry, lad, the baron will rescue your father."

The sound of gears locking in place, the ticking of a clock spring and a low hiss drew everyone's attention to the doorway. A bronze-plated mechanical cobra quickly slithered across the floor. Its black eyes sparked as it rushed the baron and his daughter.

"Genevieve, behind me!" Baron Kenzington pulled his daughter back as the serpent sprang from the ground and sank its steel fangs into his forearm. The serpent's eyes blazed, as electricity and venom coursed into the baron's flesh.

I threw my back against the wall to get away from the automaton. Fear seized me as it had in my father's office.

Twisting the handle of his cane, the Grand Master drew a hidden sword and struck the serpent just behind the head. He flung the automaton against the wall. It fell to the floor and the Templar smashed it with his boot. Oil ran like blood into the cracks of the wooden floorboards.

Genevieve screamed, "Father!"

The baron fell into a chair, gripping his arm. Genevieve rushed to his side. I heard a scuffle outside. Lord Marbury and the Grand Master bolted toward the front door. I pushed through my fear and followed. Finn wrestled with a man in a long black coat and derby hat. The henchman broke free of the Irishman but the Grand Master's sword quickly found its mark.

Genevieve cried, "Someone help!"

I ran back into the dining room and found the baron slumped over the table with his daughter clinging to his shoulder. His shallow breath and vacant gaze stunned me. Rodin landed on his shoulder and nudged his chin.

The men came back in the house and froze in the doorway. Lord Marbury sent Finn to fetch the doctor.

Grand Master Sinclair shook his head. "The KGC are on to us."

I looked at the chaos swirling around me. These vile henchmen were following the men trying to rescue my father. *Or were they following me?* I didn't know, but the possibility crushed me and I staggered back. *If Baron Kensington is poisoned, who will go after my father?*

CHAPTER 7

ESCAPE

I lurked outside the baron's room hoping to overhear his condition.

"Without knowing what type of poison was used," the doctor said, "all I can do is treat the symptoms. I'm afraid he's still in danger."

"I'll send for a chemist," Lord Marbury said. "Maybe he can identify the poison."

"What the baron *needs* is some Four Thieves Potion." Grand Master Sinclair hit his palm with a fist. "That stuff cures anything."

"We need real answers, not medieval superstitions," Lord Marbury sighed.

Grand Master Sinclair's voice softened. "Have faith my friend, all will be well."

Lord Marbury's tone trembled as he said, "Who will go after the professor?"

"I will send word to the Order. Another Templar will be sent." Sir Archibald put his hand on the Lord's shoulder. "Don't worry, friend, you've done your service. I'll not ask you take them on again. Once we've heard from the chemist, I'll visit the Tinkerer."

Just outside the door, Genevieve leaned against the

chair rail that separated the blue-flowered wallpaper from the white paneling. The flickering light from the nearby gas lamp danced on her tears.

She looked so sad and yet so beautiful.

I ached to help her. An idea crept into the back of my mind. I took her hand. It was soft and cool like a shaded stone. She tensed. I tensed. I pulled and Genevieve followed.

My heart jumped into my throat as we ran to the Blue Room and shut the door. "I want to help our fathers. I want to go with the Sky Raiders to Gibralter."

Genevieve spun on her heel and pulled her hand from mine. "This isn't like lurking in corners!"

"Maybe Col. Hendrix has the antidote. It had to have been his poison, so it makes sense. I'm going to find him, find my father, and get the antidote to save yours."

"You're bloody mad."

"Maybe, but I have to do something. I can't just sit here. I can't just go back to Eton and sit in class like everything is fine!"

Genevieve was quiet for a moment. She studied me like she had never seen me before and then said, "I'm coming with you."

"You can't, you're a girl!"

"Either I'm going or I'm telling Lord Marbury what you're planning," she said, a defiant glare in her eyes and obstinate hands on her hips. "What's it going to be?"

I wanted to argue—my father would never forgive me if I endangered Baron Kensington's daughter—but to be honest I was more afraid of what she would do to me if I said no. "I'm…"

"You have no choice. It's a woman's perogative." Genevieve slowly stepped out the door, then leaned back in. "Prepare yourself. I'll return in a moment."

"Dress warmly," I said, but Genevieve had already disappeared. The room seemed emptier without her.

I scoured the drawers for anything I could use on our journey. There wasn't much. I only had my school uniform and the books and papers in my leather book-bag. The rest of the room didn't hold much, unless I needed something blue. In the armoire, I found a pair of khaki pants and put them on with the white shirt and black vest from my school uniform. I pulled all the books from my bag except for my science book—all the equations and tables might come in handy. Then I rewrapped some food I'd swiped from lunch and stuffed it in as well.

I spun around as the door opened. My eyes widened. Genevieve wore dark gray pants and a blue peacoat over a man's shirt and suspenders. Her auburn hair, pulled tight, had been stuffed underneath a flapped cap and she carried a saber.

Rodin sat on her shoulder with his wings tucked back and his tail wrapped around her like a bronze necklace.

"You look like a man." I blurted out. I had never seen a woman in pants. The dark grey fabric of her pants clung to her, I tried to look away, but my eyes wouldn't move. I snapped up and shook my head. "You shouldn't be dressed like that."

Genevieve chuckled. "I like pants and you've never felt the cold English wind while wearing a skirt."

"But—that's not what I meant."

"Besides, the look on your face is priceless." Tucking up a stray tendril, she tried to harden her expression. "So, do I look more like a man?"

"You do… a good-looking man, I mean." My words stumbled. "If you get caught, you could get in a lot of trouble."

"I know it's dramatic, but a ship is more likely to take two boys."

I took a deep but stuttered breath. "Let's go before they catch us."

I stepped up to open the window and a strong pain wrenched my stomach as if someone twisted my insides into a knot. The feeling was just as in my father's office, or before the mechanical monster appeared. I doubled over and couldn't shake the nagging voice in the back of my mind that kept screaming *run*.

Genevieve peered through the window at the dimly lit street below.

Fear seized my guts into a tighter knot, and I clung to the heavy curtain fabric. "They've come back."

"Men in long dark coats and derby hats are slipping through the shadows." Genevieve pulled me back from the window. "How did you…we have to warn the others!"

We ran to the top of the stairs. Lord Marbury, Grand Master Sinclair and Finn stood below.

I gripped the railing. "KGC henchmen are right outside!"

All three stood stunned for a brief moment. Then Grand Master Sinclair ordered, "Hide upstairs and don't come down." He turned to Lord Marbury and unsheathed the blade from his cane. "Get Kensington to the underground trolley. Finn, you and I play hero."

Finn nodded. "I'll grab the shotgun."

As Lord Marbury slipped away to gather the baron, Finn ran for the den.

The front door burst open.

Col. Hendrix charged in but let his henchmen meet the old man's sword cane. "I'm here for the boy!"

"You cannot have him, you bronze abomination!" Sinclair's Scottish drawl shook the house.

Col. Hendrix looked up and roared, "Upstairs!"

Genevieve grabbed me by the shoulder and pulled me toward the Blue Room.

As we entered, I closed the door and Genevieve ran to the window. A loud gunshot echoed through the house. I hoped it was Finn with the shotgun from over the fireplace.

The sound of crashing metal stormed up the stairs. I looked around for a place to hide, but it had to be Col. Hendrix, only moments from smashing in the door.

Over the clashing swords I heard the Grand Master. "Alexander, run! Get to safety!"

I joined Genevieve at the window as she lifted the sash. "If Sinclair wants us to go, it must be bad."

She pointed to a narrow ledge made by the elaborate molding and whispered, "The downspout can be used as a ladder."

"Sounds like you've done this before."

A sly smile came to the soft lines of her face. "Maybe."

"I think we're going to get along."

I took a deep breath to calm my heart, then gripped the wall and took the first step onto the ledge. Genevieve followed and we slid over to the downspout. The treacherous footing made each step a cautious one, but fear of failing kept me glued to the wall. The thick metal bands that secured the copper downspout acted as a ladder to the safety of the street below, and soon we were on solid ground.

I looked back at the window. Col. Hendrix ripped the curtain down. He leapt from the second story and landed hard but upright on both feet. Two of his henchmen jumped but crumpled to the ground.

Genevieve pointed toward the docks, and we disappeared into the dense fog.

Col. Hendrix kicked one of his henchmen. "After 'em, don't let those little var-mits get away!"

Another blast from the shotgun filled the night sky. The chilly, damp veil of thick, white mist obscured everything except the sound of metal clinking on cobblestones.

London was huge, bigger than any place I had ever been, and I couldn't keep this pace for long. Breathing heavily, Genevieve and I slowed to walk along a row of merchant ships.

Col. Hendrix and two of his henchmen ran around a corner. He couldn't see us yet, but it would only be a moment. I grabbed Genevieve and dove behind some wooden crates with barrels stacked beside them.

Genevieve gripped her heaving chest and whispered, "Where do we run? I thought we would have lost them by now."

"Yeah, me too." I hoped my heart would stay inside, but it was pounding so hard, it seemed as if it might leap from my throat. And then a metal foot stomped on the wooden dock. We froze.

The Southerner's guttural voice came from the other side of the crates. "They're around here. Search everything."

I whispered to Genevieve. "Let's slip into the water."

"No."

"What?"

"It's disgusting down there."

"Well, it's better than ending up with him."

"He might have the antidote."

I couldn't argue with that.

Genevieve stood up and charged at Col. Hendrix with her hand on the hilt of her saber. "Give me the antidote for my father!"

I yanked her back behind the barrels. She struggled, but complied.

Col. Hendrix's voice sounded like sandpaper. "I ain't got it."

The gears and metal clicking and clanking got closer. We looked at each other and dove off the dock. The icy pin pricks on every part of exposed skin made me want to scream.

We clung to the thick pilings and pulled ourselves along the ropes that tied the ships to the docks.

Just above the water, I saw an aero-dirigible's hull moored to the airdocks. As I looked closer, I realized it was the same one the baron had visited earlier.

I grabbed hold of the Sky Raider's vessel. Genevieve climbed inside and then I pulled myself to the open hatch. I dared to take one last look for Col. Hendrix and saw him pointing from the docks. I quickly slipped inside.

Shivering from our short swim in the Thames River, we found ourselves in a corridor alongside the folded up wingsail. Beams with cutout interiors arched above us and formed the corridor, as a larger set of cutout beams formed the outer hull.

We heard raised voices and looked out at the open port. Col. Hendrix and his henchmen stood before the captain.

Col. Hendrix spit on the ground and said, "Bring me the children."

The captain spoke with a thick German accent. "Don't know what you're talking about."

"You got stowaways, and I want 'em."

"You're not stepping on my ship."

The captain threw the flap of his red coat to the side as one of the henchmen tried to move around him. He drew a small hand-canon from its holster. I noticed a cord running from the pommel into his jacket. Lightning cracked as two bolts arced into the henchman who shook violently and fell to the dock twitching.

More gunfire erupted. I watched Col. Hendrix and his remaining henchman run away. The Colonel stopped, turned around and stared into the open port, looking right at me. I feared the bronze demon would never stop hunting me.

As Col. Hendrix walked away, I released a huge sigh.

Footsteps on the metal planking alerted us to someone's approach. Genevieve and I ducked behind a series of wheels and gears that unfurled the wing. Would we get blasted by his lightning cannon too?

The sound drew closer.

I peered through the gears.

Genevieve sank as low as she could against the outer hull and tugged on me to do the same. I saw the captain's red coat and wondered if I'd made a bad mistake. Were Sky Raiders any better than the KGC henchmen? I held my breath.

The captain spotted the wet floor and spun around. "Who's there?" When he threw the flap of his coat to the side to reveal the lightning cannon, I stood.

"Wait, please don't shoot."

"You can tell your lady friend to stand up too. Nice disguise but your features are a little too soft."

We stood onto the metal planking. The captain looked over us and laughed. I wondered what was so funny.

The captain let his coat fall and crossed his arms. "You got names?"

"Alexander." I fell silent as three men came down the corridor. One wore a turban, the other dressed like a cowboy, and the third carried the biggest rifle I'd ever seen.

The three men stood quietly, examining us. Then the cowboy tipped his Stetson to the captain. "I've got a couple of men at the gun-ports in case they come back, and we're ready to depart on your order, captain." He spoke with an odd combination of Continental accent combined with a southern American drawl. "You want me to drop 'em in the drink?"

"Get us up into the skies. Those guys are coming back." The captain pointed at the soaked girl. "And you are?"

"Genevieve Kensington."

Her harsh tone surprised me, and I saw a wet plunge in our future. The men laughed, except for the young Indian man, whose narrow eyes studied her.

A flash of bronze darted through the port. Rodin landed on Genevieve's shoulder, his spread wings and snarling open jaw made it very clear they would have to go through the ferocious little dragon to hurt her.

"What the hell is that?" The startled captain asked.

Genevieve stood like a proper English noblewoman and announced, "He's my dragon. Now, if you please, may we have the honor of knowing whom we are addressing?"

The men laughed again. "I am Baldarich, captain of this vessel and raider of the sky." He smiled and bowed. "What brings you to my ship, other than your displeasure with your previous *watery* accommodations? Two young lovers running away? No, I don't think so. Too determined." He looked us over and ran his fingers along his sideburns and mustache. "I want the truth or you can feed the fishes."

Genevieve's brow lowered. "You were taking a man to Gibraltar, we were sent to replace him."

The blue-turbaned teenager, dressed in a matching tunic over white pants, stepped between them. "Captain, I know this girl."

From the look on Genevieve's face, I could tell she didn't know him.

"I know her father, Baron Kensington." The Indian man appeared to be slightly older than me. "They have the same spark, and he, too, had a dragon of bronze."

"What a small world we live in." The captain leered at us. "Now where is your father?"

I blurted out, "My father was kidnapped and I am trying to rescue him."

Genevieve said, "And *my* father was going to search for *his* father, but was attacked and poisoned before he had the chance. I now seek his cure."

The Indian teenager approached Genevieve. Rodin shifted but seemed to smell something familiar and eased his stance. With a look of concern he said, "I am sorry to hear of your father. May my gods and yours bless his health."

As Genevieve bowed her head in thanks, I asked,

"Captain Baldarich, will you please take us to the Port of Gibraltar? I don't have much to offer, but I'm certain that Queen Victoria would reward you."

The four men laughed, and the cowboy slapped his knee.

Genevieve stepped forward. "If you'll grant us transport, I can pay you when we arrive back in England."

Captain Baldarich crossed his arms. "We're on our way to Gibraltar; I could take you there. For a price."

"Captain, I wish to aid this girl," the boy in the blue turban said. "Her father helped smuggle me out of India."

"I understand." Baldarich nodded. "Well, young lady, this is going to cost you—to Gibraltar and back, plus fighting. 'Cause you know there is going to be fighting. But we are having a deal on saving damsels in distress, and I owe this guy a favor or two. It will cost you a thousand Pounds Sterling. Same offer I made your father."

I sighed and leaned against the one of the corridor arches. Where would we ever get that kind of money?

Genevieve smiled and nodded. She stuck out her hand. "Deal."

The captain laughed and clasped her hand in his. "Welcome to the Sparrowhawk!"

CHAPTER 8

THE SPARROWHAWK

Baldarich gestured toward the cowboy. "This is my first mate, Ignatius Peacemaker, fastest draw this side of the Atlantic." The cowboy tipped his hat to us as the captain turned to the man on his left. "That's Hunter, and this beauty is Gretel, his elephant gun. The man you really owe is my boatswain, Indihar Singh. He's in charge of the crew so you call him Mr. Singh."

I gestured toward the boy. "But he's a kid?"

Baldarich laughed. "That's why he's so good. He's a Sikh, only seventeen, but he's the best warrior I got, and the kid *knows* how to airsail."

I nodded to the three men, relieved to have found some help. The dripping wet Genevieve curtsied in her men's clothes.

Baldarich leaned toward Ignatius, "Get us out here, have bunks prepared and let Gustav know there'll be two more for dinner." He started to walk off, but stopped and turned around. "Mr. Singh, get them something dry to wear."

Mr. Singh bowed. "Please, this way."

Genevieve and I followed as the other two men walked off in a different direction.

The hull opened beside us and the long yardarm swung

out and unfurled the wingsails. The Sparrowhawk lurched. Genevieve and I grabbed the brass-accented wooden handrail to keep from slipping. The outer door closed, leaving open pits where the wingsails had been.

Mr. Singh simply swayed and continued on. Turning back, he smiled. "Your sky legs will come in time."

The bow rose and I found myself walking uphill. I heard the whirring and *chug chug* of the engines echoing behind me. I couldn't wait to see the Sparrowhawk ascend into the sky. Flying had always been my dream, but until now it had remained only in my fantasies. Now it would be real. And flying with Sky Raiders, too!

Mr. Singh led us down narrow steps to the cargo hold and gun-deck. Crates filled the center, marked with the fleur-de-lis, a golden, stylized, three-pedaled lily, one of the symbols of France.

"Wow, cannon."Two cannons sat on each side of the gun-deck toward the front, but I stopped next to a contraption that looked like a bunch of guns bound together. "What is that?"

Mr. Singh smiled. "A six-barreled, hand-cranked, rapid fire Gatling gun. Captain picked them up after your country's civil war."

"Can I crank the handle?"

"No." Mr. Singh opened the door to the forward compartment and they entered an open room with crates of cannon balls, ammunition, and other supplies for the gun-deck.

The floor sloped upward and I realized we stood at the front of the ship. My broad smile couldn't hide my excitement.

The Sikh smiled and nodded to Genevieve, "I apologize that we don't have better accommodations, but I don't think you should bunk with the rest of the crew." He bowed to us and said, "Ignatius will bring clothes and I shall return to give you a tour of the Sparrowhawk."

"Mr. Singh, I'm afraid this will not suffice." Genevieve looked around at the room. "I cannot stay here. He's a boy–it simply isn't proper."

"A boy?" I shook my head. Why didn't she just say a commoner and really dig the knife a little deeper.

Mr. Singh bowed to Genevieve. "Perhaps I can build a wall between the two of you."

"I wouldn't want to be an imposition."

"It would not be a problem."

I crossed my arms. "I still want to know what the problem is?"

Mr. Singh walked over and tugged on several hammocks hung on the walls by ropes woven through the bunched canvas grommets. "Here is your bed. Flip this latch and your hammock will slide over and anchor to that beam."

I flipped one of the latches on the port side and the canvas unfurled. "I've always wanted to sleep in a hammock."

Mr. Singh nodded. "You will feel like you are floating."

Genevieve asked. "This room is for storage, right?"

"Yes."

Genevieve looked around with a furrowed brow. "But this is also where we sleep?"

"Yes"

Her jaw clenched. "Does everyone sleep this way? Surely you have room set aside for sleeping."

"No, you are not the captain and only he has his own room."

Genevieve's expression remained stoic. "I will just have to manage." She bowed. "My gratitude for your assistance, Mr. Singh."

As the door shut behind Mr. Singh, I hopped in the hammock, letting my feet dangle.

I noticed Genevieve tried to hide her smile as she watched the water drip from my clothes. She took a piece of canvas and arranged a place for Rodin, tucked up in the narrowest part of the bow.

The little dragon picked at it with his claws, and with a final wiggle of his butt, settled down into a comfortable spot.

I kicked off my sopping boots. "We have luck on our side."

"I suppose." Genevieve cocked an eyebrow and shook her head. She went through her bag, and carefully folded her coat. "But nothing is going the way it was supposed to."

"I think this is a good thing. I've always wanted to travel in an aero-dirigible." The Sparrowhawk leveled off and my hammock swung on its hooks. The buffeting winds pushed the whole craft up and down, and side to side as the unceasing whistling permeated the hull. "Moving though the sky will take some getting used to."

The door opened and Ignatius Peacemaker walked in. He tossed me some clothes, then walked over to Genevieve and set a bundle before her. "We ain't got much in the way of women's clothes but we recently *borrowed* a few crates from a French merchant ship."

Genevieve nodded. "Thank you."

Ignatius left, and Genevieve picked through the clothes. I threw off my wet shirt and reached for a rag to wipe off. I looked at her, fumbled for the door and tripped over a crate of cannonballs. "Ow!" I rubbed my leg. "Sorry, you change. I'll be outside ... sorry."

Closing the door, I sat on one of the cannons, and felt the chilling draft whip around me. I rubbed my arms to keep from shivering.

The door opened, Genevieve stepped out and smiled. "Room's all yours. You should really get out of those wet clothes."

My head snapped up. I did a double take, and tried to keep from staring. She looked so different from the ladies

I saw walking around London. White pants tucked into high, brown leather boots rose above the knee with a flap at the top. A dark-brown leather corset with three brass-buckles covered a white top. A long, blue military overcoat gave her a noble appearance. Her fingers toyed with her locket's silver chain. Whipping my gaze away, I ran for the room.

Pulling my bundle of clothes apart, I found dark brown pants, a white button down, and brown boots. After dressing, I needed a belt. I took a leather strap from the wall and buckled it around my waist, but several feet remained. Without a proper knife to cut the strap, I kept wrapping it around myself—up over my shoulders and then down my right leg, where I buckled the end just above my knee.

Looking down at my new attire, a surge of confidence stirred deep within. I stood a little taller. I'd never liked school uniforms, too constraining, and I could almost hear my schoolmates' taunts. It made me smile; stiff suits were not my style.

Genevieve waited for me by one of the cannons. Her eyes widened. I walked up to her and asked, "So is the strapping too much?"

"No," she quickly replied.

I smiled. "You look good, like a soldier, but in a noble way."

Her face lit up, but Mr. Singh interrupted and bowed. Genevieve returned the gesture and I tried, but my bow lacked their grace.

"I am to show you the Sparrowhawk. Your duties will be assigned later."

"Duties?" Baldarich fired one last burst

Mr. Singh laughed. "Come, the captain is waiting."

I ascended the stairs to the main deck, the middle of the three, and walked forward toward the bow. We passed a room with a two long rows of hammocks stacked atop each other on the curved outer wall. From the other side, I heard pots banging as heavy footsteps thundered from the galley. I wanted to peek, and the smell was very enticing, but Genevieve pulled me along.

Mr. Singh walked by a small door in the bow. "This is the forward gun-deck."

I wanted to see but we continued. "The Sparrowhawk is well armed," I remarked.

Mr. Singh smiled. "The captain is good at acquiring things."

Genevieve shot Mr. Singh a look with one eyebrow raised. "Things?"

"All kinds of things."

He led us aft to the engine room, through a corridor lined with several large tanks. Three immense engines, their pistons and cranks revolving in syncopated rhythm, drove the vessel through the sky. Steam pipes twisted around the walls and ceiling, their segmented copper sections and brass fittings reminding me of my anatomy classes back at Eton. A man climbed through the rotating gears and propeller shafts but Mr. Singh continued before I saw him clearly.

Genevieve stepped forward. "Pardon me, how did you meet my father?"

Mr. Singh smiled with a pleasant expression. "It was a few years ago. Your father traveled throughout the Punjab fighting a rebel threatening the region."

"I remember that trip."

"The day the rebels exterminated my family, I drew my Kirpan." He patted a curved dagger tucked into the sash around his waist. "I charged in to avenge them and would have been killed, but your father saved me. He smuggled me to some traders traveling the Silk Road. From there I made my way to Europe."

"I don't remember that part. He never told me that story."

"Have you gone back since then?" I asked.

"No, I believe my holy path lies elsewhere."

We climbed the narrow stairs to the top deck, and Mr. Singh pointed to the crawl spaces on either side of the shortened corridor. "Those lead to the helium containers, the large humps on both sides of the Sparrowhawk's back. That will be your first duty in the morning, to inspect the tanks for leaks."

I stared at the small hatches, wondering what lay behind them. Was it dangerous? Could I get hurt? Was it goopy? It sounded like more interesting work than polishing brass fixtures. Mr. Singh passed a ladder leading to a small, round space above. I stopped. "Where does this go?"

"The conning tower and out on top of the vessel."

I wondered if I could stand on top while it was moving. That would be fun.

We passed two rooms on their way to the door at the end of the corridor. It opened onto the bridge of the Sparrowhawk.

My heart soared as we entered. My eyes darted from one side of the room to the other. I stood on the bridge of an aero-dirigible. *I wonder if they'd let me fly it?*

Mr. Singh pointed to the man in the brass pilot's seat. "This is Coyote."

With both hands Coyote gripped the large wooden wheel like any ship of the sea. He cast a glance over the shoulder of his long, dark gray coat that draped all the way down to wooden deck.

He looked thin but remained hidden beneath the bulky coat. I wondered if Coyote might be a gentleman, but his clothes weren't nice enough. "Are you from a western state?"

"I'm busy and you're distracting me."

I cringed. "Sorry, it's just that your name is—"

"I know what my name is, kid. Have a seat and enjoy the ride."

I watched the pilot adjust our flight path not only by turning the wheel from side to side, but pushing it forward and back as well. Three copper throttle controls rose up next to his seat, and Coyote kept moving his gaze from the clear skies to a panel with a lever, switches, and dials.

Several connected panels of glass allowed me to see the arcing blue horizon, and brass-ringed portholes gave me a view of what lay to either side.

On the port side of the bridge, large and small brass dials, shiny knobs, and switches displayed the engines' status and other gauges. On the starboard side, a map of Europe had been spread across a large flat table. Beside it, a wall of cubby holes each contained a different map.

In the center, raised on a small platform, the captain's chair sat behind a small brass railing. Four copper pipes rose up in front of the railing and bent toward the captain's chair.

As Mr. Singh, Genevieve, and I approached, the captain leaned forward, opened the hinge of the farthest left tube and called out, "Gears, this is the bridge. I want all three propellers by dinner."

A voice echoed back through the tube. "Aye, aye captain!"

Captain Baldarich turned and welcomed us with a smile. "I see you got dry clothes. I didn't think we had anything for a lady."

Genevieve smoothed out her jacket with her hand. "Ignatius said they were from the French crates you *borrowed*."

"Ah yes, let us thank the French." Captain Baldarich laughed and Genevieve smiled. "So tell me, why do you need my vessel?"

I walked around the bridge in awe. "My father and I moved to London last summer, he's teaching at Eton College. It turns out he was summoned by Queen Victoria to help translate some ancient texts about a great evil that rises up every so often. A secret society, the Knights of the Golden Circle, kidnapped him so he'll help them unleash that evil."

Captain Baldarich toyed with his moustache. "Sorry I asked. I hate to tell you, kid, but the world's full of ancient evils. Could you be a bit more specific?"

The smile drained from Genevieve's face. "According to my father and his colleagues, every time a certain comet appears it heralds the four horsemen."

"You mean from the Bible? The four horsemen of the Apocalypse? From what Ignatius says they only come at the end."

She glared at him with a cocked hip. "The four horsemen are older than that. Apparently they have sown destruction through every age. My father used to tell me tales of our family's heroes. I always thought they were just stories, until now."

My family marked me as a commoner, especially with her bloodline's long history. I certainly would never know the queen or be able to make such a claim. She truly came from a different world. I'd often been made fun of at Eton by the boys with distinguished lineages, their two favorite lines, calling me a commoner among great men or a traitorous colonist.

Captain Baldarich stood and opened all four speaker pipes, "Well men, we're off on a great quest!"

CHAPTER 9

THE TALE OF CAPTAIN BALDARICH

Genevieve and I followed the smell of spiced potatoes, bread, and beef stew to the galley. A long table left only enough room for the crew to squeeze around with forks in hand. The sound of the chef rooting around the kitchen accompanied the delicious aroma.

My stomach grumbled and roared like Rodin. The little dragon looked down from Genevieve's shoulder and cocked his head to the side. Everyone laughed as my stomach rumbled again and the captain slapped my back.

"Don't worry lad, Gustav will take care of that for you." Baldarich turned to the doorway and yelled. "Hurry, our guest might pass out soon."

A thick German accent echoed from the kitchen, "Coming right up, captain!"

I stepped back as the dirtiest man I had ever seen walked in from the corridor. Black grease and soot covered everything except his teeth, which glowed like moonlight in the middle of his midnight-colored face. He started to sit as Gustav emerged from the kitchen. The portly man in a white apron speckled with stew broth yelled, "Don't you dare!"

Gears froze, his backside hovering inches above the

bench. In German he said, "You're worse than the Kaiser. I just want a quick meal before heading back to the engines."

Mr. Singh stepped between them. "Gears, Gustav, no arguing. Many are hungry, including the captain."

A vain bulged on Gustav's forehead. "Listen Donkeyman, I'll not have you getting grease all over my food!"

"Your food is already greasy." Gears sat down and a cloud of soot rose up around him.

Gustav slammed down the pot of stew and handed out bowls to everyone but Gears. "You don't get any, you dirty wrench-rocker."

Shaking his head, Captain Baldarich turned to Gears. "Go wash your hands; I don't want soot in my soup."

Gears left behind a happy Gustav who turned his attention to the newest guests of the Sparrowhawk. His scowl vanished like a passing wind, replaced by a large smile as he filled our bowls. In broken English he said, "Good stew for growing bones."

I drained my bowl and moaned in delight as the tender beef fell apart in my mouth. I savored the last of the squishy potatoes, carrots, and other vegetables in the salty broth and looked around the table to see what else I could eat.

Everyone filed out of the galley and made their way into a large open area on the main deck. The crew who weren't on duty sat around on crates and in a few hammocks hanging from the hull. One man played guitar, and another struck an empty barrel like a drum.

Captain Baldarich sat beside me and Genevieve. He ordered Coyote to the bridge as Gears continued past them, looking eager to get back to his engines. The captain leaned back against the wall.

I looked up at him and asked, "How did you become a Sky Raider?"

The crew laughed and clapped their hands, as Baldarich leaned in and gave me a long hard look. I started to think

I'd asked the wrong question until the captain slapped my shoulder, almost knocking me over. "It's a grand tale. I used to serve in the Kaiser's army."

"You were in the army?"

"I was friends with the Kaiser! He'd arranged a promotion because I was going to marry a noblewoman. But her family found a better offer. You see, I'm Schwabish, from the Black Forest, and they wanted someone from a higher class."

"Couldn't the Kaiser help you?"

The crew laughed again. It seemed to be a very funny story to them. Baldarich smiled and grabbed my shoulder. "It was the Kaiser who stabbed me in the back. A few of her family did the deed, but he sanctioned it. I've got three nice scars to remind me of the Kaiser's generosity. I'd show you, but there's a lady present."

"I'm sorry." I felt horrible for asking. "So how did you get this great ship? Did you win it in a card game?"

"Nah, I stole her from the Kaiser."

"You stole her?"

"My last job was overseeing the aero-dirigible's construction. I call her my Kaiser compensation." The captain slapped his knee and went to fill his goblet.

I looked around and saw Hunter leaning against an interior wall. Separate from the others, he watched everyone with a keen eye. I felt his gaze often, but when I would look over, he always turned away.

Across the vessel, Ignatius chuckled through the captain's story as if he'd heard it many times before. He sat with a barrel in front of him and his gun-cleaning tools arranged in perfect rows.

Ignatius pulled the first two Colt Peacemakers from the back of his belt and laid them on the barrel. The next two from the front, two more from holsters under his shoulders, one from each thigh, and even one from each boot, but I didn't see where the last two came from. Twelve pistols in all; I had never seen a man carry more.

Mr. Singh sat on a bench beside Genevieve and asked, "Did you ever travel to India?"

"Yes, and I hope to return one day."

Mr. Singh smiled. "If India is in your heart then I am certain she will call you back."

Genevieve nodded. "My father told me much of the Sikhs. He admires your people—their skill as warriors, as craftsman, and particularly their zeal for life."

Mr. Singh said, "Your father is a great man."

Watching the two of them brought this weird feeling to the pit of my stomach, so I glanced over and watched the crew instead. Already, they had accepted me more than all my classmates at Eton. I'd made no friends since coming to London, but these men were more inviting than I ever imagined possible.

The captain started to sing in German. The others joined in, which led to a song that cursed the Kaiser. I joined in, singing in German, which delighted the crew and Genevieve, who smiled and nodded along with the beat.

Rodin perched on her shoulder.

Ignatius turned to me and asked, "So what can we expect from this bronze-plated bad guy and his secret order of knights?"

"He's mean—tough enough to spit nails—and has a wicked arm with hidden weapons."

Ignatius shook his head. "And you think you're going to be able to defeat him?"

I wanted revenge more than anything, but I hadn't thought about what I'd do when I found the mechanical monster. "I'll make him tell me where my father is and then toss him overboard."

Ignatius laughed and most of the crew joined in. At first, I wondered what was funny, but quickly realized they didn't think I could do it. The more I thought about it, I wasn't too certain either, but their laughter made me want to test it on one of them.

"Good luck with that." Ignatius picked up the Colt he'd just finished cleaning. "My advice, boy—shoot him and then ask your questions."

Hunter turned to the captain. "What they need is training; it'll be suicide otherwise."

Genevieve stood up, her hands firmly planted on her hips, "I've trained with sword and shot since I was a girl. My father insisted."

Ignatius smiled. "Dad wanted a son?"

She eyed him with an icy stare, but before she could answer, Captain Baldarich stepped forward. "Hunter has a good point. If you're going to help your fathers, both of you will need some training. Not lessons from papa, but real fighting skills." He turned to Ignatius and Hunter. "You two will start training them in firearms." Baldarich smacked Mr. Singh's shoulder. "Then you'll work on their sword skills."

I didn't know what to say, but it sounded exciting. Genevieve's gaze narrowed. Captain Baldarich said, "Now get to bed you two, you'll need your strength for tomorrow."

Genevieve and I wandered down to the gun-deck. I opened the door for her and we drifted to opposite sides of the room.

Genevieve took the man's shirt she'd worn before and put that on as she removed the corset. Removing her boots, she climbed into her hammock.

She turned to me and asked, "Will you turn down the kerosene lamp?"

"Of course." I walked over to the lamp and adjusted the knob so the flame barely glowed. I returned to my hammock and climbed in. "I have a good feeling. This feels right. Oh, and Genevieve, if it means anything, I saw your father in action. If he trained you, then I bet you're a great swordsman. Swords-woman. Whichever."

"Thank you, Alexander. That means a lot."

CHAPTER 10

TRAINING BEGINS

The door flew open and slammed against the bulkhead. My hammock flipped and dumped me onto the deck. "That was a good dream," I grumbled, struggling to my feet.

Genevieve chuckled from under her coat.

Mr. Singh glared. "Meet me on the top deck and do not make me wait or your duties will double. Training comes after lunch. If you want to eat, I would not suggest doing double duty."

Mr. Singh left and Rodin stretched, arching his back and shaking off his sleepy haze from his head to the tip of his tail. Genevieve scratched behind the three bony horns protruding from his head. Rodin curled into her hand and what passes for a dragon's smile came across his snout.

I threw on my boots and wound the leather strap around me. I wasn't going to miss lunch or double my work.

Genevieve waited for me to go and then dressed, joining me minutes later on the top deck. Mr. Singh waited in front of the two crawl spaces he'd pointed out the day before.

"Check the helium bags. Look for leaks." Mr. Singh opened the hatches. "This section isn't insulated, so it'll be cold and windy. Crawl through and climb in between the bags. Take these patches and glue."

I nodded and crawled in head first. The wind howled against the hull. It deafened and chilled me to the bone. I moved along the metal planking, excited to see what kept this aero-dirigible afloat. The crawl space ran along the spine of the vessel before opening up above me. Three huge bags, taut to the point of bursting, were secured to the inner bracing by thick metal straps.

Determined to please Mr. Singh and the captain, I squeezed around and felt all the seams of the helium bags. On the third one, I felt a small blast of air, and noticed the bag wasn't as taut as the others. Pulling the patch I'd tucked into my leather strap, I applied the glue to the bag. I smoothed the treated canvas patch over the leak and cleaned up the excess glue with my finger. Unable to feel the draft of escaping gases, I crawled back out and found Mr. Singh and Genevieve waiting.

I smiled big and said, "I plugged the hole on the back bag."

Mr. Singh corrected me, "You sealed the number drei portside helium container." Then he showed us the tanks located just outside the engine room to check the pressure in the bag I'd repaired.

Gustav called us for lunch with a cowbell.

I devoured my meal, a mix of salted meats and bread, but all I could think about was the training that would follow. Genevieve looked less enthused but still accompanied me to the top deck after lunch. Captain Baldarich waited with Hunter and Ignatius. Mr. Singh walked behind us and nodded to the captain as we arrived.

Baldarich hit Ignatius's shoulder, "See what this kid has."

"With pleasure." He threw off his duster and raised his fists.

My excitement drained, I wanted to learn, but Ignatius looked *too* eager. I raised my fists, but the little voice in the back of my head kept screaming this was a bad idea. I'd only fought the school bully twice and had lost once, but that was over a year ago.

Ignatius swung and I dodged it, which felt good and I missed the second punch, but not the knee that accompanied it. Doubled over and struggling to breathe, I stood up as much as I could and readied to fight. The voice was right—bad idea. My gut seized up and I couldn't breathe.

The captain grimaced, along with the others standing beside him. "Come on kid, that's not how you fight. Use your surroundings. Keep moving, keep your arms up, and for god's sake keep an eye on him."

Ignatius chuckled. "You might as well crawl back to the crib if that's the best you got. Try this."

As the cowboy took his next swing I ran toward the wall, not wanting to get hit again. Ignatius laughed, but I stepped on the railing and sprang off, punching him in the face.

Captain Baldarich clapped his hands. "Excellent, that's how you fight." He stepped between us as Ignatius charged me. "Let's see if the kid can shoot, then we'll see how they handle the blades."

Hunter opened the door and the wind rushed in whipping their long coats against them. I stared out at the clouds, the vast ocean below and the majesty of the endless blue above and below shrunk me to a pea. I saw the curve of the horizon, the very shape of the world.

Hunter grabbed a couple of treated canvas balloons and filled them with helium. He brought us to the door. Using a modified shot-put launcher mounted to the wall, he flung the balloons into the open sky, where they drifted away on the wind. Taking a rifle that leaned against the wall, Hunter handed it to me. "Focus your aim, steady your breathing, and when you're ready, ease the trigger, don't jerk it."

Baldarich laughed. "Pretend it's the Kaiser."

I raised the rifle and took aim. Easing the trigger, the rifle exploded and kicked like a bucking bronco. The balloon popped, spraying a cloud of black dust through the sky.

Hunter smiled. "I filled them with soot."

The captain chuckled, "Nice shot, kid!" He turned to Genevieve. "Your turn, let's see if the little lady can shoot."

Genevieve walked over and took the rifle from me. She opened the breach, popped the shell out and took another cartridge from Hunter. Once loaded she raised the rifle and in a determined voice said, "Pull." Ignatius and Hunter nodded to each other.

Hunter loaded the next balloon and flung it into the air. Genevieve waited, letting it drift away and then fired. She handed the rifle back to Hunter. Captain Baldarich and I went to the door and looked out. A puff of black hung in the sky and the captain laughed.

As they turned around, she stood with her hand on her hip, "As I said, my father trained me—in skeet and sword."

Next the captain had Mr. Singh test us. Genevieve used the saber she'd brought with her. It was beautiful with a silver hilt and an oval piece of lapis lazuli in the pommel. She and Mr. Singh fought in the enclosed space, and I watched in awe. I'd never seen two better swordsmen.

The captain handed me a cutlass with a bronze hilt and leather wrapped handle.

Mr. Singh popped it out of my hand with the first move and it clattered against the metal planking.

I picked it up and tried to surprise the Indian warrior, but Mr. Singh parried it aside and slapped me on the back. After several more attempts, I finally handed the sword over to Mr. Singh.

"I think I need more work on the sword. Can I go back to shooting things?" I grabbed the black club from my bag. Grooves cut into the cold steel handle hid the mechanics of the club. "Maybe this would help?"

Captain Baldarich stood up and walked over. "Where'd you get a Thumper, kid?"

"I took it off one of the guys who kidnapped my father." I looked at it. "Why do they call it a Thumper?"

"Here." The captain took the club and unhinged the handle. "You're in luck, I took this from a guy a week ago. It's a special kind of percussion cap." He slipped it into the pommel and closed the breach. "Here you go kid, point this out the door and I'll show you."

I took the Thumper, pointed it out the door and Hunter flung a balloon. As it crossed my aim, I pushed the button and the cap inside ignited. The thick end of the club slid forward like a piston. A concussive force blew out the end, flew through the air and shattered the balloon. The recoil knocked me into the railing. My wide, excited eyes drifted from the small dark cloud to the club. I unhinged the breach and the smoldering brass cap fell to the deck.

"Wow." I hurt in three places but didn't care.

The captain chuckled. "Just imagine if you hit the bad guy."

CHAPTER 11

THE PILLARS OF HERCULES

I sat in the sun's warm glow as it poured through the port window, studying the Thumper held firm in my hand. I used the leather strapping wrapped around me to secure a leather holster I'd made to my right leg. I checked to make certain it laid flat. I was having more fun than I'd had in years, but thoughts of my father's captivity brought me out of the clouds.

Genevieve strolled up and sat on the same ledge. I holstered the club and liked feeling its weight pulling at my side. Pushing my hair back I said, "You're an amazing fighter. Why did your father train you so well?"

As I mentioned her father, her face sank. I kicked myself for mentioning him because I'd just been struck by the same pain and didn't like passing it along to her.

She steeled herself and rose to meet my gaze. "For generations, men in my family have been knights of the crown. My grandfather said we're related to St. George the Dragon Slayer. Everyone—men and women—must be able to protect themselves and, if need be, protect the crown."

On cue, like a Shakespearian actor, Rodin flew in and landed between them. Genevieve scratched his head, and his tail whipped about.

"How'd you find Rodin? Did your father fight his mother?" Rodin whipped my leg and I let out a groan. "Sorry, is that a sore subject?"

Genevieve smiled and pulled the dragon into her lap. "No, he's just being playful. Rodin actually understands quite a bit of English. My grandfather found his egg in a treasure horde. He thought the bronze egg wrapped in studded-leather bands was a medieval relic. I don't know when his mother lived, but he didn't hatch until I was born. We assumed he was the last of his kind, but when my father and I were in India, we heard stories of dragons in the Himalayas."

"That's amazing." I had read stories from throughout the millennia about dragons. When my father taught me new languages, I often tried to find stories that piqued my interest rather than boring tales of some pharaoh's failed crops. I hadn't found a culture anywhere that didn't have a dragon.

Genevieve pointed through the bolted-brass window on the other side of the vessel. A large rock rose up from the sea, and I realized the Sparrowhawk had pitched ever-so slightly downward.

Sporadic patches of green shrubs covered grayish-white stone. The port-city nestled at its base had a single main road but its busy docks were packed with people. Seagulls gliding on air currents circled the top of the rock around the airdocks.

I turned to Genevieve and asked, "Where are we?"

"The Rock of Gibraltar, isn't it beautiful?"

I pressed against the window. "I've always wanted to see the Pillars of Hercules; he struck them with his sword so he could travel to Hades."

"It's a British colony," Genevieve said. "It's been years since I was last here, but my father always insisted on stopping before sailing on into the Mediterranean."

The airdocks, a set of moorings atop a ridge just below the mountain's peak, came into view as the Sparrowhawk made the last turn of its final approach. The vessel landed on a mesh of metal planking as large iron docking clamps gripped the vessel. The clattering echoed through the hull and across the docks.

Mr. Singh charged by where we were sitting, accompanied by several airmen. The crew threw open the bay door and extended a crane stowed in the ceiling. A couple of airmen opened the large cargo bay doors in the floor as more opened the doors of the floors below.

Baldarich came from the bridge and surveyed his crew's work. He nodded to Mr. Singh, who bowed in return, and then approached Genevieve and I. "Just stay out of their way, and don't go near the cargo doors. You might fall all the way to the bottom and that would mean I don't get paid." He turned back to Mr. Singh. "Don't unload all of this until I've negotiated the price with the dockmaster."

"Aye, captain." Mr. Singh turned to a man maneuvering the large iron arm. "Get that crane secured!"

Genevieve and I chased after the captain, catching him on the docks. I tugged at his coat. "Can we come with you and see the city?"

"No. I have to sell the stuff we acquired and buy new supplies." He shook his head and smiled. "Alright. You can go ashore, I suppose. You can't get in too much trouble here. Stick together and stay out of people's way. Be back in an hour."

As we ran off, I called out, "We'll be back, promise."

Rodin flew after us as Genevieve and I ran past some swarthy-looking men working to secure a zeppelin. I wondered if we shouldn't have asked Ignatius to join us as we scoured the island looking for clues to my father's kidnappers. Once we got off the docks, we slowed and walked down the mountain road as Rodin flew above us chasing the seagulls. I gawked at every detail. White buildings topped with terra cotta Spanish tiled roofs, brightly lit by the sun. The sweet smell of the salty sea, the narrow streets filled with every race of the world, the docks holding ships from every harbor—it was beautiful.

We passed through the market where the strong aroma of Moroccan spices drew me closer. Golden trinkets from North Africa and ceramic relics from the holy land lined every shop. I stopped at a man selling blades from Toledo, Spain, as Genevieve drifted over to the Italian silver jewelry. We passed stands with food I had never seen before. I smiled at Genevieve and swiped a pomegranate from a distracted vendor. Ducking into an alleyway between two buildings, I split the fruit in two and handed her half. She grinned and bit into the fruit. Its juices ran down her fingers and chin. I took a bite and laughed using my cuff to wipe off the juice. I felt free, free from responsibility and free from my burdens.

And then a sandy-brown fuzz ball, a Barbary macaque, leapt down from above and swiped my fruit. Genevieve laughed as I chased the monkey around the alley. It screeched at me and then sprang to a window sill on the second floor.

"Wait," she said. "You can't hurt them. A legend says if the monkeys ever leave so will the British, much like the ravens of the Tower of London." She handed me the remainder of her half. "Here, have a bite of mine."

"I wasn't going to hurt him, just scare him. Thanks."

We shared her fruit and watched the macaque, which was quickly joined by several others. Genevieve and I laughed at the antics, as all tried to sneak a bit of pomegranate from the first monkey. Bounding around the alley and up the building, they sprang from one spot to the next, screeching and calling as they tried to get some fruit. Rodin dove and scattered the troop. The little bronze dragon delighted in chasing them, but Genevieve called Rodin to her shoulder so he'd stop annoying the monkeys.

"We should keep an eye out for any leads on my father," I said, bringing us back to the reality of why we were in Gibraltar in the first place.

"Agreed, Gibraltar was where my father was to start looking," she said.

Slipping between two buildings, we stayed off the main road, hoping to avoid any problems with the city's inhabitants. We walked beneath a stone archway, a strange circular arch that didn't appear as old as the stone buildings on either side. Symbols etched on the back of the stone caught my eye, a mix of several languages and symbols.

A door at the end of the alley started to open and Genevieve pulled me into a nearby doorway. A tattooed man with dots covering his face in a lined pattern and a thin, lanky frame stepped into the alley. He wore a black vest and pants with a dirty white button down underneath. A sickle blade sat on the belt at his left side, while a club with a chained-cord hung from the other. He wore a flat, wide brimmed hat and coughed, a deep repetitive hacking that had settled in his lungs. He removed a handkerchief from his pocket and dabbed the blood from the corner of his mouth.

The man headed out through the back of the alley and missed us huddled in the doorway. He was no gentleman, more likely a pirate, and I wondered about his tattoos and what he was doing here. Knowing that the Knights of the Golden Circle were interested in Gibraltar, I also wondered if he could be involved with them. He was dressed in black, after all.

We slipped over to the door but it had no handle and couldn't be pushed open.

I studied it while Genevieve and Rodin watched the street. I looked for a hidden switch or another way through the thick wooden door. And then I noticed it. Above me, in the corner of the doorway, a small golden circle had been screwed into the stone. Genevieve looked at me with a nervous gaze. Tense and anxious, I leaned against the door, listening for any sounds within.

She whispered, "Hear anything?"

"Nothing."

I stared at the golden ring and tried to push it, turn it, pull it, but it remained anchored. Genevieve watched in amusement. I snapped a look at her and she shook her head.

"Check the rest of the door, it's probably meant to distract you." Genevieve pointed to the hinges. "See if you can lift the pin."

I pulled the pin and heard a click from behind the door. Pulling it further, I heard the latch release and the door opened. Genevieve smiled in triumph.

We entered a small room tucked on to the back of the building. A circular rug lay in the center and a chest sat against the far wall. We looked around the empty room, and I walked over to the chest. As I passed over the rug I heard a change in the sound of my steps. Genevieve flipped back the rug revealing a pattern of stone tiles on the floor in the shape of a pyramid.

Stepping on each stone, the top one rocked while others remained firm. We pulled on the tip, lifting just above the other tiles and slid over. A narrow circular rod-iron staircase led down into the shadows but the soft glow a flickering flame illuminated the way. We slipped down the stairs and found ourselves in a small chamber underneath the alley.

One wall had an upside-down semicircular arch mirroring the one above. I realized that the two arches made a circle and I brimmed with excitement as Genevieve turned up the flame on the gas lamp hanging at the bottom of the stairs. Stacked books and papers strewn on several desks around the room called to me. I ran over and began carefully filing through them. Genevieve walked over to the only wall without a desk and looked at the mosaic mural.

I scanned over books about astronomy, geology, minerals, history and a variety of other subjects. There had to be common thread that linked them and I thought hard trying to figure it out. I found a set of papers labeled 'The Sungrazer Comet' and saw the thread.

The papers outlined the core of the comet, a diagram showed that it was ice but with a dark core at its center. The diagram also showed that it was not one block of ice but several bound together surrounding this dark core. A pencil line led to the side of the page where an annotation was written—'unknown metallic compound.' There was more at the bottom.

I read it aloud. "The comet used to return every seven hundred years, but in 372 BC Aristotle prevented the horsemen from appearing by stopping the comet from passing over the sun. In doing so it broke apart."

"Alexander, you have to see this mosaic."

I walked over and looked at the wall; it was a map of the Mediterranean and the Atlantic. Everything looked in place but then I noticed the Azores were much bigger and further out to sea than they should be. I turned back to Genevieve and pointed to the paper. "It looks like they've been studying the comet."

Her shoulders drooped and she looked around the room. "I bet this is the place my father was supposed to find."

I nodded. "I think it is."

"We shouldn't stay long."

I couldn't agree more, already the voice in the back of my mind screamed to leave. My nervous laugh broke the tension. "I don't think my father has been here, all of these books were written in English."

"You do have a keen eye."

"You've never been in my father's house. Pick up a book

and you first have to figure out what dead language it's in before you can read it."

Genevieve chuckled and I turned down the gas lamp before we ran up the stairs. I slid the stone back into place as she dropped the carpet over the pyramid. We headed back through the archway, in the opposite direction from where the tattooed man had gone.

CHAPTER 12

RUNNING AROUND THE ROCK

Passing through the market, a flash of bronze and spark of electricity caught my eye. Down a dark, narrow alley, I saw Col. Hendrix in his black coat and bowler hat talking to a woman with long, black curly hair and the man with the tattooed face.

Genevieve yanked me back out of sight.

I drew the Thumper from its holster and opened the breach. I loaded one of the two shells from my pocket and peered around the edge of the building. Anger welled up inside me, and I wanted to charge down the alley, throw that abomination against the wall and demand to know where my father was, but even I knew that was foolhardy.

Col. Hendrix handed the woman a small leather bag. She smiled with delight, peered inside, and drew up a handful of coins.

Hendrix said. "I'll rejoin the ship as soon as I've checked the island."

The dark haired woman bit down on a coin. "Don't worry, I have my end handled."

Hendrix turned toward me. I snapped back, but my knee struck the drain pipe. A symphony of sound echoed along the narrow alley. I gripped my knee trying not to scream in every language I could think of and peered through the chipped wall.

The woman spun on her heeled boot, her leg jutting out the high slit of a full, black skirt. The sun glinted off the silver skull-and-crossbones that decorated her black corset. She snatched the pouch closed and asked, "What was that?"

"Trouble," Col. Hendrix said. "Get out of here. I'll handle this."

She motioned to the tattooed man. "Tobias, go with him."

I heard the sound of gears locking in place.

Genevieve tugged at my sleeve. "We need to leave," she whispered.

Nodding my head, we fled as the Colonel and Tobias stepped around the corner. I turned, saw the Colonel raise his mechanical arm. A gun barrel extended out the sleeve. "Run!"

"What do you think I'm doing!" Genevieve sprinted down another alley and up a set of stairs.

I followed, but turned around as we reached the top. Col. Hendrix swung the lever under his arm and cocked the rifle. The tattooed man carried a sickle blade.

I fired. The concussive blast slammed into the wall as the two men ducked.

Genevieve and I ran across a square heading for the road that led to the airdocks. I loaded the final percussion shell.

I looked back, but didn't see anybody, perhaps we'd lost them. Then Genevieve screamed. I spun around.

Tobias' tattooed face stood in front of me with his sickle in his right hand and a club in the other. Both covered in black leather gloves. A cord from the club wrapped around his back. He coughed, wheezing to catch his breath like a singing bird.

Genevieve drew her saber and blocked the sickle just as I raised my Thumper, but it was knocked aside by the thick serrated blade extending out of Col. Hendrix's sleeve.

"So predictable," Col. Hendrix sneered. "Come to find your pa?"

"Where is he?" I demanded.

"Near enough to tease you, but far enough, that you'll never find him."

"I want him back." My knees wanted to crumble, but I refused to falter in front of this monster.

"Foolish boy," he hissed through the bronze plates on his face. "Why don't you come with me, I'll take you to him?"

I paused, and for a brief moment the offer sounded like the best idea yet. I could go with Hendrix and, once reunited with my father we could sneak out and meet back up with Genevieve. But who knew what they'd do to Genevieve in the meantime and my father wouldn't listen to me long enough to escape on my terms anyway.

"What are you thinking?" Genevieve tugged at my sleeve and whispered through gritted teeth. Thank goodness she returned me to reality. I shook my head. Going with Hendrix was not an option. This needed bolder action, Baldarich style.

I raised my Thumper and pushed the trigger; the concussive blast threw the Colonel back against the wall, but didn't hurt the bronze armor.

"Now you're gonna get it," he growled.

Genevieve dodged Tobias' curved sickle blade, but couldn't avoid the club. It struck her shoulder sending an electric jolt through her body. She screamed in pain and knocked it away with her saber.

Then two shots rang out, echoing throughout the stone alleyway. One struck the club sending it spinning from Tobias's hand. It swung down connected by the cord and struck him in the knee. He cried out as it sparked and grabbed the club with his gloved hand. He violently coughed and a trickle of blood appeared at the corner of his mouth.

The second shot knocked the bowler hat clean off Col. Hendrix's head. Everyone turned toward the shots and saw a man in a long dark-brown duster, backlit by the sun.

Ignatius's face and two six-shooters caught the fading light, and he fired two more rounds from each gun. Dust kicked up from the ground next to Col. Hendrix and Tobias. The tattooed man ran off, but Col. Hendrix kicked me away as the serrated blade slid into his sleeve. I heard the grinding gears and sliding metal as the rifle barrel extended out from the colonel's cuff. Hendrix raised his arm and returned fire. Ignatius spun out of the way and fired.

In the confusion, I grabbed Genevieve and ducked behind a short wall. We darted up the stone stairs crouching to avoid the gun battle around us.

When his first two pistols emptied, Ignatius holstered them and quickly drew two more from his belt, sending a torrent of lead at the colonel.

Genevieve, Rodin, and I reached the top of the stairs and heard Ignatius call out in his Southern-mimicked European accent, "Keep running up the rock, I'll deal with this varmint."

Col. Hendrix fired again. "That's var-mit, yah European city-lover. If you ain't from the South—just shut yer mouth."

Ignatius holstered the second set of pistols and drew two more from shoulder holsters under his coat. I scanned the smoke shrouded street below, but the Colonel was gone, only his bullet-riddled bowler hat remained.

"Captain sent me to fetch you, good thing too, I don't think he was expecting you'd run into metal head," Ignatius said.

I holstered my Thumper. "Thank you, Mr. Peacemaker."

"You saved our lives," Genevieve said as she sheathed her saber.

Ignatius tipped his hat with one of his pistols. "My pleasure. Now let's get you two back to the ship."

CHAPTER 13

THE STORM VULTURE

Genevieve and I, with Ignatius right behind us, ran on to the airdocks as Mr. Singh stowed the crane inside the Sparrowhawk. Mr. Singh stepped up to the captain who casually leaned his elbow against the iron mooring clamps. "All is loaded."

I couldn't believe it. No one frantically prepared to leave.

Baldarich smiled and clapped his hands. "Excellent." He shook his head as we tried to catch our breaths. "Did they anger a vendor?"

Ignatius removed his hat and wiped the sweat from his brow. "No, I exchanged a few shots with their bronze-plated friend."

I pointed down the hill. "He paid a woman with black hair and some tattooed faced guy a bag of gold."

The captain's expression changed and he snapped up from the mooring. "Did she have silver skull-and-crossbones on her corset?"

Genevieve nodded. "Yes, she headed off and the two men chased us."

Urgency crept into the captain's voice as he said to Ignatius and Mr. Singh, "We're leaving! Fire up the engines and make this bird ready to fly." He pushed me and Genevieve onto the gangplank. "Get onboard and hope she doesn't see us."

I asked. "Who?"

"The dreaded Sky Pirate Zerelda, captain of the Storm Vulture." Baldarich checked the skies above and ushered everyone onto the Sparrowhawk. "She's the Anne Bonny of the European skies."

Mr. Singh began barking orders to the crew. "Baton the hatches and prepare the wingsails for deployment."

Ignatius ran for the bridge as Genevieve and I followed closely behind. Genevieve pulled me over by the maps.

Baldarich ordered Coyote, "Get me in the air." He flipped open the farthest left copper tube and yelled, "Gears, stoke the engines, be nice to her."

The frantic pace of everyone around me brought a tremble to my legs, this woman must be scary. But we were leaving, and I might lose this chance to rescue my father. I charged over to the captain. "We have to find Col. Hendrix's ship."

The captain ignored me.

"My father will be on that ship."

Coyote primed the engines, powering them in reverse and slowly pulled away from the moorings. Baldarich checked Ignatius who nodded and held up his thumb. I stepped in front of the captain, and though I feared getting punched out of the way, I stood my ground.

Baldarich loomed over me. "I highly doubt that, kid."

"Excuse me captain," Genevieve said. She walked over and stood beside me. "May I remind you that you are being paid for your services and have been chartered to find Professor Armitage? What is the point of traveling to Malta if he resides on a ship in the harbor below? Besides fleeing is exactly what this Zerelda will be expecting."

I looked around the bridge and saw Ignatius and Coyote

staring at the captain, Genevieve's words had challenged him, and they awaited his response.

Captain Baldarich smiled, put his hands on his hips, and threw his head back with a cackling laughter. "You both have spirit, I'll give you that. Coyote take us down; look for one leaving the harbor with its guns out."

Looking out the windows I watched as the wings unfurled. The Sparrowhawk dove over the harbor and skimmed the top of the high-masted merchant ships.

Rounding the Rock of Gibraltar I saw a ship with its gun ports open and a frantic crew running around on deck.

"Captain." I pointed toward the harbor. "There it is."

Baldarich looked out the window and smiled. "Coyote, bank right three degrees."

"Aye captain."

"Ignatius, get to the gun deck. Aim for the sails. I want to slow them, not sink them."

"Aye captain," Ignatius ran from the bridge, his dark brown duster billowing behind him.

Baldarich turned to Genevieve and me, "You two watch those dials and let me know if any of them go past the red lines."

I replied, "Aye Captain."

Excited to feel like part of the crew, I rushed over to the wall of large brass dials. The hands of the largest dials showed the three main engines running at sixty percent. The needle began to rise and I kept a keen eye on the red line at ninety percent.

I looked over the other dials and scales. Three marked Oldruck, monitored the oil pressure of each engine. One labeled Kraftstoff displayed fuel levels and looked full. Then I turned my attention to the dials labeled Helium-druck, which were well above the red lines.

The captain let out a guttural cry that startled me. "Bring the guns around."

"Aye captain." Coyote turned the wheel and stepped on one of the petals below him. The vessel banked to the right.

Captain Baldarich flipped open the farthest right copper tube and yelled, "Fire!"

The cannons roared and shook the deck under me. The rapid popping of the Gatling gun quickly followed.

I wanted to run to the window and watch the battle, but I'd been given an assignment. I worried about my father, but knew that stopping ships and not sinking them was a specialty of these Sky Raiders.

As we continued the turn, Genevieve sat in the chair and steadied herself with the brass railing that extended off the engineer's station.

The Sparrowhawk shuddered and lurched. I fell, slid across the bridge, and slammed into the map table.

One of the needles suddenly drop and Genevieve said, "We're losing engine one."

"Damn, that's the one on top." Baldarich flipped open the furthest left copper tube and clearly heard German cursing. "Gears, status report!"

"Some lead shot the size of my arse just ripped through the steam pipes, captain!"

Baldarich's head snapped up. "It's the Storm Vulture, take evasive action!"

Coyote pulled back on the wheel and the Sparrowhawk rose into the sky. I started to roll backward but caught the leg of the map table and pulled myself back to my feet. I returned to Genevieve's side.

Baldarich flipped open the furthest-right copper tube. "Ignatius, load the port guns. Prepare for a broadside." He walked over to Coyote. "Bring us alongside, and be quick about it."

Coyote nodded. "We'll get there captain."

I pressed against the port window encircled by bolted brass and saw the Storm Vulture flying alongside but traveling in the opposite direction. A very different design from the Sparrowhawk, it had a cylindrical fuselage with four propellers attached to the back of two fixed wings that sat below a large blimp. The front of the fuselage was made of square plates of glass that even extended to the underside. I saw Captain Zerelda standing defiantly, ordering her crew at a frantic pace.

Baldarich stroked his moustache, and winked at me. He opened the middle-right copper tube and said, "Mr. Singh, retract the wingsails. Coyote, dive and bank to port."

The Sparrowhawk lurched forward as Coyote pushed the wheel and spun it to the left. I watched the wingsails retract, the taut canvas folding over in the wind. Puffs of smoke lined the length of the Storm Vulture. Cannon balls soared just over Sparrowhawk.

I turned toward Captain Baldarich standing calm amidst the battle. The man had the steeled nerves of a naval captain and the swagger of a pirate.

The outer hull beside me exploded inward as an iron cannon ball ripped in and soared straight through the other side. I tumbled backward but was uninjured.

"Zerelda, you crafty minx. She saved a cannon knowing I'd duck." Baldarich leaned into the furthest-right copper tube. "Hunter, get topside." He yanked me back onto my feet. "Go to the conning tower and help Hunter raise the deck gun, hurry boy." Then he leaned back to the tubes and said, "Mr. Singh, I need those wingsails before we drop out of the sky."

I glanced at Genevieve who shut off the fuel, and monitored the other two engines. She looked at me with concern, I nodded and ran off.

The Sparrowhawk banked in the opposite direction but I continued down the corridor without missing a step. Perhaps I'd finally found my sky legs.

As I reached the conning tower, Hunter ran up from

below. We ducked into the little chamber that held a deck gun mounted on a vertical track.

Hunter grabbed the chain. "When the hatch opens pull this. I'm heading topside to man the gun. Once it's fully deployed, just keep feeding shells into this hopper. Got it?"

I took the chain. "Got it."

Hunter ran out the hatch and climbed up through the conning tower. I watched the hull. As it opened, sunlight poured down and a strong wind buffeted the hatch behind me. I pulled until my muscles strained and the cannon started to rise, but it took all my strength, and the rushing wind fought every heave.

Hunter called down from above, "Hurry, the Storm Vulture is turning around."

I pulled until the metal-grating base banged against the hull. Hunter slid a lever and locked it into place. Within moments he had loaded the first shell and the cannon fired. As Hunter opened the breach, the empty shell casing fell and I threw myself against the wall to avoid it. The next shell ran up a conveyer belt from the hopper and I checked to make certain another waited to take its place. Three more shells sat in the hopper. I held my ears as the cannon fired again.

A shadow chased away the light coming through the metal grating above. Running over to the conning tower, I looked up and saw the Storm Vulture above us.

Climbing the ladder I stuck my head out and felt the wind whip my face like sand paper. Through my biting vision, four grappling lines from the Storm Vulture sank into the vessel.

The doors on the bottom of the Storm Vulture opened and a large metal coil with two steel prongs extended out. I heard a crackling sound and the whirring of an engine. Huge bolts of lightning shot from the Storm Vulture and struck the Sparrowhawk. Everything sparked as the electrical current ran throughout the hull. The shock jolted me and I was tossed from the ladder. I fell down through the conning tower and smashed onto the planking below.

Captain Baldarich ran toward me. "You okay? I want you and Genevieve to hide with the Helium tanks."

All I managed was a strained, "Aye captain."

I struggled to my feet and ran for the bridge. I grabbed Genevieve by the shoulder. "Come on, the captain has ordered us to hide."

"Wait, we should help," Genevieve rose to her feet, but pulled away from me.

"I know, but the captain insisted."

Genevieve paused, but finally agreed and we ran to hide. As we passed the conning tower, I looked up and saw the Storm Vulture getting closer by drawing in the grappling lines.

I kicked open the hatch and we crawled inside. Slipping back beside one the large helium tanks we crouched together and listened as pirates landed on the hull above.

CHAPTER 14

THE CREW IS INTERROGATED

I counted at least twenty people landing on the hull above. The Sparrowhawk only had a crew of fifteen.

Genevieve moved closer to me and the smell of her hair filled my senses and made my mind spin until I'd almost forgotten about the crew.

I snapped back to reality when I heard Captain Zerelda's voice. It came from below in the engine room as she gathered the crew of the Sparrowhawk in the narrow confines surrounding the engines.

Zerelda's Dutch accent reverberated against the inner hull. "Bring Ignatius here, and you two keep scouring the ship, Baldarich and those two brats have to be here somewhere."

I crept over to a sliver of light shining into the compartment from the engine room below. A missing rivet in the seam allowed the two pieces of sheet metal to separate. I peered down into the engine room and saw Ignatius being dragged before Captain Zerelda. Blood gathered in the corner of his mouth and a large purple bruise formed beside his eye.

The sight nearly knocked the air out of me and my hands shook in anger.

One of Zerelda's men tied Ignatius to a support beam, and stepped aside. Tobias approached. Reaching behind, he pulled a long club connected by a cord and wound a crank on a small box on the back of his belt. He chuckled and leaned within a few inches of Ignatius. The gunslinger spit in Tobias's face and laughed. Tobias plunged the club into his stomach and it sparked with electricity.

Ignatius screamed, but laughed when he pulled it away. "Afraid to bruise your fists?"

"I'm asking the questions here." Tobias slammed the club back into Ignatius's gut with a smile, relishing the pain he caused as if it were the London symphony. "Where did Baldarich take the kids? Where are they hiding?"

Ignatius smiled and pulled against his bonds. "Is that all, it tickles."

Tobias plunged the club back into his ribs, the crew of the Sparrowhawk protested but their pleas went unanswered.

Genevieve tapped his shoulder and I slid back to let her see. I wondered what fiendish torture that pirate scumbag would come up with next. Genevieve gasped, and I wanted to know what happened, but couldn't ask. Genevieve rolled back away from the crack and I quickly replaced her.

I didn't like seeing my new friends being tortured. The gunslinger protected me. They all did. I couldn't believe they would. I was scared beyond all reason and wished that I could give of myself the way they did.

Zerelda grabbed Gears and strung him up to the same support beam as Ignatius.

She stepped in front of the two captives. "I want answers, so I'll ask politely, where is your captain hiding with the two little brats?" She waited a moment but no one answered. "Electricity, it's the future you know. The joyous wonder of this new age. It's beautiful. Lethal when you need it to be, and can heal many an ailment, but I like it best as a motivational tool."

The man with the tattooed face first struck Ignatius in the neck and then slammed the heavy club into Gears, just above his belt. Both screamed in pain, but neither said a word.

Captain Zerelda pointed to Coyote. "Let's see if I can get *him* to talk."

Tobias threw Coyote into the little storage unit and shut the door behind Zerelda.

I pulled away from the crack, unable to continue watching.

Genevieve looked at me and the usual fire in her eyes had faded, replaced with sadness, and unease. I wanted to turn myself over to Zerelda, to end the torment of people I had started to call friend, but that would make their noble effort worthless. I slid closer to her, the scent of her brought me comfort but the next screams made me cringe.

Zerelda's words ran through his mind and I realized she was still looking for the captain. I whispered to Genevieve, "She thinks the captain is with us."

Genevieve's amber eyes lit up. "We should try and help him."

"But we don't know where he is. Maybe we can create a distraction."

Genevieve nodded in agreement, but as we started to creep away a hand reached out from behind one of the helium tanks and snatched my shoulder. I started to scream, to fight, but a hand crossed over my mouth silencing me. Genevieve whipped around, her expression made me stop fighting.

Baldarich sternly whispered, "I told you both to wait here."

I pointed to the crack and whispered, "But they're killing them down there."

Captain Baldarich leaned over the crack and spied on the situation below. I leaned over him and tried to see too.

Zerelda stomped her heels on the grating as she charged out of the storage room and over to the boiler.

"Maybe some cooking will soften those tongues of yours." Zerelda yanked on the exhaust handle of the boiler. "Have I told you about the joys of steam?"

A blast of white hot steam burst from the nozzle and engulfed the two men. They screamed as the burning vapor seared them. Baldarich cringed and clenched his fist until the skin on his knuckles turned white. I saw the vapor rising through the crack, but still Gears and Ignatius said nothing.

I heard Zerelda as she stormed out of the engine room and said, "If they won't talk when they're in pain maybe they'll talk when another's in pain. Bring the Sikh."

Genevieve and I slipped over to the hatch and Baldarich followed. We heard Zerelda one floor below and slipped over to peer through the seam of the cargo doors. Zerelda appeared with Mr. Singh. She ordered her men to tie a rope to his legs. I wondered what was happening but Baldarich twisted his fist in his palm.

Zerelda leaned close to Mr. Singh's ear. "One chance. Tell me where they are."

Mr. Singh, his turban removed, had been forced to his knees before the pirate captain. His long dark hair whipped around his face as he stared with unwavering courage. "As part of my faith, I must resist tyranny in all its forms. I am ready to meet my god, are you?"

Zerelda pushed Mr. Singh out the cargo door with her boot heel. "Say hello for me."

Genevieve gasped.

Baldarich turned to the two youngsters and cracked his knuckles until I thought he broken them. "Damn that sky-witch! We're taking back my ship."

CHAPTER 15

RETAKING THE SPARROWHAWK

Captain Baldarich pulled me over to the conning tower. "When you hear all hell break loose I need you to cut the grappling lines. Take this bowie knife." The captain handed me a huge knife with a curved tip and walked over to Genevieve. "You and I need to create a diversion."

Genevieve unsheathed her saber. "I'll distract Zerelda."

"No you won't," Baldarich silenced himself to a whisper. "She's too dangerous."

I nodded. "I agree."

"If someone doesn't distract her she'll organize her men and we'll all be captured. Danger isn't something we can avoid."

I waited for Baldarich to tell her how crazy she was, but from the way he stroked his moustache, I knew he was thinking about her argument.

Baldarich slapped my back. "Get in place."

I nodded, grabbed a pair of brass and leather goggles and quietly climbed the conning tower's ladder. Genevieve followed Baldarich to the stairs. I slipped onto the Sparrowhawk, and the fierce wind whipped my hair.

The Storm Vulture hovered alongside and the grappling

lines drooped across the sky, connecting the two vessels like clotheslines hung between buildings.

Leaning over the edge, I saw Mr. Singh dangling just above the waves. It wrenched my heart to see my friend treated like a bag of tea.

An idea struck, like the lightning gun on the underside of the Storm Vulture.

Grabbing hold of the nearest grappling line with my hands and feet, I shimmed over to the other vessel. Halfway across, I dared to look down. Fear seized me but I couldn't stop. Several crewmen heaved Mr. Singh out of the water and then released the rope plunging him back into the Mediterranean. After dragging Mr. Singh through several waves they hauled him up several feet. I heard Zerelda yelling and moved faster.

I climbed onto the fuselage of the Storm Vulture. As I looked around I noticed the hydrogen tank connected to the fuselage with metal straps but a latch secured the strap. I pulled the bowie knife from the leather strap that wound around me.

The flash of sharpened steel drew my eye inside the open cargo doors on the Sparrowhawk's main deck. Zerelda smacked Gustav in the back of his head with the hilt of her sword sending him sprawling to the deck. Then she pulled Hunter close and kicked him toward the open cargo door. I hoped the captain would strike soon.

Being careful not to alert the crew still inside the Storm Vulture, I slipped over to the nearest latch. I pried it open with my bowie knife. It snapped back, whipping by my face. I jumped back. "Whoa! That was close." I looked around, but no one investigated. No one on the Sparrowhawk noticed either.

I slid along the side of the Storm Vulture and used the knife to unlatch two more. As I moved to the fourth strap, I saw a cloud of steam erupt on the main-deck of the

Sparrowhawk. Baldarich's signal.

I saw Genevieve step through the billowing steam cloud. Bolts of lightning from Baldarich's hand cannon arced behind her.

Genevieve raised her sword. "Captain Zerelda, your time is through."

Zerelda emerged from the white wall of fog. "Baldarich, you sent a girl to die."

Genevieve's sword cut through the steam. "I know what I'm doing."

"We'll see."

Genevieve ducked and avoided Zerelda's cutlass only to have her attack blocked by the sky pirate.

Genevieve fought well, really well, but I cringed as Zerelda's sword missed.

"Aarrhhh." Zerelda swung her cutlass wildly but a calculated Genevieve met her every stroke.

She fought just like her father had at Eton.

A bolt of electricity coursed between Genevieve and Zerelda, one of the captain's shots I bet. I had to stop watching. I had a job to do, too.

The Storm Vulture listed to one side and the strap next to me snapped from the pressure. I had done enough. Now I needed to get out of there.

I ran and leapt onto the grappling line. Snagging the rope with my arm, I struggled not to fall. I wrapped the braided line around me and secured it under my armpit.

Then I did the dumbest thing I'd ever done: I cut the rope behind me.

The wind rushed past me as I swung like a pendulum toward the Sparrowhawk.

"Alexander!" Genevieve's voice cut through the air. She'd seen me jump. As I dangled below the Sparrowhawk, I shoved the bowie knife into my leather strap and climbed, hand over hand, up the rope.

I grabbed hold of the yardarm of the wingsail and pulled myself onto the stretched canvas. Through the open cargo door all I saw were shapes darting through the dissipating clouds of steam. All I heard was the ringing of steel on steel and the stomping of shoes on the wooden deck. Sword fights and hand-to-hand combat. I hoped my friends could hold their own. I had one more task.

"Zerelda," I yelled at the top of my lungs. "Your ship is about to plunge into the sea!" I climbed up the ribbing to the first grappling line and cut it free with my knife. The Storm Vulture shook and lurched in the sky. I looked down at the deck. Zerelda screamed, and I smiled. I cut the next two grappling lines, and the crewmen of the Storm Vulture flooded out of the conning tower. I saw Tobias and knew I was in trouble, but I had to keep going. I had to cut the last line.

Tobias looked up and drew his pistol. I dove and grabbed hold of the last grappling line to keep from sliding off the Sparrowhawk. Shots rang out but flew overhead. I pulled myself back atop the vessel and drew the Thumper from my holster. Too far to strike Tobias, I hoped the flash would make him run.

I popped up and pushed the trigger, the loud shot made the men drop, and the concussive blast knocked the tattooed man on his backside. Several crewmen grabbed the drop lines they'd used to board the Sparrowhawk, and leapt off as they desperately tried to get back to the Storm Vulture. Tobias jumped onto one of the lines and swung out over the sea. I stood and grabbed the last grappling line as Zerelda emerged from the conning tower.

She raised her revolver and fired down into the conning tower. She reached for a drop line, but they were all gone. "Mutinous cowards!"

I looked at the grappling line and then at Zerelda. All that stood between her and escape was me. Her jaw clenched as she saw the Storm Vulture pitch downward, hanging by only a couple of straps. Then her eyes widened in rage, and she raised her revolver and pointed it at my heart.

With nowhere to run and no place to hide, my heart pounded in my ears, and I couldn't draw a breath. Terrified, I squeezed my eyes shut

A click. An empty chamber. A stream of curses. And then I opened my eyes as Zerelda charged with her cutlass raised. I raised my Thumper and bowie knife. A club and knife in a swordfight, those were bad odds.

I tumbled backward as she swung and quickly righted myself to prepare for her next attack, but instead of pursuing me, Zerelda grabbed the grappling line.

She glared, her eyes pools of seething anger, as if molten lava hid behind them. "I'll remember this, *boy*. I'll remember you."

Zerelda cut the grappling line with her cutlass and swung out over the water. She soared in an elegant arc over to the Storm Vulture, and her crew pulled her to safety.

I couldn't believe my plan actually worked. I ran for the conning tower and slid down the ladder to find Genevieve. She and Hunter leaned out the cargo door. I called her name and she spun around.

"Alexander!" She pushed her wind-blown hair out of her eyes and smiled. Her relief that I was okay was obvious, but she had other things to worry about, too. "I'm so glad you're safe." She returned her attention to the cargo door. "Indihar!"

Remembering that he still dangled in the Mediterranean Sea, I leaned out as far as I dared and saw Mr. Singh just above the waves. Genevieve's hand went to her mouth and I noticed slack in the line. Mr. Singh looked deep in concentration. He was levitating just above the white tips of the water.

"How is he doing that?" I asked.

Hunter smiled. "Indian magic, he is a powerful and mysterious warrior."

Genevieve nodded. "When my father and I were in India we heard tales about men who could twist into amazing shapes, levitate, and even disappear."

Hunter grabbed the rope and tossed part to me. "Help me pull him up."

Hunter and I drew the rope hand-over-hand until Mr. Singh grabbed hold of the cargo door and pulled himself in.

Mr. Singh dripped water on the metal grating and his long hair clung to his face. He smiled at the three of us and said, "Thank you. I thought all the blood in my body was going to start coming out my ears." He turned to me and extended his hand. "I witnessed your actions on the Storm Vulture, very brave."

"Brave," Genevieve said. "Foolish is more like it! You could have been killed."

"*I* could have been killed? *You* were the one in a swordfight with a pirate."

Genevieve scoffed and put her hands on her hips. "I've trained with the blade, you … you could have slipped and fallen into the sea."

Hunter chuckled. "Both of you are too young to care about the danger, but that's probably why you survived. It's good to have you back on board, Mr. Singh."

"It is good to be back. Luckily, my god did not want me this day."

Hunter closed the cargo door as the Sparrowhawk pulled away from the listing Storm Vulture. The four of us headed for the bridge.

As we entered, Captain Baldarich hugged Mr. Singh like a bear. "That sky-witch couldn't drown you!" Then he turned and grabbed me. "You damn fool, that's the bravest

and dumbest move I've ever seen. Wish I'd thought of it."
He tried to calm down and made a grand gesture of bowing
deeply to Genevieve. "Wonderful skill milady, I salute you.
And Zerelda's damn good, too."

Genevieve curtsied and I sighed, relieved to have
Zerelda's Sky Pirates off the Sparrowhawk.

Baldarich spun on his heel and said to Coyote, "Good
you're mostly unhurt. Head for that bank of clouds to the
North. We'll use them to cover our escape."

Coyote pulled back on the wheel, though he winced in
pain. "We're leaving captain."

I walked up to the copper tubes. "She got away, I
couldn't stop her. She said that she'd remember this, that
she'd remember me."

"That's not the last we'll see of her," Baldarich winked.
"But it'll take her days to fix what you did. You bought us
time. Maybe your dad named you right after all."

I smiled.

My father and the ship we were following had vanished,
but I wondered if he was even on it. I had a feeling in my
gut he wasn't. The baron's voice crept into the back of my
mind—they needed my father in Malta to translate. Just
thinking the word reassured me. Malta was where I would
find him.

Genevieve put her hand on my shoulder, "I'm sorry we
didn't recue your father."

"It's okay; we'll find him in Malta. I know we will."

CHAPTER 16

MALTA

Genevieve and I joined in to help as the crew worked feverously to finish the repairs. We both felt like Sky Raiders now and were grateful everyone on the crew seemed to feel the same.

I held the outer hull plating in place as Ignatius welded, turning my head and squeezing my eyes shut to avoid the intense light. Each flash reminded me of the Storm Vulture's lightning cannon and made me wonder what Col. Hendrix was paying Zerelda for. As the metal liquefied and filled the seam, my mind wandered to the island of Malta. *Where was my father? Was he being tortured?* I couldn't shake the nagging feeling of dread, but I couldn't let myself get obsessed, either. My priority had to be my father. I had to find him, rescue him, and get him back home. And then Genevieve. I had to help her find the antidote to her father's poison, too. I had to help her because….

Ignatius pulled the torch away and lifted the dark-lens goggles to his forehead, "Hey, the plate's slipping."

"Sorry," I shook my head and held the plate firm. "My mind wandered." I looked over at Genevieve who was helping Gears repair the steam pipe.

Ignatius chuckled. "I see why."

"What? No! She's a noblewoman. I mean…." I stumbled over my words and looked up as she wiped sweat and grime from her face. A smudge of grease crossed her cheek and a slight smile brightened her face when she saw me looking at her. "No," I blushed and turned back to Ignatius. "I was thinking about my father."

Ignatius shook his head. "Yeah, my father makes me smile like that, too."

The gunslinger fired up the welding torch again, lowered his goggles, and returned to sealing the hull.

Gustav came into the engine room carrying a large platter balanced on his shoulder. "Stop working everyone, I have treats for the brave champions of the Sparrowhawk," he bellowed, trying to be heard over all the activity. He walked straight over to Genevieve. "Ladies first. For your amazing swordfight with the sky-witch." He displayed the platter before the young noblewoman with an air of gentility I'd not thought possible. "Potato bread smothered in a honey-butter glaze, my specialty."

Genevieve wiped her hands with a rag and picked one of the rolls. "Thank you, but I only kept her busy."

"A hero's modesty," Gustav passed over Gears, who reached with his grimy hand to snatch one, and laid the platter before me. "You're next, young man. You get two for your brazen, foolhardy, and incredibly brave attack on Zerelda's ship."

I looked to Ignatius who nodded his head. I let the steel plate go and grabbed two rolls. I bit into the first one and moaned in delight. It was so good, so rich and sweet. I closed my eyes as I devoured the first one, but took my time with the second, savoring every flavor on my tongue. They smelled like grandma's house and tasted like ambrosia.

Gustav smiled and put the platter in front of Ignatius as Gears tried to reach for another.

The hatch swung open and Captain Baldarich strolled

in. He saw Gustav's platter of rolls and rushed forward, forcing Gears to divert around the damaged engine. "Potato rolls! And you drizzled them in honey butter. This is why I'll never have another chef."

Gustav smiled and swung the platter around. "Only the best."

Captain Baldarich snagged two rolls and pulled Genevieve and I closer. "Gustav is the best chef I've ever known, he probably would have served the Kaiser if he'd been born to a higher station. But the Kaiser's loss keeps my belly round."

Gustav chuckled and offered the captain another roll. With a sweep of his free hand, he looked around the engine room at the sweaty, greasy group and said, "Who wants to serve the Kaiser when you can see the world and meet a much better class of people?"

We all laughed and Baldarich swiped two more rolls. He tossed one in his mouth. Gears came around the engine and reached for one, but Gustav swung the tray away from him again.

Baldarich, his mouth crammed with rolls said, "Gears … just who I was lookin' for." He held up his hand and swallowed. "Can we repair the engine on route?"

"Yeah, I think I can get her running. Give me half a day and one of those rolls. I'll have her purring like a kitten."

Gustav eyed Gears, and Baldarich asked Ignatius, "We all patched?"

He lifted the dark-lens goggles and smiled. "Aye captain. There wasn't as much damage as there could have been."

Captain Baldarich swiped another roll and stopped at the door. "Ignatius, I want you to verify that all the repairs have been made. I want everything water tight. Gears, get that engine purring. I want all three engines by the time we get to Malta." Pointing his roll at Genevieve and I he said, "You two, clean up in here, and thanks for all your help. Gustav, give Gears some rolls and then make another batch."

The captain left and Ignatius followed. Gustav huffed and stood with the platter on his shoulder. A few inches short, Gears took the needle-nose pliers from his belt and snagged a roll, but before Gustav could walk away, he tossed it to his open hand and snagged one more. Gustav swung around and saw the smug look on Gears dirt smudged face. Gustav begrudgingly smiled and left as the contented engineer stuck his head back into the engine.

I couldn't help but laugh at Gustav and Gears, Baldarich and Ignatius, men whom I now considered my friends, and pledged that I would live up to their example. For a start, I made certain I thoroughly cleaned the welding torch and placed it in the storage locker. As Genevieve picked up the tools she and Gears used to fix the steam pipes, I stepped over and swung around the pipe in front of her. As the hot metal seared my palms, I let go and jumped back, waiving and blowing on my hands for relief. Genevieve laughed as I danced around, but she reached out to check my palms, a hint of concern in her eyes. I smiled to make light of it, but I'm sure my "smile" was nothing more than a pained and red-faced grimace. I tried to cover up the mistake by leaning oh-so-nonchalantly against the hull and ignoring the red blooming on my skin. The injury could have been much worse and was probably only a first-degree burn. The real injury I suffered was from third-degree embarrassment.

Rodin flew through the door and fluttered around Genevieve. He landed on her shoulder with a roll tucked between his claws. Rodin tore into the top of the bread where the drizzled honey butter pooled. Genevieve and I looked toward the door wondering if Gustav would be running through.

No knife-wielding, yelling chef appeared; the little dragon was safe.

We slipped down to our room on the gun-deck and sat on the crates. Rodin flew over to his spot and tucked up with the last of his roll.

"I didn't think he'd like bread. I assumed he'd be a meat-eater."

"Don't let him fool you, he wanted the honey. He has a taste for sweets."

I laughed. "We have a lot in common, then. I like sweets, too."

Genevieve was quiet, and I wondered what she was thinking. I shifted in my seat trying to think of something else to say, but I was afraid anything that came out of my mouth might be mushy or sound stupid, so I said nothing. After a moment, she spoke again. "I wish you could have seen Zerelda's face when she saw her ship."

"I heard her, for sure. She sounded none too happy."

"You've made an enemy of a dangerous pirate, aren't you afraid?"

"Nah, I don't plan to become her friend, and besides if she comes around again, you'll be here to protect me. You and your sword."

"You Americans, so cavalier, so free, sometimes I envy you." She got up and climbed into her hammock. "Instead of sword fighting, I'll end up having to attend to my husband's courtly obligations, imprisoned in bejeweled high collars and caged in whalebone corsets."

"Never!" I jumped on a crate and drew out an imaginary sword. "You'll end up like Shakespeare's Kate."

"You call me a shrew?" Genevieve protested.

"No!" I sputtered. "I'm just saying ... you'll never be tamed by a corset, whalebone or otherwise." I chuckled. "I think Shakespeare must have had you in mind when he wrote the tale."

Genevieve closed her eyes and a wide smile crept across her face. My heart thudded in against my ribcage. I jumped and almost fell off the crate when she sat up suddenly, her hammock swaying. She looked down at her dirty hands, "I'm a mess. I'm going to wash up before dinner."

She scooted out of the hammock and headed for the door, then stopped. She turned, walked back to where I was still standing on the crate. Puzzled I gazed down at her, and she rose to her tip toes, slipped her hands along the side of my face, drew me down to her, and kissed me lightly, her full lips brushing mine for what must have been just an instant but felt like an eternity. Electricity coursed through me and I was still standing there dumbfounded and dizzy as she turned and darted through the door. My fingertips rubbed the spot where her lips had been mere moments before, and my smile grew to goofy dimensions as everything went blurry.

I now understood Zerelda's interest in electricity.

* * *

After dinner, Genevieve and I strolled up to the bridge with the captain. Ignatius sat at the engineer's station, and Coyote was at the wheel, but I noticed the crew wasn't gathered on deck the way they usually were in the evening. Tension tugged at faces, pulling smiles into grim, tight frowns. Few spoke and then only in murmured tones. What was going on?

Ignatius's eyes focused on something in the distance, and I turned to see faint dots of flickering lights amidst a sea of black. An island! I snapped a questioning gaze at the captain.

"Malta." He nodded and walked to the pilot's wheel. Scanning the darkness, he pointed to an open patch of sea. "There, put us down on that moonlit patch, the water's calm enough."

Coyote pushed the wheel forward. "Aye, captain.

Shouldn't be an issue, I could probably set down on the edge to hide us in the shadows."

"Very good," Baldarich said and turned to Ignatius. "Make certain nothing leaks." Ignatius nodded and the captain flipped open all four copper messaging pipes. "Extinguish all lights and prepare for a water landing."

I ran to the window and watched as the black water moved ever closer. The silver moonlight shimmered on the tips of the seemingly small waves. *We were really going to land on water?* This ship never stopped surprising me. What could be next?

The captain leaned into the middle-right copper tube. "Retract the wingsails and seal the outer hatches."

"The Sparrowhawk can float?"

The captain winked. "She can do more than that."

"Can it travel below the water as well?" Genevieve asked.

Baldarich just nodded and smiled as the Sparrowhawk skittered across the waves until it settled in, cradled by the water. I looked out and saw about a third of the ship submerged below the waterline. Propellers churned the water and pushed the Sparrowhawk forward, cutting through the black and leaving a frothy wake trailing behind us. The vessel moved like any other ship I had been on.

Then the farthest left copper tube popped open and Gears' thick accent echoed out. "Engines are purring captain. Engine one will be completely fixed by sunrise, especially if I can turn it off."

"Go ahead."

Ignatius walked on the bridge. "Any leaks?" the captain asked.

"Not even the patches."

"Good job," the captain said, with a quick glance toward me. We all watched as the island drew nearer, and I found myself breathing faster, hands clasped tight on the railing. The captain and Ignatius climbed up the ladder and onto the conning tower. I couldn't wait. I put my foot on the ladder and turned toward Genevieve. She gave me an excited smile, and up I went with her following close behind me. As we climbed, Rodin flitted around and finally landed on her shoulder.

The captain raised a telescope to his eye, extending the brass and wooden optics with a brisk *snap*. Ignatius kept an eye on the surrounding sky and sea looking for any trouble. I walked along the top of the vessel toward the bow and heard Genevieve behind me with Rodin's wings clicking softly as they ruffled in the breeze.

I stared toward the city of Valetta. Malta didn't look very big, but it was big enough to make finding my father nearly impossible. I sat down, and Genevieve lowered herself beside me. Rodin flew around us then soared out over the water. I felt the light pressure of Genevieve's hand on my shoulder and took comfort in it.

She leaned in, speaking into my ear as if telling me a secret. "Maybe we can sneak onto the island and ask some of the Maltese if they've seen your father?"

"I can *feel* him, almost *see* him. I know he's close." I stared at the island, but what I felt wasn't longing. More like an intense sense of knowing. "I can see the room he's being held in, it has bars on the window but it looks out to sea."

"What else do you see?"

"A white building with arches, a walkway of columns that leads to his room. He walks this way every day to go to the library. A white house, but the base is different somehow. There is another room in the bowels of the villa. It's dark … I don't want to see anymore." I rubbed my hands over my eyes and then threw my hands up and turned toward her. "This is ridiculous. How am I seeing these things? They seem so real, but how can they be? And if they are real, somehow, why am I seeing *places* instead of my father."

Rodin landed on Genevieve's shoulder with his head

cocked to the side. "I think *you* are seeing him. I don't know how you're doing it, but I think you're seeing where your father is being held." She scrambled to her feet and ran over to the conning tower. I got up and followed her.

"Captain," she said, excitement in her voice. "I know this will sound crazy, but I think we're looking for a white villa with an arched colonnade. It will have a sea view and the base is probably a darker stone."

"How do you know this?" Captain Baldarich looked down at her.

"Alexander saw it. He had a vision, and I think he knows where his father is."

"Captain, I have no idea what I was saying." I tried to stop this nonsense before we wasted time on my incoherent ramblings.

Still scanning the shore with his telescope, the captain pointed to the other side of the cove. "No idea what you were saying, huh?"

I gripped the rail and leaned over, peering into the dark. There, perched atop a cliff, was a villa glowing white in the moonlight, complete with an arched, covered walkway leading across the back with a large, plain square building on one side. I couldn't believe it, the villa was exactly as I had described.

CHAPTER 17

UNDERWATER

Captain Baldarich stepped up to Ignatius. "Have Coyote get as close as he can to that villa."

"Aye captain." The gunslinger nodded and slid down the ladder, his coat billowing like an airship's balloon.

The captain ran his fingers along his mustache and sideburns, then pointed at Genevieve and me. "You two go get ready. We're going ashore."

I motioned to the door like a gentleman. Genevieve curtsied and ran off with Rodin shadowing her. I bowed to the captain and sprinted after her.

Once in our room, I collected everything I might need to free my father. I knew I needed to carry the weapons I'd gathered, so I strapped the Thumper to my leg and slipped my bowie knife into the belt behind my back. The act of securing them to my body and knowing they were there if I'd need them was comforting—and made me feel powerful. *But could I use them again?* I'd fired the Thumper and I'd almost taken down an entire airship, but still the idea of shooting someone deflated me faster than popping a soap bubble.

I'd do whatever I needed to do to rescue my father, so I put those thoughts aside and threw on my leather coat and dumped the contents of my bag, filling it with rope and a powder charge from the room we were staying in.

Genevieve, on the other side of the room, hooked her saber to her side and slipped into her long, blue coat. She called for Rodin and he landed on her shoulder.

"You look..." I paused too long, and her face started to harden. *Oh no!* I swallowed hard. "...like a knight."

Her face softened, she smiled and looked me up and down. "You look just right."

"Right?" I pushed the hair from my face.

"Just right for a rescue mission," she nodded with that glint of fire in her eye, and I knew we were ready.

She squeezed my hand, and we ran back to the conning tower where we found Mr. Singh standing beside the captain, looking ready for war. His blue turban and tunic were impeccable, but it was the three circular chakrams—steel bladed rings—hanging on one side, the curved shamshir sword on the other, and the katar punch dagger with a gun barrel on each side of the handle that made him truly intimidating.

"He looks like a warrior," Genevieve whispered.

Ignatius stood on the other side of the captain in his dark duster and matching cowboy hat. Hunter sat atop the airship with his rifles lying next to him.

Captain Baldarich waved his hands to gather everyone around him. "I don't know how he is doing it, but Alexander knows where his dad is. He is seeing it somehow, and he and Genevieve are going to be are guides. Ignatius, don't shoot anyone until I tell you. Mr. Singh, stay silent and use your blades. Hunter is our support and back-up." He walked over and put his hands on my shoulder. "If I'm gonna get paid, I'm gonna have to keep you two safe, so here are the rules: Alexander, don't fire that Thumper unless I say so, and Genevieve, use that sword to protect the two of you. But no heroics. Understand?"

Genevieve and I glanced at each other and then nodded.

Baldarich clapped us both on the back. "Good. Now, let's go rescue this professor."

"But how do we get to the island?" I asked. Towering limestone cliffs dominated the shoreline, and the villa perched on top looked inaccessible from the sea. This place wasn't a house. It was a fortress. Looking up at the formidable landscape, doubt began to eat away at my courage.

"It's too shallow for the ship to get any closer, the bottom would be shredded by rocks. And we don't want to risk being seen rowing toward shore in the small boats." The captain pointed toward the crewmen arranging coiled hoses. "So, we walk."

"Walk? How?" I asked. Then the crew brought large brass helmets on deck, heavy metal-clad boots, and stretched out thick canvas suits with lead-weighted belts set atop them.

"Put these on over your clothes."

"What are they?" Genevieve asked.

"I bought them off a Venetian merchant who claimed they were designed by Leonardo DaVinci. I doubted it, but it was a good line, and they work great." Baldarich bent to pick up one of the suits. "They're waterproofed with a coating of oils and saps. Keeps you as dry and as warm as possible. Sorry," he looked at Genevieve, "we don't have lady sizes."

"I will manage." She smiled.

I climbed into one of the suits. The bulky, stiff material scratched my skin, but appeared sturdy enough to keep out the sea—and the sea creatures. Like an oversized collar, a heavy brass ring and rubber seal sat on my neck and shoulders, making it hard to stand upright.

I looked over at Genevieve. The oversized suit swallowed her, bunched up around the metal boots and hanging from every part of her. Mine didn't fit much better and standing next to her, we sent the crew into fits of laughter.

Once suited up, Baldarich bent down. "Looks don't matter. Down there, the water will make you buoyant, hence the heavy boots and belt. But there are a few rules. One, stay on your feet; falling over will make the helmet fill with water. Two, watch your hose, don't let it snag on anything. And third, it will be dark, and you'll see things you've never imagined, but I doubt anything can hurt you. So don't go insane down there. Got it?"

Genevieve and I nodded.

"Good."

I really wanted him to elaborate on the dark, creature-filled deep that I could all too easily imagine. Thoughts of sharks, giant squids, sea monsters, and other creatures swam into my mind, but I kept my mouth shut. There was plenty under the water that could hurt me, even the water.

The captain stepped up with one of the brass helmets. "This ring locks onto the suits. I'll warn you it's heavy, but once you get underwater, you'll hardly feel it."

Baldarich placed the helmet over my head and locked it in place. The last of his instructions echoed through the cavernous dome. The captain was right. It pressed down on my shoulders and made me unsteady enough to fear tumbling into the sea. Holding on to the conning tower, I tried to look at the others. I stared out through a small circular window, but couldn't see much. Turning my head did nothing—the helmet didn't move—so I shifted my entire body, but that only made me wobble on the pitching deck. Gripping the conning tower as if it would anchor me to the world, I waited for the others to get ready.

Finally, Baldarich plunged into the water and the hose attached to his helmet chased after him.

I didn't want to follow. As I stared at the inky darkness, Mr. Singh and Ignatius stepped off and disappeared into the depths. I looked at Genevieve.

"Together?" Genevieve asked in a hollow echo that barely escaped her brass helmet.

"Together."

We stepped off the Sparrowhawk and the churning water enveloped us in a cloud of bubbles. Falling feet first like a stone quickened my breathing. It felt unnatural not to be floating on the surface. Greeted by endless night we sank until we struck the seafloor with a gentle thump. The air filled the suit making it stiff and bulbous, and I felt like an oversized balloon. The lead weights on my belt and boots secured me to the ground, but didn't feel nearly as heavy down here. Indeed, I felt almost light on my feet and with a bounce in my step, I spent a moment getting accustomed to moving underwater. After a few moments, I felt safer than I thought possible.

Peering up through the window atop the helmet, I saw flashes of color drifting in the current and the silvery moon shimmering on the surface. Genevieve came up beside me, and together we moved toward a light bobbing in the dark.

Captain Baldarich raised a large battery-operated lantern and held up his thumb to see if we were all right. I returned the gesture and Genevieve tried, but had trouble getting the oversized glove to cooperate.

The wildlife on the sea floor stunned me. Creatures clung to the coral and strange plants swayed in the current but remained anchored to the rocky outcroppings. I could feel the rhythm of the waves lapping against the cliff. Several small but brightly colored fish circled my helmet. What on the surface seemed like a barren desert hid a myriad of life below its watery veil.

I wanted to explore and could stay here forever, but I had a mission.

We plodded along the sea floor marveling at the sights, heading ever closer to the shore, ever closer to the surface. I climbed up a small rock shelf and almost fell backward as the biggest creature I'd ever seen lunged toward my head, jaws open, jagged razor-sharp teeth bared. An eel. The long, sinewy animal whipped out from a crevice and my heart nearly stopped. But, just as quickly as it appeared, it retreated back into its den.

Captain Baldarich shut off the light as we approached shore. Slowly the surface grew closer as we ascended the rocky shoreline. The waves pushed the suit but the lead weights made it easy to withstand them. When my helmet finally broke the surface and the beads of water ran down the window in front of me, I wondered what it would be like during the day. I would have to go diving again, next time with sunlight filtering below the surface.

Once on shore, we slipped out of the suits, heavy brass helmets, and oversized boots, and then reconnected the pieces so it looked like flattened versions of us lying on the beach. After the captain tugged his hose three times in short succession as a signal, the crew back on the Sparrowhawk retrieved the suits by drawing them back by the hoses. Now we were on the shore with no way to get back to the ship. It was time to find my father.

We'd come to this island for a reason, and it was time to get serious about that mission. I couldn't let my father down. I heard the soft whir of Rodin's wing beats and turned as Genevieve held out her arm and Rodin flew in and landed. Genevieve's expression was one of grim determination, and I was glad she was with me.

CHAPTER 18

THE GOLDEN CIRCLE

Captain Baldarich led us up the side of the cliff using a switch-back trail. It was the only way from the sea, and I hoped it would be empty this late at night. The captain was cautious and we all followed his example, treading softly and keeping our eyes and ears open for any unusual sights or sounds.

We finally reached the top of the cliff and slipped along the arched colonnade I'd seen in my vision. As I approached the large square building, I saw bars on one of the windows above. This was the place. I felt it with every step.

We crept as silently as possible. Noises came from the far side of the other building. I knew my father was near. *But where? And where were his kidnappers?*

We entered through an unlocked doorway and found the villa full of rooms with contrasting styles. The first room was lavishly decorated with Greek murals while the next looked as barren as that of a cloistered monk. We walked through the rooms on the first floor, but confronted no one. No guards. No servants. No one.

We came to a staircase and the captain turned to look at me. He pointed up with a questioning look, and I nodded. So he led the way and we headed up to the second floor where we discovered a door with bars in the middle.

The captain peered in and motioned to me. Inside I saw an empty cot, a tattered blanket, and a straw-strewn floor. A cool breeze carried the aroma of the sea from the opened window.

I pushed the latch and the cell door opened with the squeal of grinding metal. I walked into the empty room.

Baldarich leaned into the cell and whispered, "Now where?"

"He's either in the library or the dark place."

The captain stared me in the eye and said, "Your call, kid."

"The dark place."

"You sure?"

"No, but I've got a feeling that he's not in the library. Not tonight."

"Yeah," Baldarich said. "I doubt he'd be in the library at this time of night."

"If we were back at home, he'd definitely be in the library. Or in his office." I stepped out into the corridor.

"So where's this dark place?" Ignatius asked.

"Down a long flight of stairs. That's all I know."

Genevieve spoke up. "What about that stairway tucked away near the colonnade where we first entered?"

"I saw it, too. That must be it." Mr. Singh said.

Baldarich placed his hand on Mr. Singh's arm. "You lead the way."

Once back on the first floor, we walked toward the room we first entered. It was lavishly decorated with fine antique desks and tables. At first I thought we might be in a library, but there were no books—only trinkets.

I ran my hand over a beautiful bronze astrolabe perched on a shelf. I walked under an orrery, the planets spinning around a brightly lit sun atop a marble pillar. On a nearby table sat a spiked manacle with chains, but the spikes were arranged around the inside. I bumped a table and saw a golden chain with small studs and claws arranged like charms. It looked like a medieval torture device, and I didn't want to know what it was for.

Genevieve pointed to a large map, a mural painted on one of the walls, and I stopped in my tracks. I suddenly knew where we were. This villa was the home of a Knight of the Golden Circle.

I stepped forward to examine it more closely. It was a finely rendered map of the world with three golden circles overlaying much of it. The detail of it amazed me. One of the three circles was painted around the American south: Confederate country. The second circle enveloped the first along with Mexico, Central America and the American West. The third encompassed the other two and all of Europe and the Mediterranean Sea.

Perhaps the mural showed spheres of influence. Maybe the goals of some grand plan, but beside me a beautiful, immaculately painted, carved wooden globe with a shining golden line encircling the equator made their ambitions perfectly clear. Complete domination of the world.

Baldarich pushed Ignatius and the others. "Keep moving. He's not here."

I nodded and shuddered. This room gave me a sickening feeling that crawled up my spine. I wanted to get my father and get out of here. We moved out of this wretched museum and back out to the colonnade.

Tucked back in a corner, a stone stairway descended into oppressive darkness. My nerves were completely on edge, warning me against descending into the black, but I didn't allow myself to hesitate. We started down and were met by a foul, putrid stench that choked my senses and made me hold my breath. Everyone stopped. Even Rodin coughed and turned away.

"What is that smell? Genevieve said.

"Whatever it is, it isn't good." The captain sniffed and frowned. "But a foul odor won't stop the crew of the Sparrowhawk." He primed his lightning cannon, looked back at each member of his crew, and headed down the steps.

As we descended a few steps, the light from above faded and we came across a kerosene lantern hanging on a peg. The captain adjusted the lantern's knob, coaxing the flame inside, then handed it to me. I held it up to illuminate the stairwell, but what I saw made me wish I hadn't. A coating of green slime covered one wall and the worn stone stairs bowed in the center as if they'd been trod upon by countless souls over the millennia. This place was old. Maybe older than any place I'd been before.

We continued until the darkness surrounded us and only the light of the lantern kept it at bay. When the stairs leveled out, we found ourselves in an open area encircled by several doors. I ran to each one and looked through the small barred openings. In the third cell, a man was curled up on the floor in the corner. His shirt, stained with mud and dust, was no longer white.

I tried the door handle before Baldarich could stop me, but it wouldn't budge. The rattle woke the man in the cell. He rolled over and threw himself against the back wall. I was shocked by the reaction and held the light up hoping to see more.

"Dad? Is that you?"

The man scrambled to his feet and rushed to the door. I froze, but Baldarich yanked me back. Thick glasses I didn't recognize covered my father's dirt-smudged face. He still wore the same shirt and pants from the night he was kidnapped. I pushed past Baldarich and my father reached through the bars and cupped my face in his hands. Tears ran down his face leaving tracks on his dusty skin. "Oh, Alexander, I am so glad you're okay. They told me you'd been snatched up." Elated, I gripped my father's hands in my own. Despite the wooden cell door separating us, I hadn't felt this close to him since my mother's passing.

"Snatched up? No, we're here to rescue you."

"Where are the keys?" the captain said. "We're getting you out of here."

"The only set is with Lord Kannard."

Baldarich studied the lock and then extended his hand through the bars. "Captain Baldarich of the Sparrowhawk."

"John Armitage," my father said.

Baldarich asked, "Why are you down here? We found a cell upstairs in the villa that looked like where you'd been held."

"I refused to translate. Kannard hopes being stuck down here will change my mind. He's right."

"Let's get you out of here then."

"Thank you for taking care of my son, but why bring him here? Are you with Baron Kensington or Lord Marbury?"

I leaned closer. "No, we came on our own. Lord Marbury and the Grand Master have bigger problems. Baron Kensington was attacked. His daughter and I set out to help the two of you."

"You should have stayed in London."

I couldn't believe my father was going to scold me from inside his dungeon cell. That was just like him.

Baldarich turned to Mr. Singh. "We need to find some gunpowder to blast the lock. I'd wager this Lord Kannard fellow has an armory we can raid."

"Wait!" I pulled my bag off my shoulders and fumbled inside. Pulling out the charge, I held it up for the others to see. "Here, I brought this. I didn't know what we might need."

"Good thinking, kid." Baldarich took the charge and cut it open with his knife. Then he funneled the powder into the lock and turned to the others. "Get back, and get ready."

"Wait," the professor pleaded. "They'll hear you."

Baldarich said. "Sorry. Ignatius here prefers a loud exit, and it looks like this is the only way to break you out of here."

Ignatius stepped forward and tipped his hat to the man behind the bars. "I don't mean to second guess you, captain, but are you using enough powder?"

"I'm not trying to blow the door up, just move the latch inside the lock. It'll be fine." Baldarich motioned for everyone to step back, including the professor. "Guns ready, we may have to shoot our way out of here."

Lighting the paper from the charge with the kerosene lantern, I carried the flame to the lock and then squeezed my eyes shut and covered my ears. A puff of smoke, and a loud bang echoed up the long stairwell. The lock popped, and I yanked the door open and rushed in to hug my father. But we didn't have time to waste.

Ignatius led us back up the stairwell, and, as we stepped out onto the arched walkway, we saw a man in a long black coat standing in the center of the colonnade, blocking our way.

The man wore a black shirt, pants, boots, and vest. The only things not black were the golden buckles on his boots and belt, the buttons of his long coat, and the three golden chains crisscrossing his vest. And he was not alone. Two men stood on either side of him. Whether they were guards or members of the Knights of the Golden Circle didn't matter. They were not going to let us pass.

My father trembled. "Lord Kannard," he whispered.

The man in black smiled and, with a thick Belgian accent, said, "And where do you think you're off to, Professor?"

Captain Baldarich stepped in front of my father. "The professor complained about your hospitality. So we thought we'd take him off your hands."

"I don't know who you are," he said, wrinkling his nose

as if he'd encountered a foul odor, "but you're mistaken if you think you can just walk into my house and steal my guests."

"Guests. Is that what you call your kidnap victims?"

"Use whatever word you wish, but I must insist he remain here. And now, unfortunately, it seems I must play the reluctant host to all of you. Boys, put them in chains and take them all back to the dungeon."

Baldarich held up his hand. "Since none of us are fond of chains, let alone dungeons, I'll have to insist your boys stay right where they are while we take Professor Armitage back home."

Lord Kannard laughed. "You're hardly in a position to insist on anything at all." Without turning to look at the men beside him, he growled. "Disarm them, chain them up, and remove them from my sight. Now."

Baldarich whipped back his coat and pulled the leather-wrapped brass and steel hand cannon from its holster. "Run!"

I didn't wait to be told twice. My father, Genevieve, and I ran for the cliff. I heard the crackling of Baldarich's lightning cannon and the rapid pistol fire of Ignatius's Peacemakers, but I didn't turn around. I was focused on one goal: get my father to the safety of the Sparrowhawk.

Ignatius's revolvers filled the air with the sound of gunfire, and we ran as fast as we could. At the cliff's edge, I looked down and saw Hunter standing behind a grappling gun that rose from the deck of the half-submerged aero-dirigible. Behind me, my father's heavy breathing stopped for a moment as he stood transfixed.

"Is that a boat?"

"That's the Sparrowhawk, and we've got to hurry to get on board."

"But how on earth…?"

Just then, Hunter fired the grappling gun, and a thick

line snaked toward us. The iron claw slammed into the edge of the cliff, about an arm's length from my foot.

"Slide down the line. Grab it with your hands and feet and slide as fast as you can."

"I will not."

"Dad, get down that line before the others get here."

Genevieve helped the professor snag the line and he slid to safety on the Sparrowhawk. As he tumbled onto the deck, I pulled out my Thumper, and watched Genevieve slipped down the line, Rodin chasing after her.

I watched her land perfectly on the deck as though she'd done it hundreds of times before. I couldn't believe it; she always did everything so well. Maybe it was because she was a noblewoman.

Mr. Singh rounded a rock and stopped. He whipped around and shot one of the gun barrels on the side of his Katar dagger. The captain and Ignatius ran toward me.

The captain yelled, "Get down that line, lad."

Hunter raised his repeating rifle, fired, and then swung the rifle's lever. After taking aim he fired again.

I twisted the leather strap in my hands and leapt off the cliff. Hooking the strap and the soles of my boots on the line, I slid toward the ship until, unable to stop, I let go of the strap and tumbled across the deck.

Mr. Singh and Ignatius followed.

Baldarich fired one last burst from his lightning gun and slid to the deck. "Ignatius, tell Coyote to get us out of here. Everyone else get below, now!"

Mr. Singh pulled a lever on the grappler. The iron claw released and plunged into the water as he retracted it. All three of the Sparrrowhawk's engines roared to life and we departed the cove as fast as possible.

As soon as I was on my feet, I went to find my father, who had headed to the bridge. He held out his arms and relief flooded through me as I hugged him tight. *We'd done it! We had rescued him, and we were all safe!* "Don't worry dad, we'll be back at Eton in no time."

"No!" he pulled back, alarm plain across his face. "We can't leave Malta."

I held his gaze. "You finished the translations, didn't you?"

"Yes."

"And…?"

"The answers are on the other side of the island."

CHAPTER 19

THE ANCIENT TEMPLE

Professor Armitage and Captain Baldarich stood toe-to-toe, both grim faced. I watched as my father tried again and again to convince the captain not to retreat, not to leave the island.

"We can't let the Hearts of the Horsemen fall into enemy hands," my father pleaded. He gripped the railing and looked at Genevieve. "If only your father were here, he'd explain this better than I."

She didn't crack a smile, her cheek tensed, and her nails bit into her palms.

I clenched my fist. This wasn't over, I may have my father, but Genevieve's father still needed us. We still had to find the antidote to cure him. I hoped Baldarich would give in and do as my father asked—maybe for the right incentive. He wasn't the kind of man to risk his crew for no good reason, but he was a Sky Raider and the lure of adventure and riches might be too much to pass up.

"Captain, Genevieve already promised you a large sum for bringing us here. I believe the reward will be even greater than you can imagine if you help us just a while longer."

My father looked at me with a strange wonderment

in his eyes. I don't think he ever expected to see his son negotiate with a Sky Raider.

"Captain, my son is right. If you return us to England with the hearts, I assure you will receive a great reward."

Captain Baldarich shook his head, and looked over at Mr. Singh. "What do you say, Mr. Singh? I can imagine a pretty big reward. What say we stick with this adventure a little while longer?"

"Aye aye, sir," Mr. Singh said with a grim warrior's smile.

"Professor, I'm going to hold you to that 'great reward.'"

* * *

I stood next to my father, Genevieve, and Captain Baldarich atop the conning tower. We had cruised to the other side of the island without issue, and now my father, dressed in clean clothes courtesy of the captain himself, studied the shore line looking for something. Dressed in a white shirt and brown pants—all a bit baggy from being a few sizes too big—my father no longer looked the fusty academic. In fact, the suspenders and open burgundy vest gave him a dapper appearance, and I wondered what he had looked like when my mom first met him.

I watched him with growing admiration, seeing a side of him I had never known. My father was a bookworm, stuck in musty scrolls and bent over dusty artifacts, never one for adventure. Yet now, he leaned against the railing of an aero-dirigible and studied the island with the eye of a hunter.

After cruising along the shoreline at a slow but steady pace, my father blurted out: "Stop the ship! There it is. Right there." He pointed and bounced on his tiptoes like an eager schoolboy.

I followed my father's extended finger but saw only rocks and more rocks.

"Mr. Singh!" The captain yelled, and the familiar blue

turban popped up from below. "Launch the longboat. Put yourself, Mr. Peacemaker, and three airmen in it."

"Aye, captain."

Baldarich and the others dropped below. "Let's get to the longboat."

We collected our gear, and when I went to hoist my pack on my shoulders, I remembered my father's eyeglasses, the ones he had left behind in his office. I opened my pack and pulled the out. "Dad," I said, and held them out to him as he turned. "I didn't know when I might see you again ... but I thought you might want these."

He removed the broken pair Lord Kannard had apparently given him. "These have such bad lenses." He fitted the spectacles back on his nose, tucked the legs behind his ears, and went after the captain.

"You're welcome." I mumbled. At least he could have said thank you.

We stepped onto the main-deck with Rodin flying behind us. Mr. Singh released the rope allowing the longboat to slip into the water.

We climbed aboard and I watched as Ignatius spun the crankshaft. The propeller underneath the water whirred to life and I watched and listened to the machinery, astounded at how fast we were going. I had never seen a longboat with an engine. The European gunslinger grabbed the tiller and directed the longboat right up onto the rocky beach. We all hopped out and peered around.

Then my father, back to being the single-minded Professor Armitage, ran toward what from the beach looked like a pile of rocks, but now I saw was the ruins of an ancient structure. Ignatius followed with a Colt in each hand, but the rest of us were more cautious, and Baldarich, with his weapon drawn, peered into the night as if expecting the worst.

Genevieve and I followed Ignatius toward the stone

remains. Once we were close enough, we could see megalithic stones standing upright, some covered in vegetation, some sunk deep into the rocky soil. Pulling away some vegetation, I saw a circular design etched into one of the stones.

The professor was at my side as soon as he saw what I'd uncovered. He ran his fingertips over the engraving with an excited grin. "These are the eyes of the earth mother and this here, these lines, may represent the waters of the Mediterranean."

Genevieve asked, "Who lived here? It doesn't look Egyptian or Greek."

"It's older than both those civilizations. When people used these temples the Mediterranean was nothing more than a series of large lakes. Long before Hercules smashed through the Straits of Gibraltar with his sword, the people lived in villages below, and these temples sat atop mountains. They may be the oldest buildings in the world." Professor Armitage let his fingers dance over another carved stone. "I could spend years here."

"We don't have years." Baldarich spit the words like grit. "Kannard will be coming." He looked at the toppled stones. "I've sent the Sparrowhawk up the coast to fool him."

"We need to find the entrance." My father surveyed the site. "It may be covered with stone or dirt, so look for any openings."

We fanned out over the site, poked at the dirt and checked the seams of the rock. My father and I drifted to the center of the complex where the temple would have stood. Grass grew through the cracks looking like an emerald mortar in the moonlight. The professor ran over to the edge of the circle to a pair of thin columns, two half-buried standing stones with a lintel on top. He began tearing weeds, dirt, and stones out of the way, tugging and pulling brambles and branches fast as he could.

"Alexander." He twisted around toward me. "Come look at this! I've found the entrance."

Everyone rushed to the professor's side. Ignatius and Mr. Singh pulled small octagonal lanterns from their packs and coaxed the light to life. Captain Baldarich unhooked the palm-sized kerosene underwater lamp from his belt and lit it, too. Orange and yellow flickering flames illuminated smooth stone columns as, one by one, we squeezed under the lintel and into a mysterious world from the far, distant past.

My heart thudded and I wondered if anyone else could hear it. I glanced at Genevieve, but she was staring at the surroundings with wide-eyed wonder. Walls with cutout niches greeted us as we entered a surprisingly large room. Debris littered the ground, a mix of bones, shattered pottery, and dirt built up over the centuries. A doorway at the back of the chamber led deeper underground.

With Ignatius standing right behind him holding a lantern so he could see, my father carefully traversed a couple of steps cut into the rock. Light crept over the statue of a very curvy naked woman. The headless statue with its arms crossed under voluptuous breasts had wide hips that flowed down to a pair of rounded legs standing upon an elaborately decorated base.

Professor Armitage gasped, and his hand went to his chest. "The Earth Mother, the idol worshiped by the oldest cultures known to man."

Ignatius cocked his head to the side staring at the body. "Captain, she's just your type." The captain chuckled.

"She is the first sign listed in the ancient account. The passageway should be right here." He scrabbled around with his fingers, pressing and pulling until he found what he was looking for. A loose stone. He grasped it in his fingertips and pulled. It crashed to the ground and the sound rumbled through the temple like a lion's growl. The professor spun around, and everyone else raised their weapons.

I ran over to my father. "You found it." Together we pulled away the other stones to reveal a hidden passageway. I took Ignatius's lantern and stepped into the unknown. After a moment, I stuck my head back through the opening. "It's amazing! There are steps leading deeper into the rock."

We all climbed through the secret opening, and I led them down the rock cut steps. For some reason, I wasn't afraid at all. Not of the potential danger from Lord Kannard. Not of the dark and the unknown waiting for us at the end of the steps. Instead, I was filled with so much energy, my head buzzed.

The stairs ended at a wall flanked by two statues, one of which had fallen over. The wall's flat face held a relief of four men on horses. Professor Armitage wiped the stone clean with his sleeve and studied the carving.

Each horseman looked different and had a symbol above them I couldn't read. My father decoded the symbols, and then pushed on the carving, which slid back into the wall.

A low grumbling grinded above, and the entire ceiling, one continuous slab of granite, fell down upon us. We dropped to the floor, and the slab hit the fallen statue. The granite cracked into several pieces and dust filled the chamber.

Baldarich pushed off the chunk resting above him. "Indihar, did everyone make it?"

Mr. Singh replied. "I see everyone from the crew, but not…"

"We're here," I said as I crawled from beneath the slab.

No one had been crushed, and I thanked the statue. Without it, we'd all be dead. I saw an opening at the top that had been blocked by the slab. The smooth bare walls held only the anchor holes where the granite had been secured. The dusty stone mechanics looked as pristine as the metal interlocks of a London factory.

Think you can get us up there, Mr. Singh?" Baldarich asked.

"All we need is rope."

"Who brought the rope?"

I reached in my bag and pulled out the tightly bundled coil. "I did."

The captain looked around at his men who shrugged their shoulder. He gripped his nose and shook his head. "Thanks kid. You saved my crew polishing duty."

Mr. Singh took the coil from me and placed the coil on the stone floor just below the opening. He studied it for a moment and then nudged it slightly to better position it where he wanted it. Then he pulled a delicately carved flute from the scarf bound around his waist. He handed me his lantern and the lowered himself to sit cross-legged beside the coil, looking up once more as if checking to be sure the position was just right. I glanced at Genevieve and got a questioning glance in return. We both turned to Captain Baldarich who winked as Mr. Singh closed his eyes and began to chant in a soft, reverential voice. Then he put the flute to his lips and played, swaying back and forth ever so slightly. His methodical movements entranced me, and I watched in shock as the tip of the rope moved. At first it simply poked up from the coil like the head of a snake and swayed back and forth as if mirroring Mr. Singh's movements, but then it began to rise. Higher and higher. And higher, until it reached twenty feet up, just an arm's length from the opening.

Ignatius stepped up and tugged. The rope didn't move. It was as stiff and sturdy as a pole. He nodded at the captain and then began to climb. Once he reached the opening, Baldarich motioned for Genevieve and I to follow. One after another we pulled ourselves up the rigid rope. After all of us reached the top, save Mr. Singh, Ignatius stepped to the edge and grabbed the rope.

"Your turn," he said.

Mr. Singh stopped playing, and the rope went limp in Ignatius' hand. He and the captain held the rope tight as Mr. Singh scampered up. At last we were all together again, and I was filled with relief, as if the worst was over. I held up the lantern and surveyed a long passage cut in the rock. My father stood quietly, stroking his chin and peering off into the darkness as if trying to decide which way to go. Mr. Singh pulled the rope up as Baldarich pushed us on. "Keep moving people."

I started to run toward him, but stopped in my tracks as strange and frightening sounds rang out from the entrance. Pounding metal on rock reverberated, ricocheting off the stone walls, echoing louder and louder throughout the passage. Baldarich raised his lightning hand-cannon, prepared to shoot whatever appeared. But none of us were prepared for what materialized out of the darkness.

Lord Kannard. Holding a blazing torch and riding atop a white-shrouded mechanical steed with hooves and legs of iron, Kannard was flanked by Colonel Hendrix and several other henchmen on foot and dressed in long black coats and Bowler hats with goggles around the band. Col. Hendrix raised his arm, the gears spinning and clicking as the rifle barrel locked in place.

Lord Kannard's eyes blazed in the torchlight as he smiled. "So good of you to lead me to the right temple."

"How did you get in here," my father rasped, stunned to see his kidnapper below him.

"You were so easy to follow, I'm almost glad you were rescued. Once we saw which set of ruins you headed for, the rest was easy. Now if you'd be so kind as to lead us on the final leg of our journey...."

Baldarich backed up a couple of steps. "I knew it was too easy getting away from you fools."

Lord Kannard laughed. "Who's the fool, now?"

"Lead the way, professor," the captain whispered, and my father shuddered and ran headlong down a darkened passageway. "Run," Baldarich said, shoving Genevieve and me down the passage. "Let him find his own way up here."

I ran as fast as I could, following my father's lead, and keeping up with Genevieve's long strides. Behind us, I heard laughter and the thundering echo of iron hooves slamming into bedrock as the mechanical horse leapt from the shattered debris of the entrance into the large passage with Lord Kannard upon its back. I dared to look back and terror filled this space from floor to ceiling. The machine had made the jump with ease causing its rider to cackle with delight as he charged after us.

Then I heard a sharp metallic zing of and clank and saw behind the charging iron steed, a grappling hook had snaked out from Col. Hendirx's sleeve and snagged one of the stone mechanisms from the trap. He flew through the air and landed with a lurching thud. Baldarich yanked on my collar and I turned and ran again, continued down the passage.

Behind us, Lord Kannard called out. "Miss Kensington, are you sure you want to run? I have the antidote to your father's poison."

She stopped and turned. I spun around and saw Kennard hold up a glass vial. It glittered in the torchlight.

"I don't believe you," she yelled back.

"It's now or never, Genevieve. Do you want to save your father or not?"

She took a step forward, but Baldarich grabbed her by the arm and pushed her down the passageway in my father's wake.

CHAPTER 20

THE LABYRINTH

Genevieve, Baldarich, and I ran around one corner and then another trying to catch up with my father, Ignatius, and Mr. Singh. I saw a broken sconce on the wall that would have held a torch in ancient times.

We had passed it before.

More than once.

Baldarich pushed us down another passage. "We're lost in a labyrinth."

As we ran, I tried to study the symbols marking the walls and floor, but we were moving too fast and it was too dark. Then a shot echoed along the passage.

"That's a Colt Peacemaker," Baldarich smiled. "Ignatius is telling us where he is. This way."

We turned down the first right and ran toward the sound. I started to see one symbol over and over again and realized it was the marker. I stopped as we were about to change direction.

"Captain, this symbol is the marker, the four chevrons." I looked around and found the symbol on a floor straight ahead. "Follow them and we get through."

Baldarich smiled and slapped me on the back. "Excellent!"

Iron hooves thundered behind us. Looking back, I saw Lord Kannard several junctions away.

Before Baldarich could grab her, Genevieve drew her saber and charged back toward Kannard. Baldarich cursed under his breath, and set off after her. I stared down the passage I knew would lead us toward my father, and then turned and ran after Baldarich.

"Lord Kannard, give me that antidote or I shall take it by force," Genevieve cried out. Her voice was hard, determined. But Kannard just laughed and held up the vial to taunt her.

"Come and try, my sweet."

"Genevieve, no!" I yelled, but she paid no attention.

She lifted her saber and charged the horseman. He drew a flamebrage broadsword and aimed it at her heart, the wicked, undulating blade slithering like a serpent. The iron horse charged, four hooves galloping toward Genevieve, but she showed no fear. I stared in horror, and could barely breathe as, at the very last second, she dove under the blade and leapt up as he thundered past.

Baldarich raised his lightning cannon and fired, but Lord Kannard veered and turned down another passage and out of sight. Together we chased after him until I noticed the four chevron design again.

"The chevrons," I pointed as I ran.

"Follow them!" Baldarich said, breathing heavily.

We ran until the passage opened into a cavern with a large trench gutted through the center. On the far side, my father stood before a large stone door. Ignatius and the rest of the crew took cover on a rocky ridge beside him. Kannard charged toward my father and the crew opened fire.

At first Ignatius and the others stopped him from reaching my father, but then shots rang out from the other side of the cavern. Col. Hendrix and the henchmen of the Knights of the Golden Circle had arrived. They forced my father's protectors to duck behind their ridge of fallen stones as Lord Kannard continued toward my father with Genevieve on his tail.

Baldarich stopped and aimed at the colonel, and in return, chipped stone and dirt flew up around the captain's feet as Hendrix fired back.

Genevieve swung her saber. Metal on metal rang out as she caught the mechanical horse in the leg. Lord Kannard kicked, but she danced away and struck again. His face twisted in fury. He attacked wildly, but she jumped out of the way and grabbed for his belt where the vial was tucked. The horse reared and Kannard tried to cut her in two, but again, Genevieve was too nimble for him. She kept him busy while I ran to my father's side. He studied the sealed stone door, running his hand over the etched symbol to decode it.

My father worked at a fevered pace. He stepped back and looked at a series of rocks on a ledge just above the door. He started climbing up toward the ledge. *Where was he going?* The clash of swords behind us echoed through the cavern and kept pulling my attention away from the door. I knew the symbols on the door probably triggered another booby trap, but I had to do help my friends. Seeing Genevieve in the swordfight with Lord Kannard was more than I could bear, and she was not going to be able to hold him off much longer. Col. Hendrix and the other henchman continued to rain gunfire on Ignatius and the others, and if I didn't do something fast, they would likely shoot Genevieve in the back.

Springing the trap door would cause one heck of distraction.

With one last look behind me, I pushed the symbol in the center of the stone door. Water started to seep out of the depressed edges as the sound of grinding stone echoed through the cavern. I pulled my hand back and rubbed my wet fingers together.

My father looked down at me and yelled, "No! Not that one."

What had I done?

The door burst forward slamming into me and knocking me backward as a torrent of water followed rushed into the cave like a tidal wave. A deafening roar filled the cavern drowning out all sound and blinding everyone with the salt and grit of seawater.

I gasped and tumbled, struggling for a handhold as the raging river swept over me. Through the spray and foam, I saw Genevieve drag herself onto the ledge. She looked at me, and then to Lord Kannard who struggled to stay mounted in the rising water. I kept my head above water long enough to see the dripping iron steed rise out of the water and the rider reach up to grab my father from his perch above the door.

Genevieve dove in and the water swept her toward me. I felt her grab hold of the leather strap wrapped around my body and pull me to her. Rodin darted down into the churning mix and snatched me with his claws, but he was too small to pull either of us out of the roiling river. He dove again and again to no avail, though his actions marked us for the others.

Genevieve struggled to keep my head above the rushing torrent. She grabbed a gnarled tree root sticking out of the stone wall and held fast. I felt her pull the leather strap from my shoulder and wrap it to the tree, securing us while the water continued to flow down the passageways.

Genevieve pushed me up out of the water, and Rodin snagged my pants with his toothy snout and pulled with all his might. As the water receded around us, she collapsed beside me and Rodin landed and flicked his forked dragon's tongue out, licking both our faces. Disoriented and almost drowned, I smiled up at them both and gave myself up to oblivion.

* * *

Nothing but darkness and stone. Closing in. Surrounding me like a clenched fist. I run until my breath is ragged, my chest heaving. Stumbling, I fall through darkness toward a maze cut in stone on the floor of another great cavern. A river cuts across the top of the maze and spits me out, leaving me falling, spinning wildly until I crash down on the stone floor in a sickening heap. Struggling to my feet, I look around the darkened chamber and wonder if I've landed at the gates of Hell. As if caught in Cerberus's jaws, stalactites and stalagmites grow like razor-sharp teeth, ready at a moment's notice to bite down. Ancient symbols are etched into an arch at the back of the chamber, and atop four marble pillars, I recognize four beating hearts encased in iron bands.

From out of the depths, the sound of charging horses echoes around me and an inferno fills the room. I spin in every direction seeking the source of the pounding hooves until four nightmare steeds burst into the chamber through a wall of flame beneath the arch. They smash the stone teeth, shake the ground, fill the air with the stench of death. Red eyes blaze from their bronze and iron bodies and a foul black smoke rushes from their flaring nostrils.

"Alexander! Alexander!" Through the smothering chaos, I hear my name, as a sweet voice, like a choir of angels calling to me. I turn toward the voice and float up toward it, out of the darkness.

* * *

I snapped awake and sat up, almost hitting Genevieve in the head. She leaned over me, her brow wrinkled with concern. As she fell back to avoid me, I flipped onto my knees. "Are you okay?"

Then, to my utter surprise, she snatched me up in her

arms and gripped me tight, and I found my arms wrapping around her instinctively, as if that's why I had arms in the first place. We held on to each other, and I reveled in her embrace, not only because feeling her against me was amazing, but also because I was still dizzy and unsettled from being caught in the river.

"You dragged me from the river," I said, finally. *She had saved my life!* "How many hours have I been out?" I asked. "Is everyone okay?"

"Hours, no you've been out for only a few minutes."

"How can that be, so much happened?"

"You got swept away by the water, but the captain and his crew are back near the door. Lord Kannard took your father."

"I had the strangest dream."

"What did you see?" Genevieve asked as an excited Rodin, his tail whipping back and forth, squeezed up between us, looking at me as if he couldn't wait to hear what I had to say.

Rubbing the dragon's head, I looked in Genevieve's eyes. "I know where they're taking my father, and I saw that the horsemen will be born from fire."

CHAPTER 21

THE HEART OF THE HORSEMEN

The underground river had receded and settled into its banks, and Genevieve and I made our way back up toward the door to reconnect with Captain Baldarich and the crew of the Sparrowhawk.

It didn't take long to find the passage down which Kannard had taken my father. I stopped at the entrance, held back by the putrid odor of death and decomposition mixed with the musky smell of dust and ancient stone. Everything around me seemed bizarre and otherworldly. So much had happened in such a short time that nothing felt real. I focused on my dream, on the beating hearts bound by iron bands atop the pillars. They couldn't truly exist, could they?

Light filled the chamber as Captain Baldarich stepped forward with his kerosene lamp. The passage's rough walls descended ever deeper into the rock. Staring into the darkness I knew my father, Kannard, and the secret of the four horsemen lay within its depths. With the nightmare vision fresh in my mind, the last thing I wanted to do was step into the darkness. But it was either that or admit my terror. And abandon my father. Looking into Genevieve's determined eyes, and seeing the captain and the rest of the crew willing to confront the unknown dangers before us, I felt less afraid. With Baldarich illuminating the way, I forced myself to take the first step.

I heard the hooves of the iron horse before I saw it. The sound of Col. Hendrix barking orders and my father's excited calls echoed up the passage and let me know we were on the right path.

We arrived at the end of the descending passage where the ground flattened out beneath our feet. We were at the bottom, and just like in my nightmare, the teeth of hell stood in our way. Beyond the gaping mouth of jagged stalactites and stalagmites and on the other side of a steaming fissure slicing through the bedrock, I could see the arch of cut stone looming over Lord Kannard and his henchmen. My father, his back to us, stood studying the symbols carved into the arch. Col. Hendrix had his rifle-arm pointed at my father's chest.

Lord Kannard turned on his bronze-plated steed and locked eyes with me. "So glad you could join us, boy."

"Let my father go!"

Lord Kannard threw back his head and laughed. "Ah, you are endlessly entertaining. When are you going to realize you're not in control here?"

"Father!" I called out. "Don't help them!"

My father started to turn toward me, but Col. Hendrix pulled back his sleeve, and gears twisted and clicked as the serrated blade slid into place. He pushed the knife's edge up against my father's throat.

"You are a brave young man, I'll give you that," Kannard said, "but I hold all the cards. Now tell those annoying shipmates of yours to lower their weapons."

Captain Baldarich holstered his lightning cannon and motioned for everyone to do the same. Genevieve sheathed her saber as Mr. Singh secured his Katar in his sash. Ignatius twirled his two Colts and holstered them in a one quick motion. The other crewmen stowed their weapons but I kept a hand on my Thumper.

Lord Kannard sat back as a wicked grin crossed his face. "Now Professor Armitage, if you would please continue your translations. Just remember death is not something you can control, but once I have what I want, you can determine how it affects you."

"Damn you," my father swore. He struggled to turn back toward me, but the Colonel pushed him toward the symbols. "If it was easy, you could have done it yourself."

"Why should I bother when I've got such a learned scholar to do the work for me?" Kannard said.

My father turned away from Kannard to study the symbols on the arch, and the henchmen formed a line between him and the Sparrowhawk's crew. They raised their rifles and swords, taking aim at the Sky Raiders like a firing squad. Captain Baldarich made certain to keep his crew from making any sudden movements. Everyone watched my father, who stopped several times to look at me.

Anger built within me. It wasn't fair that the Knights of the Golden Circle would succeed after everything we'd done to stop them. I studied Lord Kannard. *What was his weakness?*

The noblemen twirled the glass vial in his fingers, causing the milky yellow liquid to tumble inside. I glanced at Genevieve, her gaze never left the vial. Turning back to Lord Kannard, the gloating smile never left his face. The man delighted in toying with other people's lives, and it disgusted me.

"I know you want this," he taunted, "but what are you willing to do to save your father's life?" He chuckled. "Life is about control, Genevieve, especially for people like us. We blue bloods were born to rule these lesser men. In time you will come to understand this. Your father does."

She turned away in disgust. "I will never be like you."

"You already are, my dear. You were born that way."

My father looked up and said, "I've found it."

Lord Kannard goaded his steed forward until he was positioned between my father and me. He drew his revolver. "Reveal the hearts of the horsemen, or I will shoot your son."

"I said I would do it as long as you don't hurt him." My father looked at me and then back up to Lord Kannard. "We have a gentleman's agreement, and since you claim to be a gentleman, you must keep it."

"I will keep my end of our agreement as long as you do exactly as you are told. Now, reveal the hearts of the horsemen or your son will die."

My father turned back to the arch, reached up and pressed the symbol of a four-pronged crown, then a four-lined spiral, a double chevron, and finally the hieroglyphic symbol of the horsemen. He did it slowly, deliberately, as if filled with dread.

The sound of grinding stone filled the fissure and dust fell from the archway. Several stalactites fell from the ceiling and crashed around me and the Sparrowhawk's crew. The stone archway spun around entering the floor on one side and rising out of the rock on the other. It stopped. Four symbols were chiseled at the top of the arch. Four large urns dropped out of holes on its underside, ringing sharply in my ears with a piercing echo as they shattered on the rocky floor.

"*No!*" My father ran over to the broken artifacts and fell to his knees, his face contorted in a grimace of horror. Picking up the pieces, he exhaled. "Just simple undecorated earthenware."

He searched among the shards of pottery and within the shattered remains found a second smaller red urn and pulled it free. A mix of iron and ceramics, the base and topper were iron, and bands of iron surrounded a bulbous ceramic middle. The urn split in the center, but was locked in place by a sliding latch. "They're unlike anything I've ever seen before."

He twisted the lid from its base. Reaching inside, my father pulled up a crumbling dark red powder. Rubbing his fingers together he sniffed at the powder then touched one finger to his tongue and quickly spit on the rocks. He turned to Lord Kannard. "It's bloodbone, dried powdered blood."

Lord Kannard leapt off his horse and dug through one of the ceramic pots. He removed an ashen white urn. He clutch it close as if more precious than gold. He turned back to his iron steed and said to the crew of the Sparrowhawk, "Now you will learn the true nature of the Horsemen. For you see, the iron steed requires a heart to unleash its terror, and a rider to become a scourge of the Earth."

The bronze plates on the chest of the iron steed slid open. Inside, oil dripped on spinning gears and rows of pistons moving in synchronized precision. Kannard placed the urn in the chest cavity and secured it. As soon as he did, the urn began to glow and pulse. The bronze plates closed and a low rumble rattled from within the steed.

Kannard slipped his boot in the stirrup and swung into the saddle.

The ground began to tremble, and I wanted to scream as the iron steed's eyes started glowing with a haunting fiery light. The metallic beast grew in size and snorted twin columns of black smoke. An eerie aura surrounded the rider as Lord Kannard's skin darkened and his face hardened, his visage looking more and more like a stone statue than a flesh and blood man.

He pulled hard on the reins and his steed rose up on its hind legs, hooves pawing the air before slamming down, making the earth shake so it knocked us all from our feet. Stalactites shattered as they fell from the ceiling, sending showers of rock across the cavern floor and into the fissure.

With his arm raised high, Lord Kannard rode toward us. "Attack!" he yelled and his henchmen rushed forward. One by one, we scrambled to our feet and tried to run, but we were blocked by Kannard's men and forced to fall back further into the passage.

"Stay back!" My father yelled above the chaos, and I watched as he stepped up on a raised stone pedestal triggering the third trap.

The crevice broke open wider and wider, separating us from the iron steed and Golden Circle henchmen. The pungent smell of rotten eggs and ammonia burned my lungs, and I saw one of the men lower his torch to stare into the crevasse as it grew ever wider. The gas ignited and sent a fireball roaring up to the ceiling. Fire engulfed the henchmen and blew the crew of the Sparrowhawk further back into the passage.

I shielded my eyes and squinted through the burning air looking for my father. The Iron Horseman was surrounded by flames, but Kannard and his steed were unaffected. He thrived on the carnage, and roared in delight as his henchmen screamed and writhed in agony leaving all but Col. Hendrix alive. Through the shimmering flames, I saw my father jump down from the pedestal and rush toward the urns. But Col. Hendrix got there first and kicked my father aside, grabbed the other three urns, and leapt onto the back of the Kannard's steed. The edge of the white shroud covering the beast caught fire, glowing orange and spitting sparks as the two rode through the inferno.

They fulfilled my vision of Hell. Would we be able to stop a creature born from hellfire? Kannard wheeled his mount around so he faced us, then withdrew the antidote from his belt and held it high.

"Genevieve, I cast your father into the fires of Hell!"

"No!" she screamed and rushed forward as Kannard

threw the vial into the burning crevasse. Mr. Singh caught her just in time. He wrapped his arm around her waist and pulled her from the edge as flames licked her boots.

The Iron Horsemen raised the hooves of his steed and slammed them against the far wall of the cavern. The ground shook violently and a fracture in the wall appeared along with a new eruption of flames from the fissure in the floor. As the fracture in the wall grew, rock fell away in chunks to reveal a hidden passage to the surface. Kannard urged the iron steed forward, leaving us behind as he and Hendrix disappeared into the dark.

"Father," I yelled, my voice ragged as I coughed and choked on the smoke. Just as I was about to give up hope that he could have survived the latest conflagration, my father jumped the fissure. He dove through the fire and tumbled into the passage to land near my feet. His hair was singed, his clothes were smoking and his face was black with soot. I hugged him so tight, he finally pushed me away so he could breathe.

"I'm sorry for setting off that trap but it was the only thing I could think to do,"

Captain Baldarich shook his head. "You saved us. Almost killed us, true, but in the end we're still here and their henchmen are dead. I'd say the trap worked."

"But Kannard got away with all four urns. He'll be able to bring the horsemen to life."

"We'll find another way," I said, still holding on to my father.

"Where will they go next, Professor?" Captain Baldarich asked.

"To London, almost certainly."

"That gives us a fighting chance," the captain said. "We just have to get back to the Sparrowhawk."

Genevieve met my gaze. "Back to London without the antidote." Tears filled her eyes. "I failed."

CHAPTER 22

CHASING KANNARD

The fire extinguished and the smoke dissipated. Hell had left its cage, unleashed on the world. We made our way across the fissure and followed Kannard's path up to the surface. In the distance, we watched Kannard and Hendrix ride up a gangplank and board an airskiff. His voice rang out in the night air: "Unfurl the wingsails. Get me in the air!"

As soon as a dark figure in tattered clothes pulled up the gangplank and released the anchor lines, the sleek ship, secured by rigging ropes underneath an aerodynamic blimp, sprang into the air. Large, white triangular sails on either side of the ship billowed in the strong wind as the vessel soared away.

"Damn, he'll be tough to catch," Captain Baldarich ran past me toward the shoreline. "Signal the Sparrowhawk, Mr. Singh," he ordered.

Mr. Singh fired a flare into the sky.

"Can we catch them?" my father asked.

"They might be in an airskiff, Professor Armitage, but I have the fastest aero-dirigible this side of the Atlantic," the captain boasted.

As soon as the Sparrohawk arrived, we rushed aboard

and ran to the bridge. Genevieve and I ran to the windows. Kannard's small vessel was far out in front of us, but its white sails stood out against the cloudless sky.

With a nod from the captain, Mr. Singh ordered the crewmen into action. "Get the wingsails deployed, and trim them for speed."

I pulled Genevieve and my father over to the map table. The crew scurried around as if the deck plating were on fire. Ignatius took his place in front of the wall of dials, and began checking each one. Coyote pushed the three copper throttle levers forward and pulled back on the wheel. The Sparrowhawk titled upward as it climbed into the sky, and once the wingsails deployed, the speed increased.

Baldarich flipped open the furthest left copper tube and yelled, "Gears, I need all she's got, and I need it now." He closed the tube and turned to Coyote. "Follow that airskiff."

Baldarich pulled the telescope from his belt and extended the optics. Looking through it, he studied the airskiff and then offered it to Genevieve. Pressing against the brass eyepiece she adjusted the optics by twisting the leather-wrapped wooden tubes.

Rodin sat on her shoulder; his tail wrapped around her back. He spied the contraption extending from her eye, and with one claw batted the telescope. She patted the little dragon and handed the device to me.

I adjusted the optics and aimed it at the Kannard's ship. His crew strained the ropes of the two sails to get as much speed as possible, and Lord Kannard stared back at me through his own spyglass. I wondered what he was thinking. I saw him turn and yell at his crew. The Sparrowhawk was gaining on him, and he was none too happy about it.

Rodin reached out and swatted the telescope.

Captain Baldarich opened the middle-left tube in front of him. "Bow cannon to the ready."

A moment passed and a reply echoed back. "Bow cannon ready, sir!"

"Fire!"

The airskiff suddenly rose twenty feet with a simple adjustment of its wings and the cannon shot sailed harmlessly underneath.

The captain slammed his fist against the arm of his chair and said through the same tube, "Fire the forward Gatling and get that cannon reloaded." He shifted toward Coyote. "Stay with them."

An "aye Captain," came from both the tube and Coyote.

I watched the bullets course through the air only to be dodged by the swift airskiff. Then the cannon roared to life, but once again, they rose on the wind and avoided the shot.

Captain Baldarich leaned in to the copper tube. "Hunter, what the hell is going on down there? I need to hit this little cloud-jumper."

Hunter's voice echoed back, "It's too windy out there, captain. It's giving them the advantage. We'll need to get closer if I'm to hit them!"

My father checked the compass mounted beside the pilot. Confirming the direction, he ran to the map table. I stared at the charts wondering what he saw, and looked up to find the captain had joined us.

"I believe they are indeed heading straight for London," my father said. He looked across the map table at me. "The comet is crossing the sky now, and soon it will pass over the sun."

"When that happens, the four horsemen will be summoned," I continued his train of thought.

"Exactly," my father said. "We must stop Kannard before it's too late." He turned to the captain. "Can we catch them?"

Baldarich smiled at the land-lovers around him. "We have one advantage they don't. They rely on the winds to propel them; the Sparrowhawk uses the wind, but we don't need them. We have engines." He ran his fingers over map. "Once we hit the coast, the winds will shift and they'll have to change tack. When they do, we'll have them."

I studied the lines drawn on the map. Fascinated by the wind patterns and terrain changes displayed, I paid particular attention to the markings on the southern coast of France. The symbols intrigued me: a new field of study to learn. I had no idea what Kannard would do once he made it to London or how he would summon the other Horsemen, and I didn't want to find out. We had to stop him before he got the chance to put his plans into place. Despite what Genevieve's father or even Grand Master Sinclair thought, we had accomplished the first goal—we had rescued my father. Now we just had to stop Kannard and find another batch of antidote. All before the comet crossed the path of the sun in the sky. A wave of determination swept through me, and I was filled with a great sense of responsibility for seeing our mission through.

The captain patted my father's shoulder. "You should get some rest, professor. Unfortunately, we're not a passenger liner, so we don't have any rooms for you."

"That is not a problem. I won't require anything more than getting me to London as soon as you can."

"He can stay with us," I said.

My father narrowed his eyes and looked back and forth at Genevieve and me. "You are staying together?"

"Accommodations are scarce," the captain said with a mischievous smile. "Why don't you two show him below."

Genevieve and I led my father downstairs. As we entered the room, now segmented by a large canvas sheet, I showed my dad where the extra hammocks were stored.

Instead of sitting with us and giving us a chance to finally catch up, my father, back to being *Professor Armitage*, planted his hands on his hips and scowled. "These accomodations are unacceptable! The two of you have been sleeping down here together? I am going to take this up with the captain immediately!"

"Wait—" Genevieve and I both started. But it was too late. My father had already turned and slammed the door behind him. I shuffled back and climbed into my hammock to avoid Genevieve. Rodin flew over and landed on my stomach. I pitched forward as the claws pricked my skin and Rodin flapped his wings smacking me in the face and chest. Genevieve called Rodin back to her but he simply smacked me in the face with his tail and settled down on my lap.

Genevieve came over and sat beside my hammock. "Sorry about Rodin, but I think he really wants to sit with you."

"It's okay," I rubbed Rodin's head. "He's adorable enough to get away with it. Listen, I'm sorry if my father offended you in anyway, he hasn't been the same since my mother passed. He feels like he has to control me or I'll end up as some sort of criminal."

"I'm sorry to hear about your mother. How did she die?"

"Three years ago she became sick and died in the summer. She was only sick a few weeks."

"I'm so sorry. My mother passed away several years ago as well, an accident at sea while traveling to Egypt."

"Two of a kind." I tried to smile, but it wouldn't hold. "I'm sorry about your mother."

"I've come to terms with it." Genevieve's hand went to the silver locket around her neck and I knew she probably felt the same way I did about my mother.

From out on the gun-deck I heard the captain's voice coming from the copper tube. "There's the airskiff! Man your battle stations! Forward guns prepare to fire!"

There was no time to feel sorry for ourselves now. I looked at Genevieve, scrambled back out of my hammock, and we

ran out the door with Rodin flying behind us. We reached
the starboard gun-port and peered out at thick black storm
clouds. Genevieve tugged my sleeve and pointed to a dot in
the sky. "It's the Storm Vulture."

"Zerelda!"

"Hurry, we've got to make sure the captain knows."

CHAPTER 23

BETRAYED

I ran onto the bridge and pointed as I tried to catch my breath. Genevieve, with Rodin hovering around her, blurted out, "The Storm Vulture is here. Out the port side."

Baldarich ran to the window. "Curse that witch! Why now?"

"She's coming on fast," I gasped.

"Coyote," the captain said, "turn us away, and stay out of the range of their grapplers." He peered through his telescope, and without looking at me said, "Alexander, looks like all the damage you caused has been repaired. They look to be in fighting form." He turned to Genevieve. "Fancy another swordfight with a pirate?"

My father's eyes widened, no doubt wondering what on earth I could have had to do with damaging a sky pirate's ship and why in the world the daughter of a baron would have ever crossed swords with its captain.

I waited for the Sparrowhawk to surge forward and bank away from Zerelda's ship. Could we stay out of her reach? Would we be able to escape or would we have to fight again? The moments ticked by as blood pounded in my temple and my heart thudded against my ribs. I looked around. I should be leaning as the vessel banked into its turn, but our speed hadn't increased and we remained level, sticking to the same course we'd been on. I saw Coyote sitting with his hands on the wheel but his gaze was a thousand miles out in the stormy sky. I glanced over at the captain and started to speak, just as he turned around.

"Coyote, I said turn. Keep us out of the range of their grapplers."

Coyote rotated the wheel toward the Storm Vulture and the vessel started to bank. "I'm afraid I can't do that captain."

The captain crossed the bridge toward the pilot, but Coyote leapt out of the seat raised his arm and a small pistol slid out his sleeve and into his hand. He pointed it at the captain. "Don't make me shoot you, captain. She just wants the kids and the professor."

Baldarich put up his hands. "How much is the sky witch paying you?"

"More than you." Coyote pulled a buckler shield from under his long gray overcoat. The small metal shield had a raised center that held the concealed gun barrel. He pointed the shield at Ignatius, who hadn't moved from the engineer's station, but had a pistol aimed at the pilot.

I stared in disbelief. *How could Coyote turn on his own crew?* "If this is about money, we can get you more when we get back to England."

"Maybe you don't get it, brat, you're not going back to England." He shook his head. "Welcome to the real world, where happy endings only come at the end of a barrel."

His words hit me like a fist to my gut, and I felt like I might throw up. I had never been betrayed before, sure bullies had picked on me, friends had told their white lies that freed them from obligations, but a liar, who I considered a friend? Someone with whom I'd faced death? Never. I had been ignorant to those feelings and I wished now that it had stayed that way.

Baldarich's eyes narrowed and his voice deepened. "Coyote, I want you to think real hard about your next step, it may be a long one."

"Captain, my next step was already planned. They'll come aboard, I get paid, they take possession of the kids and the professor, and after that, fate is left in your hands." Coyote smiled, but kept his guns trained on the captain and Ignatius. "You can either turn them over peacefully, or you can be blasted out of the sky. Either way I get paid, and get safe passage off this vessel."

"Those are my only options. I see. I should be worried then?" Captain Baldarich laughed. "You disgust me; I saved you from swinging underneath that yard arm after you'd fled America."

"You yanked me off a ship during one of your raids and offered me a slightly better deal than the one I had. I'm not one your German lap dogs, I'm here for the money and we haven't been bringing in much of it lately." He looked at Ignatius. "Come on, you know what I'm talking about. Why don't we make the Sparrowhawk our new ship?"

"Sorry, I don't like Zerelda or her new friends." Ignatius spit on the deck. "Besides, I'm going to have too much fun shooting you."

I bit back the tears and stepped forward causing everyone to shift. Coyote pointed the shield at me, Genevieve pulled me back by my sleeve as Rodin slid from her shoulder. Ignatius stood up and aimed his Colt at Coyote who moved the shield back and forth between the two of us. Baldarich took a step to the side and closed the distance between himself and the pilot.

The hurt and disappointment morphed into pure rage, and I didn't care that the shield gun was aimed at my head. I marched toward Coyote, shouting, "How can you betray us? Zerelda is working for Kannard and he is evil. How can you help them?"

"Quit being so naïve, kid. I have no love for the English, and as an American you shouldn't either. So Kannard and his horsemen want to head to London and wreck havoc. Maybe they'll topple the crown, take down the monarchy. More power to them." My father raised his hand to interject, but Coyote aimed his pistol at him. "Shut up, I would love to shoot someone here, and I think you've more than served your purpose, Professor. My paymasters didn't seem too concerned if I killed you."

My father lowered his hand and looked at me, stunned and confused.

"I only want to know one thing," Captain Baldarich said. "When did she buy you?"

"When Zerelda captured the Sparrowhawk. She made me an offer I couldn't refuse. Besides you'd just shown you didn't care. First you make that damn Indian your boatswain, and then you let them take the ship and torture us, rather than give up the kids. That let me know where your loyalties lay."

Baldarich shook his head. "I liked you, Coyote, but I should have listened to my instincts and never trusted the trickster."

"Enough small talk. Raise the white flag or I'll use one of their bloodied shirts to signal the Storm Vulture."

I couldn't listen any longer; the pain ripped me from my shell. "Everyone tries to complicate this with excuses, but it's simple: you help people no matter what their country, class, or color."

Baldarich threw back his coat and said, "Ignatius. Kill him."

Coyote turned his shield toward Ignatius who fired his colt. The bullet struck the buckler and rang like a gong. The captain drew his lightning cannon and dove to the ground as Coyote fired at him without looking. The bullet went over his head; he rolled and fired. The electric bolt missed, but the look it put on Coyote's face brought a smile to everyone's face.

Rodin flew in, attacking Coyote's head. The little bronze dragon scratched with its claws and bit his ear. Genevieve smiled and drew her saber and I reached for my Thumper.

Coyote threw the dragon at the wall. Rodin clung for a moment and then dropped to the floor. Shaking his head, and spitting out several locks of Coyote's hair, the little dragon looked ready for more.

Coyote took another shot at Ignatius, forcing him to duck away and run off the bridge.

The captain cried out, "Ignatius, help me get this ship back on course."

"Aye,"

Genevieve and I ran after Coyote, and found him by the conning tower ladder.

Mr. Singh blocked his path.

Coyote still had his buckler shield raised, but had already used up the two-shot derringer in his other hand. Pushing himself against the wall, he drew a duck-foot pistol and fired. The eight barrels of the duck-foot were arranged in pairs that fanned out in a wide arc. All the barrels fired simultaneously.

I grabbed Genevieve and dropped to the deck. Mr. Singh fell backward down the stairs.

Coyote raced up the ladder and out the top of the conning tower. I leapt up and followed. I popped my head above the conning tower and looked around. I'd expected to get shot, but Coyote was running for the front of the Sparrowhawk. Climbing out onto the top of the aero-dirigible, I saw the Storm Vulture trying to maneuver overhead. The wind whipped against me and made it hard to stand. The cool moisture of the storm dampened my clothes and I shivered.

The Sparrowhawk banked away from the Storm Vulture and I grabbed hold of a stabilizing line to keep from falling.

Looking up at the sky pirates, I had the sudden feeling this was a bad idea. I didn't know what Coyote was trying to do, but Zerelda was pointing at him.

The Sparrowhawk dove to gain speed and slipped away from the Storm Vulture. Coyote tumbled forward, and I let go of the line and slid after him. My hands frantically searched for the railing, and snagged it with one hand. The Sparrowhawk leveled off and Coyote who had locked his foot into a seam sprang up and looked over the side.

I drew my Thumper and said, "Come back here, traitor!"

Coyote turned and smiled. "Kid, if you ever played poker with me, you'd know I always have an escape plan."

"That's because you cheat. I've seen you play." I wanted to pull the trigger, but I'd never shot a man point blank. I hesitated.

Coyote laughed, winked at me, and dove off the railing like a circus performer. His jacket ripped open, and a huge canvas chute opened above him, billowing in the wind. Our eyes connected one last time and he pointed to the eastern sky with a crooked, wicked smile.

I looked east and saw black dots arcing out across the sky. It was a zeppelin armada of every size and shape ready to engulf us like a pack of sharks devouring its prey. Two shots rang out, and I ducked. Below the ship, Coyote spun wildly in the air, one rope connected to his canvas chute had been severed and he gripped his leg as his pant leg turned red and blood dripped into air.

I used the rail to slide back to the conning tower and descend the ladder. Hunter stood there leaning on Gretel. Thin wisps of smoke still streamed out of the barrels and the wide smile on his face was all I needed to know where the shots had come from.

"You hit him."

"Winged him. He'll have a hell of time with that chute, and landing is going to hurt. Doubt he feels it, though. No one betrays the captain."

"He did more than sell out to Zerelda," I pointed toward the eastern sky where the black dots were slowly getting bigger. "An armada of airships is heading this way."

CHAPTER 24

THE ARMADA

"Good, you two are back." Captain Baldarich said from the pilot's seat.

In the distance, the armada stretched across the clouded sky. Huge war zeppelins towered over smaller airskiffs, and air balloons bobbed along behind them with clusters of bombs dangling on long tethers beneath the navigator's baskets. The sun glinted on gleaming brass and matte steel as they closed the distance.

Gunports popped open in rapid succession on the larger vessels as men crisscrossed the open decks in a flurry of activity.

The pirate fleet was terrifying, yet I couldn't look away. I tried to count them, but lost track, watching the flagmen relay orders with whipping arms. Then in unison the armada turned toward the Sparrowhawk.

"Let the battle begin," I whispered, hoping no would hear my fear.

"Milady, sit here." The captain stood, but still held on to the wheel. "Alexander, stand beside her, man the throttle and help her steer."

Genevieve snapped, "I can handle it," and sat down.

"This is about to get pretty nasty. I love this ol'girl, but she's a bit of a whale. She'll try to kick back with each canon shot, so Alexander will help you steady this thing. Hell, even that back-stabber Coyote would have needed my help."

I nodded, and grabbed the three wooden-handled brass throttles.

"Just do what I say and you'll be fine." Returning to his chair, the captain turned to my father. "Get me a bearing on that fleet."

"Surely you're surely not going to depend on two children to fly this airship."

"Are you going to fly it, Professor?"

My father's face turned white. The captain held his gaze. "Bearing, professor. Now, if you don't mind."

My father turned back to the map and charts arrayed on the table. "If you're looking for a fight, turn northeast, and you'll run right into them."

"Excellent!" Baldarich said as he dropped into his chair. "Starboard turn, thirty degrees, rise five degrees."

I looked at Genevieve; her puzzled expression mirrored my own. "Queen's English, please," she said.

"Turn the wheel to the right until you see it move thirty degrees on the compass and pull back a little bit until the nose is up five degrees. Alexander, push all three levers two ticks forward."

"That, I can understand." She followed his instructions as I adjusted the throttle and the Sparrowhawk soared into ever-darkening skies.

The captain barked orders into each of the copper tubes. I studied his calm demeanor, the way he commanded the vessel like an orchestra conductor. He was fearless and I was in awe of his calm demeanor. I couldn't swallow the lump lodged in my throat nor fling away the sweat pouring from my brow. Terror gripped me in its clammy claws, but passed like a swift breeze over Captain Baldarich.

I bit my lip and thought of the word fear in every language I could think of. I tried to imagine what the battle might be like, but the captain leaned in and said, "It'll be far worse than anything running through your mind. Count on that."

"How did you know...?"

"Seen that face plenty of times." The captain looked out the window and stroked his mustache.

The Sparrowhawk angled toward the armada, and I realized Baldarich studied the configuration trying to figure out what would happen in the battle before it took place.

Genevieve grunted as she turned to port. I grabbed the wheel as it jerked back to starboard. Genevieve and I fought to bring it back, as my knuckles turned white.

Baldarich pushed back his dark leather coat and his hands went to his hips. "Let's see who's come to visit. Milady, take us through."

I turned and asked, "What?"

"If you were truly on my crew, I'd dangle you outside for that remark." Baldarich spun around and smiled. "Right down the middle, please, and Alexander full speed ahead. I wouldn't want to be shot."

We repeated in unison, "Aye captain."

"Better. And try not to hit anyone."

The Sparrowhawk flew straight through the middle of the armada. Several airships opened fire, but all were off on their timing. By plowing straight through the middle and increasing our speed, the captain had thrown off the gunners.

Passing between two Zeppelins, Baldarich slammed his fist against the railing. "Damn, these two are part of the German air corps. I was hoping they'd only be sky pirates. Not that I mind sending a few of the Kaiser's lackeys to the ground."

"Is the Kaiser coming after us too?" I tried to keep my

voice from trembling.

"I doubt it. He and England are on opposite sides of a bunch of treaties, that's all."

My father brought his hand to his chin. "Kannard might have turned to the Kaiser to help with the Templars."

The captain motioned to descend and Genevieve pushed forward on the wheel. The Zeppelins opened fire, and I ducked. I knew it was pointless, but I couldn't help it. Genevieve held steady, barely blinking at the repeated booms.

We slipped past them and the two zeppelins broadsided each other with cannon fire. A huge explosion erupted above us casting an amber hue on the windows. I ducked again.

Baldarich leaned closer to the window. "Wait for it, wait for it … now! Pull up, hard."

The crumbling, fiery wrecks plunged through the clouds as the Sparrowhawk twisted between the mass of airships. My pulse quickened, and my hands were white as I gripped the levers. I had never seen this many airships, even in New York. The armada appeared endless, and in the distance I saw reinforcements on the horizon.

At first, one or two cannon balls crisscrossed in front of the Sparrowhawk as if we waded through a tennis match, but when Baldarich ordered us to turn back, the cannons shook the air like thunder. Lead shot crossed before us like sheets of rain.

The captain pointed to one of the larger ships. "Perfect, bring us alongside that one."

Genevieve and I maneuvered the Sparrowhawk.

Captain Baldarich walked over to his chair and flipped open one of the copper tubes. "Gears, I need smoke."

A voice echoed back. "But, captain, I quit after the last grease fire, I swear."

Baldarich shook his head. "I need a cloud, and I need it

now!"

"Oh! Aye aye, sir. Coming right up."

The captain hadn't fired a single shot, but had taken out several airships. I wondered, what could be next?

Thick, white smoke engulfed the windows as it billowed out from the back of the Sparrowhawk. My first reaction was fire, but the captain saw my concern and said, "Cloud powder. Gears has a great recipe. We'll be completely obscured in no time."

Genevieve nodded. "So you intend to hide in the smoke?"

"Yes and no." The captain went to the window. "Alexander, slow us down, one tick above full stop."

Stopping was suicide, but I did as I was told. All the ships closed in on our position, and soon we'd be surrounded. Any one of the large zeppelins could knock us out the sky. They were probably readying their guns right now while Baldarich acted like he was standing in a den full of sleeping bears trying to decide which one to poke with a stick. I swallowed hard and waited for the next order.

"Who will take my bait?" Baldarich asked as he watched the armada moving through the clouds. "Captain Harker! Haven't seen you since you cheated me at cards."

A medium sized airship crested over another vessel heading straight for the Sparrowhawk. Its gaudy bright colors made it stick out from the steel-gray German Zeppelins.

The captain said to Genevieve. "Prepare to dive. Straight down and then roll to the left. If you do it right we'll miss all the action above us. If not, we die a fiery death. Having fun yet?"

Genevieve smiled. "Awaiting your orders captain."

The gun ports on the large Zeppelin opened along its entire length. "Now! Alexander, full throttle."

I pushed the levers forward, Genevieve put us into a deep dive, and the Sparrowhawk dropped out of the cloud.

Wisps of white still clung to the windows as we plunged into open skies. The rest of the smoke enveloped the armada as the pirate Captain Harker and the larger Zeppelin opened fire with full broadsides. Seeing them fire into the cloud, other airships did as well, and in the chaos, round upon round slammed into the zeppelins above us.

The Sparrowhawk rolled out and slipped beneath the carnage. I couldn't believe it. We hadn't fired a shot and already it was looking like we'd won.

Genevieve straightened out the Sparrowhawk and flew just below the others airships. Looking up, I saw the battle raging as the armada fought itself. But a couple of vessels quickly saw through the scam, and dropped below to come after us.

Baldarich pointed into the sky. "There, head for that small one and get above it."

She pulled up and banked the Sparrowhawk. I watched the captain as I pushed the throttle forward and helped Genevieve control the wheel.

Baldarich flipped the cover off one of the copper messaging tubes. "Mr. Singh, prepare to fire the grappler, we're going fishing."

The captain tapped his foot as he waited. The Sparrowhawk flew over the airskiff and Baldarich slammed his fist against the railing. "Mr. Singh, fire!" He turned to Genevieve. "Wait for it."

I heard the pop of the grappler, and the whirring of the unwinding cable. Then the Sparrowhawk shuddered as the cable went taut and Baldarich smiled. "Ahead, Master Armitage. Milady, would you maneuver us over to that blimp please."

The captain laughed as we soared over the blimp. I heard a loud crashing sound and felt the whole vessel shake. They had just dragged one ship into another. Amazing. Baldarich had this armada at his whim. He appeared to move with ease and pick his targets at will.

Genevieve screamed, I looked up and saw one of the large Zeppelins rising to block their path. Genevieve pulled with all her might and I joined her. Together we spun the wheel to the left sending the Sparrowhawk into a steep bank. We barely missed the huge airship, but now several of the ships had caught on to our tactics and we found ourselves suddenly surrounded.   My stomach tightened, sensing the shift in the battle. We had dipped in and out of the fleet picking vulnerable targets, but now, Genevieve and I couldn't find any way to maneuver.

Captain Baldarich looked out the window and shook his head. "Well it was fun while it lasted, looks like we'll have to fight our way out of this one." He winked at Genevieve. "Excellent work in the pilot's seat, Milady. You'd be too expensive to keep for long, but you'll do 'til I can find another."

"With pleasure, captain." Rodin flew up and landed on Genevieve's shoulder.

Jealousy's bitter blade pricked me. I wanted to be the new pilot, but I bit my tongue, and instead turned back toward the window ringed by brass bolts. That was when I saw it. The Storm Vulture, loomed at the edge of the firestorm, her bow aimed right at the Sparrowhawk.

"Captain!"

He spun around. "That witch has the worst timing." He pointed at me. "Head down to the gun-deck and assist Mr. Singh."

"Aye, captain."

CHAPTER 25

STORMS

I ran to the gun-deck but found it empty. I began gathering cannon balls and powder charges next to the port side guns. The Storm Vulture approached from that side and from what I'd learned, we would bank, come alongside, and then the broadsides would begin.

From the copper tube above, I heard the captain's voice. "Battlestations! Port guns prepare to fire."

The crewmen charged down onto the gun-deck led by Mr. Singh. I set three pre-loaded magazines next to the portside Gatling gun. I looked up to find the Sikh watching me.

"You prepared the guns?"

I saluted. "Yes, sir, I knew we had to be ready and assumed the captain would keep them on the portside."

"Good job." Mr. Singh commanded the gunners, "Open gun-ports and prepare to fire." He shifted back to me. "Open the starboard ports as well. It will help clear the smoke."

I ran over and pulled a series of levers to snap open all the starboard gun-ports. A cold wind carrying the smell of rain whipped through the gun-deck. I ran into the forward compartment, grabbed my leather jacket and a pair of goggles. Returning to the gun-deck I saw the Storm Vulture coming alongside. Fear threatened to immobilize me, but I pushed it aside. Fear would have to wait; I had a duty to perform.

The Sparrowhawk banked toward the Storm Vulture, and I wondered what Baldarich was thinking, until I realized the distance was closing between us. In moments we would be in position to fire, before the Storm Vulture would be ready. I smiled, and made a note to remember that tactic.

Mr. Singh pointed his shamshir at the pirate vessel; the sword's curved blade and handle remained firm in his hand. "Cannon one, fire. Cannon two, fire. Gatling, fire at will."

I watched as the first shot ripped through the hull of the Storm Vulture forward of the wing. The second plunged through above the wing as the Gatling gun aerated the hull just behind it. I jumped up, cheering the success.

Mr. Singh stood stoically before the others and said, "Prepare to receive broadside."

Uh oh. I didn't like the sound of that.

The airmen manning the guns ducked behind whatever they could find, but Mr. Singh remained defiantly exposed in the middle of the gun-deck standing before the Storm Vulture.

I saw four puffs of smoke from the Storm Vulture. Cannon shot ripped through the hull beside me. Dust and smoke choked the air, splinters of wood and shards of metal exploded across the gun-deck, biting my skin as they flew by. The outer hull peeled inward as a cannon ball punched through and whipped past me. Another passed harmlessly through an open gun-port and straight out the starboard side.

Mr. Singh pointed his shamshir at the airmen. "Reload."

They returned to the cannons, and loaded their second shot as the men operating the Gatling gun opened fire. A shower of lead spewed a choking cloud from the barrel and filled the deck with smoke. The rapid fire of the Gatling ripped into the side of the Storm Vulture as fast as the men could crank the handle on its side.

The chaotic scene playing out before me reminded me of a machine, they way everyone moved in unison, each with a function and a duty, like interlocking gears. The battle frightened me to my core and made me want to cower in a corner. But I knew there were no safe places on the ship and I needed to be prepared to jump into action at Mr. Singh's next command.

Mr. Singh aimed his shamshir at the Storm Vulture again. "Fire!"

I saw a single puff of smoke from the last gun-port of the Storm Vulture, but only one. Had they held back one cannon from their broadside?

Two cannon balls connected by an iron chain ripped through the first cannon's gun-port. The chain-shot cut through the men manning the cannon.

The second cannon on the deck of the Sparrowhawk, the one I stood frozen behind, roared in a burst of smoke and fire. The force messed my hair but I didn't flinch, the horror before me locked my muscles and wrenched my insides into knots.

I tried to reach the first cannon but slipped in the oil and blood, and crashed into the cast-iron weapon and its wooden carriage. I frantically searched for the burning rope to light the wick and fire the cannon. The punk lay beside the remnants of one body, extinguished.

I looked around for another source of fire but saw nothing. The lamps that were lit now lay shattered on the deck. Mr. Singh ran to the cannon and tore a piece of his blue tunic. He dug a small shard of flint from the pouch on his belt and struck his sword above the fabric. A few sparks showered down but would not ignite the silk.

Above him, I saw the little bronze dragon soar down the stairs to the gun-deck. I called out, "Rodin!"

The dragon flew down and landed on the cannon.

Mr. Singh stopped trying to light the cloth, which blew away in the raging wind, and said, "Remember to aim."

I sighted between Rodin's legs and saw the side of the Storm Vulture through the whirling smoke. I pointed to the wick. "Rodin, fire, come on I need a fireball."

The little dragon wiggled his backside, all the way to his tail. He extended his neck and a small ball of fire shot out and ignited the wick.

Sparks raced into the barrel and the cannon hurled its shot toward the Storm Vulture. The cannon recoiled back from the blast. I fell backward and avoided being struck by the ropes which held the cannon in place.

Rodin flew toward the ceiling startled by the blast.

We looked out through the smoke and saw a new hole in the engine room of the Storm Vulture. Black smoke billowed out the side.

I clenched my fist and shouted with excitement. "We did it!"

Mr. Singh looked over his shoulder at me. "Load another; I'll get two men to relieve you."

"Aye Mr. Singh."

I picked up the tightly packed cloth powder charge and slid it into the barrel. With the ramrod held tightly in my hand I drove it to the base of the barrel.

As I ran for the ball, Mr. Singh's voice call out the dreaded words, "Prepare to receive broadside."

I looked for Rodin; he was just above me flying around the deck. I grabbed the bronze dragon, pulled him close to my chest, dove against the wall at the front of the vessel and prayed we would survive.

The gun-deck exploded as the cannon shot ripped through, showering wood and metal on everyone inside.

Shards tore into the wall above me, but Rodin and I remained unhurt. I popped up and saw Mr. Singh still commanding the deck. One of the airmen stepped around me with a small piece of metal in his arm and grabbed an iron ball.

I sat up, but held Rodin tight to my chest. The little dragon clung to my jacket and kept its wings tucked close to its body. I rubbed Rodin's horned nubs. The dragon looked just as scared as I felt. The smoke swirled, dissipating in the strong winds whipped up by all the holes and open ports. The smell of gunpowder and imminent rain filled the air, making me cough and choke.

I called out to Mr. Singh. "What should I do?" The Gatling gun's magazines had to be reloaded, more iron shot was needed for the cannons, and injured crew members needed care.

My thoughts turned to Genevieve. Was she safe? I whispered to Rodin. "Go find Genevieve, make sure she's okay."

Rodin flew off, soaring up the steps.

Suddenly, the Sparrowhawk banked steeply to starboard and climbed higher in the sky. Everything not secured, including me, tumbled backward.

I grabbed hold of the starboard cannon and righted myself. Looking out the gun-port, I saw the black clouds of the storm engulfing the Sparrowhawk. "The captain is brilliant to hide. The armada will never follow us in there."

Mr. Singh nodded. "But we could still be torn up by the high winds or lightning could spark the charges. We must trust in god."

I nodded, but Mr. Singh wasn't making me feel any better. He may put his trust in his god, but I put mine in the captain.

CHAPTER 26

CRASH LANDING

Once the rain started, I wondered if it would ever stop. It pelted the vessel and poured through the shattered hull in sheets. The sound of hail battering the airship sounded worse than the rapid-fire of the Gatling gun as the Sparrowhawk was buffeted by the storm. The wind roared through the gun-deck, and Mr. Singh and I fought through it to seal the hatches. I hoped the captain knew what he was doing, but I feared that if the armada didn't take us down, the storm would.

The gun-deck plunged into darkness between each flash of lightning. After the hatches were sealed, I helped secure the cloth-covered charges to keep the gunpowder dry. Mr. Singh stopped me from loading the last four into a chest. He grabbed two and said, "Not these. You men wipe down the barrels. Alexander, load the cannon and plug the barrels. I want to be ready if the Storm Vulture comes into range."

I joined with the other men and said, "Aye, aye."

The crew wiped the rain out of the cannons. Once dry, a relative term in this heavy storm, I rammed the charge down the barrel followed by the iron shot. One of the airmen handed me a large wooden plug and I sealed it into the end of the barrel.

"Just remember to remove it before you fire," I said with a black-humored smile.

The airmen laughed just as a lightning bolt arced inward from the outer hull and struck one of the cannon.

Mr. Singh checked the cannon and sighed. "It didn't ignite the powder, thank god." He leaned out one of the holes in the hull. "I think the lightning rods have been damaged, they're supposed to direct the lightning around the Sparrowhawk."

I wondered what would happen if it had exploded, but cast-iron shrapnel wasn't something I wanted to see.

Bolts of electricity arced past the Sparrowhawk's starboard side, but I heard no thunder and it came from below.

It wasn't the storm.

"The Storm Vulture's lightning cannon?" I asked. "What do we do when they're firing from behind and below us?"

"We pray," Mr. Singh said with his usual happy grin.

"We don't have any guns back there, do we?"

"Go tell the captain, he may not be able to see the bolts. Tell him we have a surprise waiting for those jackals."

I extended my hand. "Be careful, Mr. Singh."

We grabbed forearms. "Watch yourself as well, Master Armitage."

I ran up the stairs and found the captain. "The Storm Vulture is firing its lightning cannon from behind and below us."

"Tell me something I don't know."

"Mr. Singh has a surprise waiting for those jackals."

Baldarich nodded and a devious grin crossed his face. "Now that is good news."

"Wait with your father." The captain pointed to the professor who clung to the bolted-down map table. "I think I know how to get us out of this mess."

My father looked me over. I knew I was a mess, soaked with blood and rain, the smell of gunpowder clinging to my clothes, and scratched all over from the shivers of wood and metal that ripped through the gun-deck. Genevieve's face registered alarm and concern, but I couldn't read my father's expression other than that he was not happy.

The captain snapped his new pilot's attention back to the wheel. "Genevieve! Put the wind on our backs, and get ready to turn our side to those vultures."

Genevieve struggled to turn the wheel as she let out a hearty, "Aye, captain."

Ignatius spoke up from the engineering station. "Captain, I don't think the Sparrowhawk can handle the stress. We're already buckling."

"She'll hold," Baldarich said with a smile. "I know something that witch doesn't. The Sparrowhawk has integrated helium tanks but the Storm Vulture's flying under an external hydrogen tank. It can't handle the stress of the wind. Her external tank will be ripped away from the fuselage if she tries to follow us. Besides, maybe we'll get lucky and one of those lightning bolts will find her hydrogen and give us a fireball to light our way."

The Sparrowhawk banked to port and I grabbed hold of the map table to avoid sliding across the bridge.

The vessel lurched right and then back left, buffeted by the strong winds. Thunder roared around us, quickly followed by the rapid flashes of multiple lightning bolts. I noticed my father trying to count the seconds in between the thunder and lightning, a trick I'd been taught years ago to tell the distance from the center of the storm, but these came too close together. We were in the heart of the storm.

I found my footing, let go of the map table, and ran to the port window. The black storm clouds had enveloped us making it darker than a moonless night – except when the lightning flashed.

As electricity ignited the sky, the Storm Vulture burst through the dark, billowing clouds. I called out, "I see them. They're still behind us."

Thunder crashed and I watched as lightning struck the Storm Vulture. I wanted to cheer, but the outer hull beside me peeled back in the high winds. My nerves told me to get away from the window, but I remained until I saw the sky pirate's bank away from us. "Captain, the Storm Vulture's turned starboard."

"Genevieve, hard to starboard!" Baldarich flipped open the copper tube and yelled, "Mr. Singh, fire all starboard guns!"

The Sparrowhawk banked to the right. The guns erupted. The iron shot cut through the clouds and slammed into the front of the blimp, which blew apart in a fireball larger than any I had seen. But only the first compartment—the rest remained intact. The Storm Vulture limped into the dark clouds and disappeared.

Thunder exploded and an ache in my gut told me something bad was about to happen. I turned to Baldarich, but the sky ignited as lightning crackled around us. The Sparrowhawk lurched, shook violently, and listed to port like a ship about to sink. My stomach tightened.

Baldarich slammed his fist against the railing. "We've been hit! Was it the Storm Vulture?"

I looked back out the window. "No, they've fled into the clouds."

Gear's voice echoed up through the furthest left copper tube. "Captain, port wingsail's been ripped to shreds! Also, pressure's building in engine three. I have to shut it down."

Ignatius checked the dial and nodded his head. "It's at the red line, captain. We don't want it blowing up in this storm."

The captain shook his head. "But we can't make it through these winds without it."

I stared into the dark clouds below. "We're going down aren't we?"

"What kind of talk is that, lad?"

A rumble echoed through the hull and the Sparrowhawk lurched suddenly, throwing everyone on the bridge from their posts. Captain Baldarich fell but held onto the railing throwing out his arm, he caught my father who grabbed me by the collar of my shirt. Ignatius tumbled out of his chair and hit the wall. Genevieve tried to remain at her post but was tossed from her chair causing the wheel to spin wildly. The Sparrowhawk listed far to port before finally turning on its side. We all tumbled onto the wall and the vessel nosed over hurtling everyone against the bow. Only Rodin was unaffected as he darted around the bridge avoiding debris.

Baldarich and Genevieve struggled to climb up to the pilot's wheel. The captain pulled himself into the seat and grabbed the spinning yoke. Yelling a guttural battle cry that hurt my ears, he pulled the wheel against his chest trying to right the Sparrowhawk.

Ignatius clung to a rail at the bow of the vessel and looked at the gauges of the engineering section. "Engine three is about to blow and it looks like the other two have stopped. Cap, I'd say we're—"

"Don't say it! I've never crashed a ship, and I don't intend to start now." Baldarich's veins bulged in his forehead and his knuckles turned white. "Right yourself, you fickle beast!"

I rolled over and looked out the window I'd fallen against. We'd broken through the cloud bank, and the lights of a large city spread out below us, sparkling like the Milky Way on a crystal clear night.

Genevieve grabbed the wheel with the captain and pulled hard. Slowly the Sparrowhawk began to level off, still listing severely to port.

Ignatius ran to the copper tubes, flipped them all open,

and yelled. "Gears! If you're still alive, we need an engine now! Mr. Singh, get the port wingsail working!" He ran off the bridge, stumbling as he tried to navigate the debris and slanted deck.

I stumbled over to the engineer's station and studied the dials. None of the needles were in the places they were supposed to be. Out of the tumult, I heard my father's voice.

"It's Paris, and it's getting closer."

The captain's voice strained as he continued to pull on the wheel. "Thanks for stating the obvious, Professor. Brace for impact."

My father ran to the map table and said, "Alexander, Genevieve, secure yourselves."

I unwrapped the leather strapping from my body, and tied one end around the railing of the engineer's station. Genevieve left the captain and grabbed hold of me. I bound us together with the leather strap. Huddled side by side, we locked eyes. Then she called out for Rodin. The little bronze dragon flew down and landed beside us. Genevieve grabbed him and clutched him to her chest. I wrapped my arms around her and waited for the impact.

Paris loomed below us, too close and getting closer. The Sparrowhawk's nose still tilted downward and listed to port which caused it to continue turning no matter how steady the captain held the wheel. The winding Seine River cut the city in half and we appeared to be aimed at a large park on the western edge.

Baldarich's gritty voice squeezed through clenched teeth. "Let's hope we miss the river. I don't fancy a swim at the moment."

The captain wrangled the Sparrowhawk with all his might. Once over the river, he pushed forward on the wheel and the nose plunged into the park. The impact jolted the bridge, and Genevieve, Rodin, and I swung forward but remained secured by the leather strap. My father tumbled from underneath the map table, and the captain slammed into the wheel.

Scrapping, sheering sounds cut through the air as the metal and wood hull raked across branches, stone and grass. We finally skidded to a stop and I looked around, surprised to still be alive. I checked Genevieve and knew from her smile she was okay. We both looked over Rodin who wiggled out from between us. His grunts, snarls, and growls signaled his displeasure, but he was uninjured.

"Not my best landing," Baldarich said, pulling himself free of the wheel. "Everyone all right?"

An "Aye, captain," came from my father who gripped his forearm as he pulled himself to his feet.

I untied the leather strap. "We're okay."

"Good to hear it. Now if I can walk I'm going below to see who else made it out of that storm and survey the damage," Baldarich headed off the bridge, favoring his right leg.

Left on the bridge with my father, I said, "Your arm, are you hurt?"

"I'll be fine." He looked me over and turned to Genevieve. "I'm just glad you two are safe."

"Now what are we going to do? How do we get to London?" I asked.

Genevieve shook her head. "Getting to London isn't the problem. It's what we do once we're there. Lord Kannard will get there long before we do, and he'll have already put his plan into action."

"Then how do we stop him?"

My father clutched harder at his arm and winced. "I don't know."

CHAPTER 27

THE CITY OF LOVE

"Where are we?" I asked.

"Looks like the Champ du Mars," Genevieve whispered. "Father and I stayed nearby on our last holiday."

We were on solid ground, trailing Captain Baldarich as he surveyed The Sparrowhawk assessing the external damage. The underside had crumpled like a piece of paper, but most of the upper structure remained intact.

"Ignatius, head out with Gears. He'll know what we need, but you do the negotiating. I know it's late, but bang on a few doors if you have to. We have to get back in the sky."

Ignatius tipped his Stetson and asked, "What will you be doing, Cap'n?"

"I have to grease some palms to make sure we don't get hauled off to the Bastille for landing in a city park. Should be back by morning." Mr. Singh walked past the door and Baldarich said, "Indihar, come here, while I'm gone, you're in charge. If the Gendarmes show—afer all, how could they miss us—tell 'em to speak with their superiors before they arrest the whole lot. Just don't mention my name."

"Aye, captain," Mr. Singh said with a smile.

"You're a good man Mr. Singh. Repair what you can.

Ignatius and Gears will return with supplies as soon as possible." Baldarich turned and pointed at Genevieve and me. "You two stay out of trouble, and don't get in the way of my crew. Your father busted his arm; Hunter's setting it."

I nodded. "Yes, captain. Thank you."

Everyone set about their tasks leaving Genevieve and me standing awkwardly in the center of the city park.

Genevieve's face was shining with excitement. She leaned in and whispered. "Have you ever been to Paris?"

"No."

"You should see the city, it's beautiful. I could give you a tour."

I looked across the skyline. Then back at the ship where my father was getting his arm set. What would I rather do? Sit with him and listen to him lecture me about how irresponsible I'd been or see the sights of Paris with a beautiful girl? "I'd like that."

"Let me secure Rodin." Genevieve and I climbed back inside the vessel, and she made certain the little bronze dragon would remain tucked up in the nest he'd created in our quarters. "I'll bring you a treat if you're good," she promised with a kiss on his head.

We left the Sparrowhawk and made our way down to the stone walls lining the Seine. The flickering lights of the gas streetlamps made the water sparkle, and the rain soaked streets reflected the star-filled sky above. It was magical.

I leaned against the stone railing and watched the city go by. Carriages rumbled by, people laughed and carried on, voices filled the night with joy. The vibrant, infectious, nightlife was unlike anything I'd ever seen. "Hardly seems real that we were just in a fire fight with a sky pirate armada." I said.

Genevieve was quiet for a while, and we stood side by side without saying—or needing to say—a single word. Then she brushed her hair behind her ear and took my hand, her soft, cool skin shooting a tingle of electricity through me. "Come with me. I want to show you something."

"I am at your command, Milady," I teased, happy to have her hand clasped in mine.

She led me down a few streets to an open square. A large obelisk stood in the center with statues all around the plaza. "My father brought me here. It's the Place de la Concorde, I love the fountains."

"Wow, it's beautiful."

"The obelisk is—"

"Egyptian," I squinted to read the hieroglyphs across the street. "Created for Ramses II."

Genevieve glanced my way with a coy smile. "Show off."

"Where is the Louvre? I've always wanted to see the museum."

Genevieve pointed. "It's not far; maybe we can see it tomorrow."

"That'd be nice. They'll be fixing the Sparrowhawk for days."

"We should get back," she said.

"What? It's too early, look at this place."

"But, we should—"

"See more Paris!" I smiled and slipped my fingers through hers again. "Come on, I saw some theaters this way."

"But Parisian theaters—"

"Will be fun."

We ran through the streets until music filled the air. A long line of well-dressed men waited to enter one of the theaters. One of several tucked away along a narrow cobblestone street.

Genevieve clung to my arm. "We'll never make it inside."

"Please, you're with me." I pointed toward the alley. "Come on, I used to do this in New York all the time."

"Did your father know you frequented the theater?"

"Hah! Hardly. He wouldn't approve. Of course, he doesn't approve of anything I do."

She hesitated, but stepped forward before our fingers pulled apart. "I'm not sure about this."

We approached the side door, and I pulled it open cautiously. The bright sound of up-tempo music poured into the alley, and the smell of sweat and perfume drew us in.

"Do we dare?" Genevieve whispered, her breath warm on my ear.

"Absolutely," I said. We slipped inside and hid behind a thick black curtain at the back of the stage. A line of women danced onstage, kicking up their skirts and flashing their black lingerie to the rousing cheers of the audience.

Genevieve covered her mouth with her hand. "Is that the can-can?"

"I think so."

"It's so ... scandalous."

I smiled. "Yeah."

The women rushed off stage, and I pulled Genevieve further behind the curtain. The announcer was saying something as the audience cheered wildly. Then another woman walked past where we were peeking through the curtain and took her place onstage.

Genevieve gasped. "She's only wearing feathers!"

"Really? Let me see." I pulled the curtain wider and there she was, bare butt and all. "Woah." I could barely breathe.

Slower music began and the woman started to dance, her body undulating to the rhythm like nothing I'd ever seen before. The sweet aroma of Genevieve's hair intoxicated me and I wanted to touch it. But I dared not move a muscle.

A man in black suit with a bushy moustache saw us from the other side of the stage. He stood and, with a stubby fat cigar, pointed at us. "Time to go," he mouthed with a glowering look as he made his way around props and backstage equipment.

With a flurry, we ran out the alley door just as he reached our side of the stage, and kept running until we entered the chaos of the main street as Gendarmes raided one of the other theaters. People ran in every direction.

"This way!" We darted down another alley, slipping through the missing slats of overturned shipping pallets.

We emerged in a small corner park, and I pulled her behind a cluster of trees as the Gendarmes whistled and called for order.

"It's crazy out there!" Genevieve said. Her face was flushed with excitement and she leaned in to quickly kiss my cheek just as I turned toward her. Our lips met and, emboldened by the wild night, I pressed forward. Electricity shot through me as if I'd been hit by Baldarich's lightning canon.

She pushed away and bit her bottom lip. "I ... I didn't mean to do that."

"I did." I couldn't help the goofy smile painting itself across my face. "For a first kiss, that was amazing."

I held her gaze, then slid my arm around her and kissed her again.

She pulled me closer, our bodies pressed together, and an eternity passed.

When I pulled back from Genevieve, the smile wouldn't leave my face no matter how hard I tried. I wanted to keep kissing her, to lose myself in the sweet aroma of roses that always seemed to surround her.

She brushed back my hair. "You're certainly bolder than we first met."

I blushed. "I feel more like myself than I ever did at Eton."

"I can tell."

I ran my finger across the soft porcelain skin of her cheek. "You however, are just a bold as when we met. I don't think I'll ever forget seeing you in pants."

"And I'll never forget the look on your face."

Several distant whistles signaled more Gendarmes on the way. "We should get out of here," I said.

"I agree, but I have to find something for Rodin. You don't want to see the mood he'll be in if we don't come back with the treat I promised."

We ran down a street lined with bakeshops and cafés. We stopped at a street vendor closing up his cart and I asked in French if he had any leftover food. With a friendly smile he opened his cart and handed each of us some bread and the remaining slice of a wheel of cheese.

"Merci," she said.

We both thanked him several times and then he leaned forward and winked at me before trundling off, pushing his cart before him. His parting comment made my cheeks flush and heart pound against my chest. I handed the bread to Genevieve, who twirled off under the lamplight. *"Comment est-ce que je peux refuser deux jeunes amants?'* How could I deny two young lovers? That's what he said, isn't it?"

"Yes." My voice was barely a pathetic squeak.

She bit her lip and said, "Thank you, and Rodin thanks you."

I wanted to kiss her again, but blurted out, "I didn't know you spoke French."

"Of course, it *is* the diplomatic language."

"Let's head back," I said, not daring to look at her.

"Good idea." She started walking and I quickened to catch up. "But you have to tell me how many languages you speak?" She pulled a soft tuft of bread from the middle of the loaf and popped it in her mouth.

I looked at my feet. "I've never actually counted." My stomach twisted up in knots; this was the question that always brought me ridicule. "Some I can figure out, like Spanish and Portuguese. I don't know it, but I can get by because I know French, Italian, and Latin. The romance languages are funny like that."

"The romance languages. I always liked the sound of that."

The blood rushed from my head, and I thought my knees might actually buckle. I distracted myself by stuffing a piece of bread the size of France in my face.

"What about ancient languages?"

I held up a finger while I struggled to chew and then swallow. "My father taught me all the Biblical languages. He thinks you should read the Bible in its original form. But he made certain I also studied hieroglyphics, too. And Arabic, and he's been threatening to teach me Cuneiform and Sanskrit. You probably want to run away now."

She giggled. "How do you remember them all?"

"Must be a family gift." A tense chuckle escaped. "I just sort of understand them." I looked up; we'd arrived back at the Champ du Mars.

The Sparrowhawk remained exactly where it had landed and the crew was hard at work on the repairs. We slipped inside and went to our room. My father was asleep in a hammock but Rodin emerged from his nest. The little dragon rushed over and circled us, studying our hands as he sniffed with his nose.

He landed on Genevieve's shoulder and began rooting around to find the food he could smell but couldn't see. She smiled and held the cheese on her palm. Rodin craned his neck to reach it and she held her hand a little farther away so that he had to stand on his hind legs. He looked adorable standing on her shoulder. She brought her palm down. Rodin sniffed the cheese and greedily snatched it up in his jaws. Too big for one mouthful, he bit off a chunk and held the rest in his front claws.

The dragon cooed as he ate the cheese. Happy and content, Rodin flew back to his nest and curled up for the night. I dropped into my own hammock but wasn't eager to put this day behind me. It had started off as one of the worst of my life, and ended as the best.

CHAPTER 28

UNEXPECTED MEETING

I woke to the sound of workers pounding metal and driving nails. I dropped out of my hammock, ran my fingers through my unruly hair, and stepped out to see if I could help. A flurry of activity buzzed around the Sparrowhawk as the crew lowered the hull plating into place and stretched new canvas to fix the wingsails.

I found Mr. Singh who supervised the wingsail's repair. "Anything I can do to help?"

"Nothing right now, ask the captain."

I nodded, and found Baldarich in the engine room with Gears working on engine three. The captain pulled his head out of the engine. "What do you want?" he asked.

"Need me?"

"No, this is skilled work. It will take days to get her up in the air again. Try Indihar."

I sighed. I saw my father pouring over a map and avoided him, then went looking for Genevieve. She and Rodin were walking the main deck, and I couldn't hide the smile she brought.

"Want to get out of here? No one needs me today. You could show me more of Paris."

"We can go to the Louvre. I think you'll love it, and it's not that far."

I raised my arm. "To the Louvre."

We placed Rodin back in our room and disembarked from the Sparrowhawk. As we crossed the Seine, Genevieve stared at the ladies passing by, and I realized she stuck out in her pants. "We should get you something else to wear, just while we're here in Paris."

"I'm fine in pants."

"We *are* in the silk capital of Europe."

Genevieve smiled. "Well … maybe we could just look."

We found a dress shop with the latest fashions displayed in the window. Stepping inside, I asked in French, "Excuse me, could you help this lovely woman find a dress?"

Within moments she'd selected a light blue dress with a high collar, when she emerged from the dressing room, my mouth dropped open.

"What's wrong, is it the color?"

"No, you look amazing," I rubbed my hand over my face and smiled.

In the window behind her I saw the bronze plated face of Col. Hendrix. I froze, but didn't know if we'd been spotted. "Come on we have to go."

"Why?"

I grabbed her arm. "Hendrix is outside." Her body stiffened.

"What do we do?"

I leaned in and whispered, "We run." I went to the dressing room; gathered her pants, corset, and jacket, then stuffed them in my leather bag.

Taking her hand, I led her out the back door of the shop and down the alley before finally stopping in the shadow of a building.

She snatched her hand away and held her chest. "What have you done? We just stole this dress?"

As I caught my breath, I said, "I guess we really are Sky Raiders."

"In all of Paris, we run right into him! Do you think he's still back there?"

I peered around the corner. "I don't know. Maybe, we should find a place to hide."

Genevieve pointed. "The Louvre is right there."

We ran toward the old castle just north of the river and darted inside. I stopped and looked around in amazement. My father had taken me to the Metropolitan Museum in New York, which I thought was wonderful, but it wasn't in a former French castle. Paintings and sculptures by all the great masters filled the immense halls. Looking up at the ceiling and everything around me, I almost fell over. "It's so overwhelming."

"I want to show you something." Genevieve led me toward one of the galleries.

"Here it is." Genevieve pointed to a painting on the wall. "It's Ferdinand Delacroix's 'Liberty Leading Her People.' I think it's beautiful."

"It is." Looking around, I noticed what hung on the opposite wall. A grand painting with three Templar Knights dressed in white tunics with a large red cross over their chests.

"Alexander, thank you for being here. You make it easier to deal with my father being poisoned."

"I haven't given up on finding a cure for your father."

"Lord Kannard smashed the vial. I think I'm out of options. I just hope we make it back before he..."

"Don't say it. Chances are that wasn't the only batch of antidote." I took her hand in mine. "We'll find a way, Genevieve. We have to."

The sound of footsteps on the marble floor yanked us away from each other. A man in a long blue coat trimmed with white stitching strode toward us. He looked to be in his middle thirties and was handsome in a studious way. He stopped, bowed, and asked, "Pardon, but you are Baron Kensington's Daughter, are you not?"

I pulled her behind me. "Who are you?"

"I am the Chevalier Eustache de Moley, Nobelsse d'épé."

I noticed his ring; it bore the same cross as the painting behind me.

"My father met with you when we came here," Genevieve said. "In this museum."

"Yes, and I know what has happened since that meeting. I believe I can help you." He bowed and motioned for us to follow. "Please, at my estate, I can explain everything."

CHAPTER 29

FOUR THIEVES POTION

I was beginning to believe in the Templar's mystical nature, but that didn't mean I trusted them. Genevieve might know him, but the way he found us in the museum felt a little too convenient.

I followed the French nobleman out of the Louvre, and noticed he studied the scene with a cautious gaze. I quickly searched for the men in long black coats who had pursued us earlier, but saw only a carriage decorated with ornate gold leaf.

"Wait." I grabbed Genevieve's sleeve.

Two silver-plated mechanical steeds stood before the carriage with a white-wigged coachman holding the reins from atop his perch. A similar footman stepped off the back and pulled a small lever. The door popped open and a gold-trimmed step flipped out from underneath.

The nobleman stepped into the carriage, but I held Genevieve back and pointed to the mechanical horses. "Those are *very* similar to the one Lord Kannard used."

Lord de Moley assured her. "All will be explained."

"My father trusted you and so shall I, but we will require an answer about your automatons."

She stepped into the carriage with assistance from the

footman, but I ignored the snooty, white-wigged man. We sat opposite the French Templar, who studied us as the carriage pulled off at a leisurely pace. It quickly picked up speed, as the metal hooves clinked against stone.

My eyes narrowed. "Now about those horses … Lord Kannard has a bronze steed that looks just like yours."

Lord de Moley shook his head. "Bronze? He always did lack a nobleman's grandeur."

Genevieve narrowed her eyes. "You know Lord Kannard?"

"Of course. There was a time when we were friends. He was a member of the Templar Order, but he was corrupted. Now his highest ideal is the desire to enslave all men."

"A Templar, that's impossible!" My chest wrenched in pain as a pillar of my idealized world crumbled. "He's evil, he kidnapped my father, poisoned the Baron, and you're telling me he's your friend!"

"Used to be my friend. My mentor even. But those days have fallen into distant memory. However, he knew of the ancient blueprints and the texts your father has been studying."

I heard the pain in Lord de Moley's voice. I was reminded of Coyote's betrayal of the Sparrowhawk crew.

"You said you could help us, what did you mean?" Genevieve asked.

"I believe I can aid your father."

She leaned forward. "You have the antidote for the serpent's venom?"

"No, I'm afraid only the Knights of the Golden Circle know what poison was used. However, I have another solution. Perhaps a better solution."

The carriage turned down a tree-lined road leading to a sprawling mansion on the outskirts of Paris. The white stone had grayed with age. The grounds needed a gardener to prune back the overgrowth, but the villa still maintained its grandeur, an echo of earlier times when the king himself would have stayed within its walls.

As we entered, I noticed most of the furniture was covered in great swaths of white cloth. Deep layers of dust smothered the side rooms, but a well-traveled path wound through the halls.

"Forgive the state of my home. Had I known guests were coming, I would have notified the staff."

I laughed. "Our stop in Paris was unplanned."

"I must confess I spend most of my time in the study," Lord de Moley said with an apologetic smile. "And I would be honored if you would address me as Eustache."

How could I address a nobleman by his first name? He seemed to sense the question and continued, "I insist. I spend so much time alone, it would be nice to feel as though I were entertaining friends."

The nobleman—Eustache—opened a series of double doors using several keys tucked away in various vest pockets. I heard strange overlapping sounds as we arrived on the second floor balcony of the nobleman's study. Massive equipment and various contraptions made of bronze, brass, or iron filled the center of the room. A Tesla coil curled up in one corner, and a machine spinning half globes drew my attention to the other. On the tables, long glass tubes twisted around wood and iron stands connecting angled bottles and beakers, some bubbling atop small flames.

Two walls covered in once-magnificent cabinetry ignited my curiosity. I wanted to explore the hundreds of cubby-holes and long shelves filled with strange, labeled jars, bottles of every size and shape, odd-shaped wooden boxes, and intriguing canisters like tiny chests made of copper.

The wall we passed through was covered from floor to ceiling with shelves stuffed with books. Only the small arched doorway broke up the collection of dust-covered tomes that would have made my father's mouth water in envy. The final wall at the back of the room held two windows, one with his desk and the second his telescope. A glass door stood between them with the de Moley family crest mounted above.

We headed down a wrought-iron circular staircase to the floor below. A myriad of exotic spices and sweet aromas mixed with putrid burning beakers and a bit of sulfur that seared my throat. I wished my father's office was more like this, twisting glass, bubbling beakers, and mysterious machines—so much more interesting than just old books.

Eustache motioned for us to sit. "I've devoted my life to the Order and discovering the lost knowledge of the Old World."

Genevieve lit up. "You're talking about magic aren't you?"

I dropped onto the stool. "Magicians are just snake oil salesmen. That's what my father always says."

He paused, smiled as he cocked an eye at me and then continued. "With this new industrialized world rising over the horizon, many of the old ways are being forgotten. Sadly, the Inquisition stamped out much of the rest. So myself and a few others have dedicated decades to the study of alchemy."

"You're an alchemist?" Now he had my attention.

"An apothecary actually, a mixer of potions, and one of my discoveries a few years ago was this." He pulled a small silver box from the cabinet and handed it to Genevieve. She ran her hand over the three lapis lazuli stones at the center of a twisted Celtic design. With her thumb, she slid the clasp to the side and opened the box. Inside, lying on green velvet was a glass vial containing a strange cloudy blue liquid.

Eustache sat across the table as Genevieve and I looked up with questioning gazes. "It's Four Thieves Potion."

Genevieve stared at the vial. "Grand Master Sinclair

mentioned this. He thinks this could save my father."

"I believe it can. During the horrible Black Death, four thieves developed a potion to steal from the wealthy homes in the infected cities. When eventually caught, they had not contracted the plague, nor even been sick, and one had been cured of his consumption. Their lives were spared for the secret of the potion." He pointed to the silver box in her hands. "That took me years to develop, I read the Vatican transcripts of their trial and the supporting material of a French apothecary and doctor who worked with them. It is rare, valuable, and there isn't enough time to make more … so treat it with care." Genevieve nodded her head repeatedly.

"When your father was attacked Grand Master Sinclair sent a telegram, and I immediately went to work to make that batch. I was about to leave for England when I heard of your crash. You have until the third day of the full moon, about one week, to administer that dose to your father. He'll be weak for some time but, God willing, he should recover."

Tears came to Genevieve. "Thank you. You have my eternal gratitude. I'm certain my father will thank you when he is in better spirits."

"Yes, thank you." I wanted to know more, to ask the questions sparked by the nobleman's tale, but my thoughts shifted to my own father. "We should be getting back to the Sparrowhawk. The captain said it could take that long just to fix her, and we should probably be helping."

Eustache's expression hardened. "No! You cannot wait that long. You must leave immediately."

"How can we get to England in a week without the Sparrowhawk?" Genevieve asked.

Eustache grabbed a rusty key from his desk. "Come with me, both of you."

"I should contact my father."

"I've already sent word. Wouldn't want him thinking

you'd been kidnapped."

"But—"

"I trust him, Alexander. And my father's life depends on him."

I drew in a deep breath. Genevieve stepped through the glass door and crossed the gardens to follow Eustache. I stood in the doorway and watched as they walked past roses of every color growing with abandon on the grounds amidst overgrown flower gardens, ornamental bushes that clearly needed tending and row upon row of fruit trees. *We should return to the Sparrowhawk. We should consult with my father and Captain Baldarich.* As Genevieve disappeared around a bunch of bushes, I shoved my concerns away and ran after her.

Eustache rattled the rickety door of a stone shed on the far side of his garden. I tried to peer through the lead glass, but it was covered in dusty cobwebs and all I could see were dark blurry shapes. He slipped a key in the lock and as he pulled it open, the musty smell made me cough and sputter. Every surface within was covered in a thick grayish-brown veil. Iron tools lined the walls. A splotchy canvas tarp covered whatever filled the center. He walked up to it and yanked the corner back, filling the shed with a cloud of thick dust.

As the dust settled, a slender sleek craft, like a long boat, took shape on a trailer. But I noticed right away, it wasn't any ordinary boat built for skimming the waves. Rigging lines ran along the rails securing two large sailfins on each side of the stern. Plus a three-bladed propeller sat where the rudder should be. The craftsmanship was beautiful, but it was also the oldest airskiff I'd ever seen. I ran around soaking up every little detail.

Eustache lifted a bundle of dirty white cloth and tossed it on the craft. "She's called the Mystic Wind, and believe it or not she was the fastest airship of her time."

"But which century was that?" I chuckled.

"Oh come now, she's a fine craft. The balloon is in great shape, the only problems are the sails," He stretched out the cloth. "They're as holey as Swiss cheese. We'll need silk or canvas to fix them."

I helped him muscle the balloon into place and secured it with the rigging ropes. Pointing to a round metal box in the center of the airboat, I asked, "What is this?"

"It generates the heat that inflates the balloon and runs the propeller." He tapped a wooden handle with a brass knob. "Pull to add heat, that makes it climb and speeds up the propeller. Trim the sails and fins to steer."

I smiled and we hooked the balloon's tube to the engine. Eustache poured coal into the tank and checked the igniter.

Genevieve looked over the sails. "We'll get off the ground but, we won't go far. We'll never reach England."

I poked my head through one of the holes. "Where are we going to get enough material to patch these holes?"

"My dress!" Genevieve clapped her hands in excitement and twirled around until her skirts billowed out in a wide circle. "I'll change into my old clothes."

I shook my head at her. "Genevieve—" She turned and, for a moment, her shoulder's drooped and her expression darkened. "—That's brilliant!"

Her smile returned even bigger than before. I tossed her my bag, and she headed off behind the shed.

I went back to looking over the airskiff.

"So what do you think?" Eustache asked. "Can you two fly this?"

"Absolutely! Thank you so much. I don't know how we can repay you, but I will see you are compensated. Granted this comes from a penniless schoolboy, but I'll figure something out."

He laughed. "No need. If you truly want to repay me, save her father."

CHAPTER 30

HISTORY OF THE ORDER

Genevieve stepped out from behind the garden shack wearing her pants and corset, and I couldn't hide my smile.

Eustache quickly turned to look. "My my. Very improper for a young lady of your position. I wonder what your father will think."

Genevieve stuck her hands on her hips. "I like it."

Not only had I'd become accustomed to this look, but to be honest, it suited her more than the dress. I had to admit I liked it, too. Very much.

Eustache motioned toward the house. "It is late. Why don't we have some dinner and repair this vessel in the morning."

I dropped the hammer on the table. "That sounds great. I'm starving."

Eustache guided us through a large banquet hall that held one of longest tables I had ever seen, and into a small dining room with an ordinary wooden table and four chairs around it.

"Please have a seat. Bertrand makes the best food, and tonight he is serving one of his specialties—beef bourguignon."

I rubbed my stomach. "Sounds delicious."

A moment later the servant appeared and presented each of us with a plate covered by a silver dome. Bertrand removed the lid from Eustache's plate and said, "May I present, beef bourguignon with onions, mushroom, and petite boiled potatoes."

"Thank you, Bertrand."

The tender beef was smothered in the most delicious sauce I had ever eaten. I didn't know if this was just the first great meal I'd had since leaving America, or if I was just really hungry after all the hard work I'd done today. Either way, I couldn't stop eating.

Ice cream came for dessert. I couldn't believe it. I had tried ice cream once, on a trip with my father to New York City, but this was creamier and chocolate. I moaned as I licked the spoon clean. "This must be how ambrosia tastes."

Genevieve chuckled.

Eustache licked his spoon clean, too. "Ice cream is definitely one of the finer things in life."

We returned to the study after dinner. Bertrand brought hot chocolate for Genevieve and I and coffee for his lordship.

Eustache took a drink and then walked over to a bookcase. He removed a dusty tome. "You two might find this interesting." He set down the thick, hardened parchment manuscript. The cover, embossed in large gold print, read: Histoire de l'Ordre. "It's called…"

"It's in French." My heart quickened. "History of the Order. The Templars?"

"It tells the tale of the Templars since they were disbanded."

"What sent them underground?" I asked.

"King Philip the Fair, as he was known, conspired to rid the world of Templars. On October 13th, 1307, it was a Friday, the king had every Templar arrested. My ancestor was Grand Master at the time, and he was burned at the stake. It was horrible and has led the world to fear every Friday the Thirteenth."

I ran my fingers through my hair in disbelief. "But they were knights."

"The Templars were wealthy and Philip needed gold, but there was another reason, too. He was a member of the Knights of the Golden Circle. He had declared all of the Templars heretics, but my ancestor got his revenge. At his execution, he cursed the king saying he would join him within the year. The king died a few months later."

"Whoa."

"I didn't think the Golden Circle was that old," Genevieve said as she sipped her hot chocolate.

Eustache put his hand on my shoulder. "The current circle was formed after your country's civil war, but their roots are much older."

I clenched my fingers trying to force the chill of his words away. My father never talked about the war, and I never asked. Maybe it was different in the south, but up north, it wasn't something grownups talked to kids about. I just knew I was glad I hadn't had to live through it.

Eustache circled the room and Genevieve and I sat in two chairs covered in the softest leather I'd ever felt. "One sacred duty the Templars accepted was to defend mankind against the four horsemen and other demonic threats."

I watched him closely and nodded along with each beat of his tale.

"Just because the world turned on the Templars doesn't mean that sacred duty ended."

He stopped behind Genevieve's chair. "Great men have always stood up to evil, and the Kensingtons have been in the fight for generations."

"Really? My father and grandfather are special agents of the queen, and my father loves to tell stories of our ancestors. But some are so outlandish, I thought they were just family lore. Almost like family fairy tales."

He smiled. "Oh, they are so much more than that."

Genevieve's voice trembled. "What do you mean?"

"The last time the four horsemen appeared was in 1588. They assembled the largest armada Europe had ever seen. Admiral Kensington—your ancestor—destroyed their Spanish Galleon the *Cuatro Jintes*."

I shook the haze from my head and stared at Genevieve. "Your family fought these things before?"

"Several times," Eustache answered. "Death and destruction go hand and hand with the horsemen. A Kensington tried to stop the Black Death in the 1340's, but the Templars had been destroyed thirty years prior. With so few allies he could not hold the plague back."

Genevieve's shoulders slumped as she remembered every story her dad had told her, as if the weight of history and all those battles pressed down on her back. Then Eustache turned to me.

"The Kensington's are not the only ones with a history tangled up with the Knights of the Golden Circle and the horsemen. Turn to the title page, Alexander."

I went back to the book and flipped to the title page where an inscription was written in an elegant script. I read it aloud. "*For my friend, Pierre de Moley. A brother in arms, now it's time for you to bear the history. Your friend, William Armitage.*' There's a date, 1715."

"Bravo, an excellent translation."

I reread the inscription three times. One of my ancestors had been a Templar! I ran my fingers over the ink. I didn't have the long history of family tales. My stories didn't go past my grandfather, but here was proof of someone over a hundred years before. It humbled me.

Eustache placed the book back on the shelf. "Now we should get some sleep, we have a busy day tomorrow. Especially if we're going to get the Mystic Wind airborne."

Genevieve followed Bertrand, as I lingered a moment staring at the book tucked into its place on the shelf. Then Bertrand escorted us both upstairs to a couple of rooms at the end of a long hall. The rooms had no layer of dust or sheets covering the ornate furniture. I assumed Bertrand had been preparing them all night. The soft linens, downy pillow and mattress felt like heavenly clouds and I slipped easily into a deep sleep.

*   *   *

We rose with the dawn and after breakfast, Eustache led us out to the garden house where the Mystic Wind waited. We all began work immediately. Genevieve set to work mending the sails and within in no time, the holes began to disappear, covered instead by the luxurious silk from her stolen dress. So much needed repair that it was midmorning when we finally began inflating the balloon. All was going well when I doubled over with a pain so severe, I felt like I'd been stabbed through the stomach. Genevieve shot me a questioning glance and ran to my side.

Eustache spun around. "What's wrong?"

Genevieve put her arm on my shoulder. "Are you alright?"

"Someone's coming," I gasped. "I don't know how I know, but…."

"I'll see who it is and send them away. If not, your duty is to get this craft in the air and get to London."

"It's danger—" I started, but the pain silenced me.

Eustache stepped into the garden and Genevieve ran to a window to see who it could be.

"It's a man in a long black coat and hat. He's entered the garden from the other side," she said as I struggled to stand upright.

The nobleman called out in a stern voice. "Trespasser. I demand you leave my property this instant."

Genevieve gasped just as I made it to the window. There he was. Col. Hendrix! Striding fast through the garden, he tipped back his hat to reveal the bronze plates and sparking electric eye.

"They call me War," he said, "and I've come for the kids."

Genevieve and I saw the disgust on Eustache's face as he faced the Colonel.

"I'm afraid you cannot have them," he said and turned as Bertrand stepped from the shadows, a golden-hilted rapier in his hand.

CHAPTER 31

THE DUEL

I pressed against the window to get a better view. I couldn't hear them, but didn't need to. Their expressionless faces conveyed one message—a fight was imminent.

"So it's to be a duel, then," the colonel said.

Eustache bowed as he drew the rapier.

"I'll kill you where you stand, Frenchy."

"I doubt that, you're more machine than man now."

"Lord Kannard sends his greetings." Hendrix's wicked smile curled the corner of his mouth. "He says he regrets that you must die, but perhaps you would prefer this way. Death will spare you from enslavement."

"How kind of him to think of old friends at a time like this."

"I'll enjoy spilling your blue blood all over this garden."

"If you don't mind, may we start? I have other matters to attend to."

Colonel Hendrix retracted his bronze right hand and the serrated blade locked into place.

Eustache shook his head. "Not even a real sword, how dissatisfying." He lunged and his downward thrust barely missed the colonel. He pressed his attack only to be parried by Hendrix who countered with several slashes that pushed Eustache back toward the main house.

I wiped off the dirty window with my sleeve to get a clearer view. I wanted to help, but knew we should remain hidden—at least until the airskiff was ready to fly. Studying their movements, I tried to determine who would win, but Genevieve returned to the sail and tore a swatch from the dress to patch it.

"How can you patch the sails right now?" I asked without taking my eyes off the duel.

"Our duty is to escape. Eustache is fighting Hendrix to give us the time to finish our repairs. You heard him."

"I know, but its Col. Hendrix. We should go help Eustache."

"This is a matter of honor." Genevieve's fingers began stitching again. "We cannot interfere."

"The man who attacked my father is in the garden, and I'm hiding in a shed."

"You shouldn't be hiding. You should be filling the balloon with air in case...."

"But—" I knew she was right.

"Alexander, you know this is bigger than one sword fight."

"You're right, we have to get the potion back to London."

"I'm sure Eustache is a fine swordsman, he comes from a long line of swordsmen. We must take advantage of this opportunity."

The clatter of swords drew my attention back to the window. Eustache pushed the colonel toward the fountain in the center of the garden. Col. Hendrix leapt onto the marble ledge and his serrated blade ripped through Eustache's coat.

I gasped and gripped the windowsill. Hendrix's attacks pushed the nobleman back toward his villa. Eustache forced him away with parries, but stumbled as he blocked the confederate.

I couldn't watch any longer. I checked on the balloon.

Genevieve finished sewing the pieces of her dress over the largest hole in the sail. The balloon swelled to ever-greater dimensions and showed no holes or leaks. I looked over the engine and pushed down the lever ever so slightly to quicken the inflation. I just hoped Eustache would last until we could all escape.

Peering over my shoulder into the garden, I cringed. Eustache had been cut in the shoulder.

When the balloon was large enough to lift the boat, I anchored it with two lines and ran to the window. Colonel Hendrix forced Eustache back to the steps. Hendrix kicked the Frenchman to the stone. I feared what would happen next and ran out of the shed. I reached for my Thumper, but felt nothing.

I hadn't taken it to the Louvre.

I snatched up a flower pot and hurled it. The terra cotta shattered against Hendrix who whirled around. Eustache leapt up.

The confederate smiled. "I was waiting for you to stick your head up, kid."

"You'll not harm him." Eustache raised his sword toward the colonel. "Alexander, get out of here."

"Alexander," Col. Hendrix good eye focused and a shudder rippled through me. "I'm here to make you an offer. Come with us and become a Horseman."

"What? Me?" I felt like I'd been hit in the gut.

"Yes, you. You want adventure, right? Respect? Men with fancy titles to treat you like an equal? We hold the key to everything you've dreamed of—"

"I'll never join you!" I was shaking, breathing hard as if I'd just finished a five mile run.

"That's the spirit!" Eustache called out.

"Are you sure?" Hendrix ignored the nobleman and walked toward me. "Wealth. More money than you could ever imagine."

I didn't need money and had a big imagination. I shook my head.

"Power." Hendrix clenched his fist. "When you enter a room men will tremble."

"Do you want allies or slaves by your side?" Eustache asked me, advancing in the classic fencing pose as Hendrix thrust his arm out, holding him back with the serrated blade.

"What about that girl of yours? Kensington's daughter. Is she cowering in the shed?"

I glanced back at the shed and hoped Genevieve hadn't heard that. If she had, she'd probably come running out to join the fight.

"Enter the Golden Circle, become a Horseman, Alexander. A king of the new world. If you do, I'll spare Miss Kensington and give her to you. She can be yours forever."

Give her to me? What did he mean? My heart leapt into my throat. *What was I being offered and why?* The words made me angry, but doubt seized my mind like a clawed hand. There had to be a reason.

"Why me?"

"You're not like these pompous royals. You're a common man thrust into the world of great men, men who believe they were born above your rank. But you can be their equal. You *deserve* to be their equal. You're exactly what the Knights of the Golden Circle were created for. I know what you're thinking, that I'm bad, but you don't see I'm trying to help you."

"But you've been chasing us since we left London."

"I've been trying to reunite you and your father. I want to help you be your own man."

He was trying to twist my memories. I closed my eyes and thought of that night at Eton. The night he kidnapped my father. And I knew the truth. He wasn't trying to help me, and he hadn't helped my father.

"These nobles use you. They expect you to serve them like a dog. Do what you're told, follow their orders. But listen to me. Grow up and be a man. Rip off your collar and join us."

Eustache brought his sword down on Hendrix's blade.

"You lie." I yelled. "You attacked me and my father."

"I never hurt your pa, even when he refused me. We were nice. Would *your* Queen do the same? Become a Horseman!" Hendrix took two steps toward me.

Eustache forced himself between us. "Stay true to yourself, Alexander."

Col. Hendrix laughed at the nobleman. "Become a Horsemen or be enslaved by a bunch of barons and lords. It's your choice, Alexander Amitage. Embrace your destiny as a Knight of the Golden Circle."

My blood was boiling. I lashed out to cut through Hendrix's words. "I am no dog! No *Queen*, or baron, or lord sent me. I came on my own. I am an American, and unlike you, I believe all men are created equal. I won't enslave anyone and I'll do everything I can to stop you!"

"Including die?" In one movement, the colonel swung his arm out at me, the serrated blade poised to slice through me.

"Not as long as I draw breath." Eustache parried the colonel's blade.

For a split second, I wanted to retreat to a safe corner just like I had back at Eton, but I didn't back down. I wasn't that boy anymore.

Eustache never removed his gaze from his opponent, but said to me, "Finish what others have started, Alexander. Get Genevieve out of here, and know that it has been my greatest honor to aid you."

Without a word, I ran for the shed, hearing the colonel cackling like a madman behind me. Genevieve sat in the airboat waiting for me. She smiled and I realized she'd heard my words. I wondered what she thought, had I sounded stoic or frightened. I yanked the rusty lever to open the roof. Dust and leaves showered down upon us

I heard the clash of steel and Eustache say, "Tell my old friend Kannard, he shouldn't have sent a bronzed demon to face a knight."

Hendrix slashed his blade. "Would you die already?"

I hopped in the airskiff. "We cut free, go after Eustache, and then sail over to the Sparrowhawk. Agreed?"

"I was just waiting for you," she said.

We untied the anchor lines and the airskiff lifted off. Rodin flew in and landed beside Genevieve, she snatched him up and embraced him, but then turned to me.

"If Rodin is here, then people from the Sparrowhawk are, too. What do we do?"

Through the window, I saw my father and Mr. Singh run out of the villa and stop. I pointed and Genevieve saw them, too. We rose out of the shed to the stunned, uplifted faces of everyone in the garden. I unfurled the sails and steered the vessel toward the house.

Genevieve pointed over the side. "Look, Golden Circle henchman."

As my father and Mr. Singh stood on the steps of the villa, Eustache and Col. Hendrix fought by the fountain, the henchmen filed in around them. Mr. Singh pulled out his Katar with the barrels on either side and shot two henchmen. Eustache used the confusion to thrust his sword into the colonel, but he struck bronze and his sword snapped in two.

I pushed the lever and descended toward my father. "Get in."

He grabbed hold of the side and hoisted himself into the airship.

I leaned over the railing as one of the henchmen pulled

a revolver and shot Eustache in the shoulder, sending him toppling backward. Col. Hendrix stood over him and thrust his blade into his chest.

"No!" Genevieve and I screamed.

Mr. Singh retrieved three chakrams from his belt and threw them at the colonel. The first sharpened metal ring struck Hendrix on the right side of his head, knocking him back, and sending his hat tumbling to the ground. The second struck the henchmen with the revolver in the head and remained there as the man collapsed in a lifeless heap. The third sliced into Hendrix's left arm causing him to roar with pain.

Mr. Singh grabbed hold of the airskiff's railing. My father and Genevieve grabbed his arms and pulled. I fought back tears and yanked the lever back, powering up the propeller and sending hot air rushing into the balloon with a great *whoosh*. The airskiff soared into the sky leaving the carnage below us.

Col. Hendrix switched his right arm to the rifle barrel and raised it to take aim at our balloon, but through his pain, his aim was off and he missed by a wide margin.

Tears streamed down my face before drying from the wind rushing by. *It wasn't fair, why did he have to die?* I tried to shove the pain deep inside, but so much anger couldn't be contained. I cursed under my breath, swearing a thousand oaths of revenge as we soared ever higher. I took one last look back toward Eustache's ancestral home and thought about the book in his library, the one with my own ancestor's name in it. Then I watched as Gendarmes arrived and rushed toward the back garden. With any luck they'd arrest the colonel and his henchmen, but I doubted it.

"What happened, Alexander, and what were you doing there?" my father scolded. "We got a strange message last night and Mr. Singh and I have spent all day trying to find you."

"A brave man saved my life and was killed for it. That's what happened." I banked the airskiff to the right.

"Wait. The Sparrowhawk is that way." My father pointed toward the city.

"We're not going back to the Sparrowhawk."

"Then where are we going?"

"We're going to England," I said.

"Damn it Alexander! Put this vessel down and answer me at once."

"No." The word felt good on my tongue, and the shock etched on my father's face almost made me smile.

"Lord de Morley gave his life so we can save Genevieve's father." I looked at Genevieve and she scooted closer to me, Rodin perched imperiously on her shoulder. "We're not about to let his sacrifice be in vain." I'd never defied my father before, and I tried to keep my hands from shaking from the emotion of defying him now.

"And just how are you going to save Baron Kensington's life?"

Genevieve spoke up. "Only the Knights of the Golden Circle know what poison was used on my father and they're obviously not going to tell us or provide us with an antidote. Grand Master Sinclair notified Lord de Morley, a Templar from an ancient family, and he made a special batch of the Four Thieves Potion. If my father takes it in time, the Templars believe it will cure him."

"So," I locked eyes with my father, "we're going to England to save the Baron, and you're just going to have to come along."

Genevieve placed her hand on my arm. "You were amazing back there, Alexander. How many men could be offered such power and turn it down?"

Mr. Singh, who had been quietly taking in everything that was happening around him, turned to me. "What power?"

"Yes, Alexander, what is she talking about?" my father demanded.

I shook my head, unable to put it into words. Genevieve answered for me. "Colonel Hendrix offered Alexander the chance to become a Horseman, but he refused."

Silence. I glanced back and saw the two men's stunned expressions.

"How long will it take to get to London?" my father asked finally.

"As fast as the Mystic Wind will carry us."

CHAPTER 32

RACE BACK TO LONDON

I trimmed the sails to catch more wind. We soared above the patchy farmland of the French countryside. It was exciting to fly the Mystic Wind, to feel the air whipping in my face, and become one with the currents.

Mr. Singh helped me read the wind, but my thoughts never lingered far from the vision of Eustache. I would not let him down.

My mind drifted to the Sparrowhawk and her crew. "Do you think…?"

Mr. Singh nodded. "They will be fine."

Genevieve sat against the bow, and I watched the waves of her hair whipped about by the wind. She used her hand to push it down but her focus was on the sliver box in her hand, she hadn't let it out of her sight and I understood why, it held her father's salvation. After a while, she stuffed her hair down into her collar with one hand, never once letting go of the box.

Beside her, Rodin clung to the bow, with his wings billowing in the wind, a fitting masthead for the airboat.

My father sat hunched down in the middle of the airskiff, his arms tightly held against his chest trying to stay out of the strongest winds. I wondered what he thought of me. Was he proud, or just calculating what punishment would be levied back at Eton?

I pushed the thought away. Soon, we'd save the baron and life would return to normal. The Templars would deal with Lord Kannard and Col. Hendrix. I would return to Eton. But that meant returning to the responsibilities I'd fled. I didn't know what consequences awaited me; I only knew they'd be severe.

I checked the propeller to avoid my father's gaze. It hadn't been used in years and looked stressed to the breaking point. With my attention focused behind him, I saw several glistening shapes on the horizon. "Indihar, we have a problem."

The Sikh turned. "I see them."

"What is it?" my father asked.

"I don't know, but I count seven of them." I reached into my bag and retrieved a leather pouch. I removed two lenses wrapped in linen and a thick, leather hide with several holes on the ends and a toggle and loop in the middle. Setting the lenses in the holes at the ends of the leather hide, I wrapped them up and secured it in the center. I raised the telescope and studied the glints of light behind them.

"Zeppelins." I saw seven silver-skinned dirigibles, with more airships behind them. "I'll head for those clouds, maybe we can lose them.

I handed the telescope to Mr. Singh. He nodded and then said, "We can't get too high or we'll freeze. This skiff is built for speed, not altitude."

He passed it to Genevieve. After looking she handed it to my father who took it and then looked up with a scowl on his face.

"Alexander, this is my telescope! I told you to put it back."

"Just punish me when we get back to London."

I trimmed one of the sails and pulled the lever all the

way back. The Mystic Wind soared upward into a large, fluffy cloud. I reached out and let my hand cut through the white mist. Water dampened my fingertips as the vapor danced in circles around the airship.

Genevieve sat beside Indihar staring into the endless white world.

I checked the fuel level, hoping we still had enough. I couldn't tell, but hoped it would last until we crossed the Channel.

I asked Mr. Singh. "Can we outrun the Zeppelins?"

"So long as the winds remain at our back we'll have no problem."

Genevieve looked to the stern, to the endless clouds behind them. "But why are they heading to England?"

I had been thinking the same thing.

Mr. Singh cast a glance over his shoulder. "That many airships, has to be the German Army. Perhaps part of the armada the Sparrowhawk tangled with."

Genevieve's browed furrowed in concern. "An invasion? That's foolish, we'll blast them back across the Channel."

Professor Armitage shook his head. "Not if the British army is busy with the Four Horsemen."

Genevieve's hair whipped about in the wind. "Do you think the Knights of the Golden Circle are in league with the Kaiser?"

"I don't know, but Europe is only bound together by a few shaky treaties."

Mr. Singh nodded. "It is what I have feared. In the chaos incited by the arrival of the Four Horsemen, the Kaiser will attack."

We all sat back against the sides of the boat and silence enveloped the Mystic Wind. I continued to fly, even when Mr. Singh offered to take over. I found it therapeutic, it kept my mind off the all the problems that would greet us when we landed.

We crossed the English Channel under a star-filled night. The moon grew larger, and we all gazed at the tailed star, the Sungrazer Comet hanging on the western horizon. I had read many stories, from the Middle Ages to the Romans, Greeks and even Babylonians, that portrayed comets as harbingers of doom.

However, I also remembered my science classes. The works of Isaac Newton, Copernicus, and Galileo said comets were just travelers through the cosmos, circling the sun in huge orbits, greater than even Jupiter and Saturn. I wondered what this one would bring, scientific enlightenment or death and destruction.

Around midnight as I stretched and yawned, Mr. Singh took over. I slid next to Genevieve who had been quiet through much of the flight. We didn't talk; I simply lay beside her and stared into the night's sky. She looked up into the stars, but then her focus fell once again on the vial she carried. We drifted off to sleep, with Rodin curled up between us.

I woke suddenly and grabbed the rail as the Mystic Wind shook and shuttered. I looked back at Mr. Singh who struggled with a sputtering engine and a deflating balloon. I slipped to the Sikh's side and helped him with the controls. Below lay the city of London, an interconnected web of brick and cobblestone sprawling out from both banks of the winding Thames River and covered in a thick gray fog.

Genevieve and the professor woke with the next shudder.

I checked the fuel, but it was gone. I looked over the city for a good place to set down, but the crowded city afforded few open spaces.

Genevieve rubbed her eyes and pointed toward the center of London. "There is my house. Can we make it? We can land in the garden."

I stood up, raised my hand to shield my eyes and followed her gaze. "Mr. Singh, think we can get another few miles out of her?"

"Yes, but I would say a prayer that we survive the landing."

I pumped the lever to see if I could get any hot air into the balloon or the propeller. It didn't help, but it made me feel better.

Mr. Singh trimmed the sails to catch more of the tailwind. I opened the side door on the engine and called for Rodin. The little dragon crawled over and looked at me with its head cocked to one side. I pointed to the engine, puffed my cheeks and blew, trying to demonstrate. Rodin twisted his head to the other side and stepped forward. Wiggling his backside he breathed deeply and released a little roar and a thin column of fire. The heated air filled the balloon and caused the propeller to spin twice as fast, but the effect only lasted a moment. The Mystic Wind lifted, hopefully enough to land at the house.

"One more time," I said. Rodin cocked his head at Genevieve who nodded.

"We're depending on you, my friend," she said. Rodin concentrated on the open door, repeated his little backside wiggle and let loose one more jet of flame. I patted him on the head and he looked up proudly, then flew back to sit on Genevieve's shoulder.

I took my hand off the lever, no use in worrying about something that didn't work anymore, then slid over and helped Mr. Singh pull the rigging lines to keep the vessel under control. The Mystic Wind skirted the pointed roof of one stately home, and scraped a few tiles off another as it slid toward Genevieve's house. The right keel-fin smashed into a weathervane decorated with an archer, decapitating the figure and shattering the wooden stabilizer. The vessel dropped suddenly as it leapt off the roof and slammed into the cobblestones below. The boat twisted and spun around, the sails caught on the lamp post and the deflated balloon smothered everyone aboard.

I pushed the heavy fabric up creating a space underneath. Genevieve clutched Rodin, and to my side the young Sikh extended his hand with a large smile.

"Not quite the garden, but a fine landing nonetheless, Master Armitage."

"Thank you Mr. Singh." I pushed aside part of the balloon that covered the last of the vessel and my father. "You okay?"

"I'll be fine."

Genevieve pushed the front of the balloon back and turned to see several men standing around the vessel. "Alexander, I think you should get out of there."

"Coming," I struggled to climb out from underneath the balloon. The Mystic Wind was surrounded by determined men with puzzled expressions. They had rifles, pistols, and swords aimed at me as the other three people crawled out from below the balloon. I pointed up to the roof and said, "I'll pay for that."

Lord Marbury and Grand Master Sinclair stepped out of the Kensington house. I waved and could tell from the puzzled looks on their faces that they weren't expecting me. The two men scanned the scene and huge smiles came to their faces as they saw Genevieve climb out. Even brighter expressions emerged when they recognized my father.

"Professor Armitage! Oh my, it is good to see all of you," Grand Master Sinclair said as he hugged Genevieve. "We've been hearing all kinds of strange reports over the telegraph."

Lord Marbury shook my father's hand. "John, we're so glad that you're back safe and sound."

"Thank you Lord Marbury. I believe I have my son to thank for that."

Mr. Singh bowed to the two men, and I stepped forward. "This is Indihar Singh. He is a friend of the baron's and has helped us tremendously on our journey."

Grand Master Sinclair asked Genevieve in a hurried tone. "Did you find an antidote?"

"No, but Lord de Moley gave me a vial of Four Thieves Potion."

"de Moley! I knew that old French aristocrat would come through." Grand Master Sinclair grinned and clapped his hands. "Why didn't he come with you? He was supposed to be here days ago."

"He won't be coming," I said, my voice tight with anger and pain. "He fought a duel with Colonel Hendrix, and gave his life so we could escape."

Sinclair and Marbury looked at each other. Their faces betrayed their weariness and concern. "There is no greater sacrifice for one of our Order. May he rest in eternal peace."

Lord Marbury walked over to Genevieve. "Let us get that potion to your father, so Eustache's sacrifice is not in vain."

"Yes, where he?" Genevieve asked.

"He remains in bed, in his room."

We ran inside with Rodin fluttering above Genevieve's head. She raced upstairs and found her father in his bedroom with Mrs. Hinderman checking on his fever. Genevieve ran over and threw her arms around him. I smiled, knowing she was probably breaking all the rules of decorum for nobility.

The baron's reddish skin tone came from the fever that racked his body. Bundled under thick blankets he shivered as his daughter pushed back a lock of hair from his face. Beside him on the nightstand a forest of glass bottles held the latest in medicine, chemistry, and home-made remedies.

On a small table at the end of the bed, a microscope sat beside several slides lined up in a wooden stand. I looked at the scene and guilt hit me like a canon shot. I'd been running around with Genevieve having the time of my life while the baron and my father suffered at the hands of the Golden Circle. Sure, we had rescued my father and now had a cure for the venom slowly poisoning Baron Kensington, but that didn't even out the score. I'd been having fun. Despite the danger. *Or because of it?*

Genevieve poured the vial of Four Thieves Potion into a glass and with Ms. Hinderman's help propped her father up and moved the pillows to support him. He winced from pain as they lifted him, but the baron, with a strong resolve and stoic demeanor, tried not to let it show. He drank the oily blue potion, and gagged on the bitter remedy. Ms. Hinderman then rubbed the potion on the bite marks. Genevieve encouraged him to drink the whole vial and the others came in as he finished.

As we waited to see what the potion would do, I thought of Eustache and his courage. His sacrifice. I thought of everything he'd said to me while he fought Col. Hendrix. *Stay true to yourself, Alexander,* he'd said. *But how, Eustache? How do I do that?*

After a while, the baron's color began to return to normal and he threw off one of the blankets. Grand Master Sinclair, Lord Marbury, and my father appeared in the doorway.

"Good to see you've risen from death's door, Maximilian," Sinclair said.

"Only you would think so, Archibald." The baron coughed and gripped his chest; his daughter put her hands on him to help ease his pain, brigning a smile to his strained face. "Thank you, my dear. I am so relieved you've returned."

Marbury and I pulled chairs around and we all sat with the baron while Mrs. Hinderman brought in tea. She arranged the tray on a table beside the bed.

"So tell me about this adventure the two of you wandered off on." The baron said.

Genevieve hesitated. I knew our tale would have to be a slippery slope of half-truths if we were to stay out of trouble. Otherwise I was likely to be thrown in the Tower of London and Genevieve shipped off to a convent. I walked over, picked up a cup of the strong smelling black tea, and began.

"It's a crazy tale, really. But we joined the honorable band of Sky Raiders you were going to use, and they graciously helped us find my father." Hardened jaws and narrowed glares told me no one believed me. "Okay, so we owe them money for taking us to Gibraltar, Malta, and Paris. Oh, and we also owe them for fighting with us, and for destroying their ship while trying to get us back to London. Indihar was the boatswain, he's been amazingly helpful."

"Indihar Singh?" The baron's face brightened. "Why didn't you say so? Where is he?"

"Waiting outside," Sinclair said.

"Well, bring him in! What are you waiting for?"

I ran to the hallway and returned pushing Indihar before me. The baron studied the Sikh and then a large smile broke out across his face. "How are you? Look how much you've grown."

"I am well and very glad to see that god has been generous to you."

"Indihar Singh, a Sky Raider. Someday you'll have to tell me that tale. To think you and my Genevieve joined up with that scoundrel Captain Baldarich. I suppose you could do worse—as scoundrels go, he's a right honorable chap." He chuckled and Genevieve's face nearly glowed with joy. Her father's laugh was surely music to her ears. "Please know that any debt you felt you owed me is repaid. My daughter's safety is all I could ever ask for."

"No debt has been repaid. Your daughter and the professor's son didn't really need me. They faced battle bravely, sought wisdom wisely, and stood up to tyranny over and over again."

Lord Marbury and the baron looked at Genevieve and me as Grand Master Sinclair asked, "Battles?"

I shifted, wringing my hands. "Little ones, more like disagreements really."

Lord Marbury and the baron shook their heads, but the Grand Master studied the two of us. I wondered what the old man's lingering gaze meant. Was he angry, or sizing us up for the next part of this adventure?

Lord Marbury sent for the doctor who checked the baron's vitals, listened to his heart with his stethoscope, and felt his forehead for fever. Taking a sample of his blood he studied it under the microscope and then turned to the others. "His heart is stronger and his breathing has improved. He's still very weak, that will take time to pass, but I believe the venom has been neutralized."

My heart soared, but I knew it wasn't over. Somewhere in the city, Lord Kannard lay in wait. The comet hung in the sky, and the four Iron Horsemen waited to unleash their terror upon the world. Sinclair put his finger to the side of his nose and then pointed at me with a wink. I wondered what it meant, but was almost afraid to find out.

CHAPTER 33

BAD NEWS

I stared at the walls of the Blue Room late into the night unable to stop thinking about Genevieve. She wouldn't leave her father's side. Every thought made me happier but filled me with a thousand questions. We were out of danger—for now—and I wanted to tell her how I felt. Maybe she already knew. Maybe me saying the words out loud would bring her the same happiness I felt whenever she looked at me.

Tomorrow, I pledged. Tomorrow I would tell her. Tomorrow.

I finally drifted off to sleep only to have happy dreams of kissing Genevieve turn into haunting images of a city consumed by fire, under siege by a hail of brimstone. A vision of the Iron Horsemen, four fiery bronze steeds ripping through London as the Sungrazer comet smashed into Parliament. An explosion, so large it punctured the clouds and tore every building from its foundation.

Death beyond any scale I could imagine.

I fought to lash out in my dreams. "You will never succeed!" But even my determined heart wavered as the black cloud engulfed me. Smoke blackened the sky and choked out the sun. London grew dark and then darker.

The cloud that smothered me hardened to iron and formed manacles around my wrists and ankles.

I snapped awake in the morning, shocked and confused by the blue blur surrounding me. A bedspread came into focus.

Pushing back the haze, I rubbed my eyes and tried to sit up. I heard people in the hall and below me on the first floor; I looked at the window and then saw bright, quite unwanted sunlight. Morning was long gone.

My school uniform was still in the armoire, but I dressed in the clothes that made me comfortable: khaki pants, white shirt, and dusty black vest. I wrapped the leather strap around me, uncertain if it brought me security or I just liked it. Either way, today I needed the confidence.

I hopped down the stairs two-at-time and found several men in the dining room. I heard Grand Master Sinclair, Lord Marbury, my father, and several other men whose voices I didn't recognize. They talked about Genevieve's and my adventure. From their tone I knew they weren't pleased, but this time I didn't just charge in. This time, I crept toward the doorway, leaning closer to listen. But a noise from the second floor drew my attention, and I turned to see Genevieve and her father approaching. Not wanting to be caught lurking, I ran for the front room and right into Finn, who stood inside the doorway eating an apple.

"Finn, hi, I was just looking around."

"And I'm Saint Finn," he said with a smile. "Don't worry about it, kid, you can hang in here while they decide what to do."

Moments later, the men left the dining room to greet the baron and his daughter. Finn and I wandered closer to watch. I saw several people I didn't know, but from their dress and stature I could tell they were nobles.

One was certainly a Templar. He had the cross on his ring. The man was my father's age with a short ponytail and long red coat just as I imagined the British of the revolutionary times would have worn. The baron shook the man's hand.

I turned to Finn. "Who is that?"

"That's the Duke. He's the father of Genevieve's betrothed."

The word pierced my chest like a sword. "Betrothed?"

Of course, how could she not be? The nobles managed their lives just like their estates, with precision and exacting standards. Pain ripped through my chest. I struggled to breathe and leaned against the wall.

Finn shook his head. "You like her. I understand, but lad, you'll have to learn your place. These people live in a world you'll only dream about. They're blue bloods; her whole life was planned from day one. Sorry kid, find yourself a good American girl." Finn smiled, his bright red eyebrows rose up and down in a gesture I didn't quite understand.

"What? Yes, of course, I knew that. Please, at school I'm surrounded by nobles. It's nothing like that." My face was hot and I tried to not clench my jaw. I wanted to put my fist through a wall.

I turned back to the men in hall, trying to forget what the Irishman said. The baron was still weak so they shuffled him into the conservatory. I wanted to hear what was being said, so I slipped out of the room with Finn and crossed the hall. The men inside talked about the events of the past few months. I leaned against the wall and listened.

"My daughter was foolish for leaving the way she did," the baron said, "and Professor Armitage, you have my apologies that we did not take better care of your son."

"The fault is not with you, Baron Kensington. My son is headstrong, and didn't think his actions through. I'm just glad he and your daughter returned safely."

"Yes, no doubt due to the heroic efforts of our friend, Mr. Singh."

I burned with anger. Now I *really* wanted to slam my fist into the wall. How could they sit there and say such things? How could Genevieve sit in there and listen to them without saying a word?

I heard the Duke's snooty voice. "I do hope she's outgrown this need for adventure. Your son as well, Professor. These are serious matters facing the crown, and the last thing we need is the interference of children."

That did it! Angered erupted beyond anything I'd ever felt before, and I couldn't listen one second longer. I burst through the door so hard it slammed against the wall and bounced back almost hitting me. I slammed it again and stormed in. Everyone stared at me as if I had horns sprouting from my forehead but I didn't care. I strode forward and took command of the center of the room, just as I'd seen Captain Baldarich do on his ship.

"How dare you speak about us as if we're mere children? As if we somehow *interfered* in your grand plans—"

The Duke shook his head. "Not only children, but insolent ones at that—"

"I'm not done, Your Grace!" I pounded my fist on the table. "You responsible adults allowed the Knights of the Golden Circle to kidnap my father and then did nothing to save him." I gestured to Genevieve's father. "Were you there when Baron Kensington was was struck by that serpent? No!" I turned to Marbury and Sinclair. I struggled to breathe, as if they'd sucked all the air out. "Genevieve and I took matters into our own hands. We found safe passage to Malta. We figured out what the Knights of the Golden Circle were planning. Together with the crew of the Sparrowhawk—yes, Sky Raiders!—we rescued my father from Lord Kannard's dungeon. With the help of Eustache, we repaired an airskiff and delivered the potion that saved the baron's life. And you sit in here and call us children."

My father stomped his foot and reached out to grab me.

"Alexander, that is enough!"

I glared at him and stood my ground. "No it isn't. You call us children, but you know what I see? I see nothing but old men content to concoct plans in secret, content to watch England burn, while the Horsemen unleash their evil."

"ALEXANDER!"

I turned on my father. "You'll not silence me today. I have fought and bled for this cause. I'm not a knight nor am I a member of some secret club you have to be born into." I turned to the Duke, father of Genevieve's betrothed. "You hope Genevieve is done with her adventures? Why don't you speak to her directly? She's in the room. She's not a piece of furniture. She proved that when she singled handedly fought off Zerelda, the captain of the sky pirates, with a brilliant bit of swordplay. She proved that when she pulled me from a raging underground river and saved my life. She proved that when she mended the sails on the airskiff so we could escape Colonel Hendrix and his henchman. I'll not let you talk down to her or me. I don't care whose father you are, what order you command or what horrors you have witnessed. Do you think for one moment that we did not face the same or worse? And one last thing," I turned to Baron Kensington. "Indihar Singh is a great man and he well deserves praise. But know this, you owe your life to your daughter and Eustache de Moley."

I stopped, my chest heaving as if about to burst. I awaited their challenges, their mockery, and their dismissal, but until it came I was not moving.

The baron coughed and my hard heart shattered. I'd just yelled at a sick man. I looked at Genevieve expecting her to appreciate my defense, but her eyes blinked back tears. She looked shocked and a bit horrified. *Was she upset I had broken decorum and insulted the aristocracy?* I suddenly wanted to apologize. To her father. Not to anyone else. Never to them.

I would not take back one word of what I said to them.

The room was quiet. Everyone stood in stunned silence. The Duke was appalled and Lord Marbury's face looked stunned, but I was surprised to see Grand Master Sinclair had a broad smile on his face. Red and flushed, my father was livid. I thought for a moment that he might bend me over the table and paddle me right there.

From in the hallway outside the conservatory, Finn clapped his hands together and laughed. A knock at the front door jolted everyone out of silence. Finn and Mrs. Hinderman greeted a man who said, "I have a message for Lord Marbury."

Mrs. Hinderman led the man into the conservatory. He entered and I relinquished the center of the room to the messenger, who wore a fine suit and carried a leather briefcase with the royal coat of arms embossed on the front.

The messenger stopped in front of Lord Marbury and bowed. He unlatched the brass lock on his briefcase and flipped open the top. Retrieving a bound scroll from inside, the royal messenger handed it to Lord Marbury. Then departed without waiting.

Lord Marbury broke the seal, unrolled the scroll, and read over the message. Concern knitted his brow as he glanced at Grand Master Sinclair, the baron, and the duke. "There were a series of thefts, the same night the professor was attacked. One concerns me; several of Nikolas Tesla's papers on loan to Oxford were stolen."

Sinclair looked at everyone in the conservatory. "It is time to finalize our plans for the defense of London."

The duke stepped forward. "Her Majesties Armies are ready to fight. Most are outside the city, but some are stationed within London. The constables will be ready to act as well."

From his chair, the baron said with a labored voice, "They won't be enough, the power of the four Iron Horsemen is beyond the power of rifles or swords."

I reclaimed the center of the room. "Genevieve and I have seen the full power of the Iron Horsemen. Lord Kannard shredded bedrock with a single stomp of his steed's hooves. One almost destroyed us on the island of Malta. I can only imagine what four will do to London. Also, the Kaiser is sending soldiers. We saw the Zeppelins as we flew here."

"The Kaiser?" Grand Master Sinclair said. "What is that pointy helmet doing sticking his bushy mustache where it doesn't belong?"

"Perhaps the Golden Circle has something on him," the duke said. "Perhaps his attitudes have changed."

Sinclair looked at the Duke. "Perhaps he's just a pompous ass." He turned to the others. "Lord Marbury, return to Buckingham Palace and see what you can find about these papers."

Lord Marbury nodded. "I'll borrow Finn, if it's all right with you, Max?"

The baron nodded and Marbury departed, calling for Finn as he stepped out the door. Grand Master Sinclair turned to the others, "We leave for the Tinkerer's Shop at once and you two," he pointed to Genevieve and me, "are coming with us." He walked over to Indihar who had been standing quietly on the edge of the gathering. "You as well, lad."

The duke stopped the Grand Master with his cane pressed across the old man's chest. "I think I should get Her Majesty's Royal Armies ready to face the Kaiser's soldiers, don't you?"

"Yes, yes. You do that. And good day to you, Your Grace." The duke released Sinclair and I watched him walk away. I didn't like that man. At all. Maybe it was the fact that his son was set to marry Genevieve. Maybe it was the comments he'd made about our journey. Maybe it was his face. But something about that nobleman made my skin jump like a flea-infested dog.

Grand Master Sinclair leaned over Baron Kensington. "We'll take the electric trolley to slip out of here without being noticed. Can you make it, old friend?"

"I wouldn't miss it. I'm fine, feeling better all the time."

Genevieve helped her father. The Grand Master followed the two of them with Indihar, but my father grabbed me by the arm and held me back.

"You're not just getting away with that little outburst from earlier. Is that understood Alexander?"

"Yes, sir."

My father held me tightly. "I taught you better than that."

"Yes, sir," I repeated.

He loosened his grip on my arm, and we followed everyone into the kitchen, through the secret passage in the pantry, and down the narrow stairwell.

"What is this place? I thought I'd explored all the secret passageways in the house," Genevieve said to her father.

"Another one of those things I was going to tell you about when you were older."

She huffed. "Typical, what's a secret society without its secrets."

The trolley car pulled up as we stepped onto the brick platform. Genevieve looked around at the circular passage and the odd car with the antenna reaching up to the ceiling. She was intrigued and excited, and I was glad to see her sense of adventure was still there.

We all stepped into the trolley car and sat on the lush semicircular seats. Grand Master Sinclair closed the door, and we flew down the track.

CHAPTER 34

THE TINKERER'S SHOP

I tried to speak with Genevieve, but she still attended to her weakened father so I kept my distance.

The trolley car stopped beside a large iron door. Sinclair ushered everyone off onto the brick platform. Removing an ornate brass key from his vest pocket, he unlocked the door and slid it to the right. The old Templar struggled with the massive door, so I helped him pull. A long hallway extended into darkness, but as we reached the end, we found only one door. It was labeled 636.

Sinclair yanked a nearby lever, and a bell ring in the distance. The old Templar pulled on one of the hinges and the door opened in the opposite direction. The false hinges reminded me of Gibraltar. A mechanized circular staircase twisted up through the ceiling like a corkscrew, rotating as if a giant drill tried to escape this underground tunnel. We stepped on and the stairs it carried us through the brick-lined passage. Lights in the risers of every third step lit the way.

I let my fingertips run along the passage wall, fascinated by the rough brick.

"Pull you hand back before it gets mangled," my father scolded.

I flattened my palm against the surface and let my whole hand drag along as we moved ever upward.

Reaching an open section several levels up, Sinclair stepped off the stairs and the others followed. I wanted to keep riding, but hopped off in turn.

A short passage took us to another large metal door, and as Sinclair stepped onto the metal grate, the door slid open. Almost like magic. As we passed through, I looked up and saw the large mechanism that controlled the door and another grate on the other side. It had a clunky, homemade feel, not the factory built products that came off the new assembly lines.

We entered the lowest floor of a metal shop. I stepped into another world, a world of iron and steel, a world that dwarfed me as I walked amongst large pieces of scrap metal and unidentifiable machinery. The smell of oil and burning coal filled the air and the sound of a hammer pounding on metal echoed from all directions.

The center of the shop rose three stories to a metal roof with windows ringing the top. The dull light of an English day filtered through the soiled glass. The sun reflected off the shiny brass and seemingly ignited the dust which sent sunbeams crisscrossing through the open space. The hues it produced gave this place an ethereal look like the paintings I had seen in the Louvre.

Sinclair pointed to the floor above. "There he is! Come, the lift is over here."

We moved to the back where a large metal plate connected to two iron eyebeams ran up all three stories. Two large wheels geared to an engine clamped around the eyebeams.

We all stepped on and Sinclair said, "Alexander, take us up."

At the base of the lever I saw two symbols, a plus and a minus. Assuming plus meant up, I pushed a small lever up. The metal plate lurched and slowly moved up the eyebeam tracks. As the lift pulled up to the second floor I shifted the lever back to center and it stopped abruptly.

Sinclair led us to the main work area. Tables, anvils, and a forge filled the space, along with other equipment I had never seen before. Some looked handmade, like the forge, which glowed bright orange and the heat radiated clear across the room. Other pieces like the train-engine-sized furnace had been scrounged from factories around London.

Seated at one table, hunched over a cylindrical iron mechanism, a man in a dirty white button down, suspenders and a thick rubber apron wrenched a bolt into place without even acknowledging that people had entered his shop. He finally whipped his head around as Sinclair cleared his throat. He had a few extra pounds and a second chin, his raven-hair ringed his head in a band, and his bushy mustache twisted out to points laden with enough dust and metal shavings to turn it gray. His goggles held a complex set of multiple lenses that amplified his eyeballs like a frog.

I smiled as the man's large pupils darted back and forth. His tool belt carried the standard wrenches, screwdrivers, and a measuring stick, but also oddities I'd never seen before. A spanner to pry things apart, a rod with magnets at each end, and attached to his belt, a steam powered drill with thin hoses that led to another device on his belt before larger tubes ran to a series of tanks beside the table. They were the most amazing tools I'd ever seen. My thoughts drifted to Gears; he would love this place.

Grand Master Sinclair stepped forward. "Everyone, I'd like you to meet the Tinkerer, you're standing in his London workshop. This is Professor Armitage, his son Alexander, and you remember Baron Kensington, and his daughter Genevieve. The Tinkerer has been helping prepare the defense against the Iron Horsemen."

"I've finished it, too," the Tinkerer said in a thick Scottish accent. "We're all set. You have to see this, Archibald. It's my masterpiece."

The Tinkerer led us to the front of his shop. He walked with a limp in his right leg, a metal brace hinged at the knee. A paint-speckled gray canvas tarp covered an object taller than the balcony above it, and I had to stop myself from reaching out to peek under it. Curiosity overtook me. The tarp hid a secret I desperately wanted revealed. I had a sudden feeling in my gut that I'd been on this whole journey to stand here, before whatever lay hidden. I sensed destiny, a chosen path, but I tried to mask my excitement and not be the giddy schoolboy leaping up and down. That was how the duke would expect a child to behave, and I was most definitely not the duke's idea of a child.

With a grand sweep of his arm, the Tinkerer pulled the tarp, unveiling an iron machine in the shape of an armored knight. Covered in plates like some kind of medieval armor, it stood the height of two men, with a red-crested plume of horsehair running down the center of its helmet. The right arm extended down to a three-fingered hand, but the left was permanently bent at the elbow. Covering the entire forearm was a large shield with a Templar cross in the center. Behind the shield lay a cannon and several other devices. Thick legs led to wide tracks on each foot.

The Tinkerer pushed on a release pin and the chest of the mechanized machine swung open. He tilted the helmet's visor up and I saw inside was big enough for a single man to sit.

The Tinker pointed. "The operator stands on the knees and reaches through the arms to the controls in the elbows. His head fits in the helmet and is covered by the visor. This is the only exposed part of the operator when the Iron Knight is in combat. I even padded the seat for comfort."

I stared and tried in vain to keep my mouth closed. This was the most magnificent machine I had ever seen, better than the aero-dirigibles, even greater than Lord Kannard's Iron Steed.

Grand Master Sinclair slapped the Tinkerer on the back. "That boy wants to be a knight!" He chuckled as he walked over to me. "In time, maybe. But this isn't for you. It's for Baron Kensington."

My heart sank, sinking to the floor along with the rest of my hopes.

Of course it wasn't for me. I was sixteen and nothing more than the son of a professor. Not an aristocrat from a noble line of ancient heroes. I wanted to kick myself for being so naïve, for thinking that a simple kid could achieve the greatness set aside for others.

I looked at the baron, sweat still clung to his brow and he leaned against his cane staring at the machine. He didn't look well enough to carry the burden. I wondered if my chance would come after all, but reminded myself that the Templar order had many more knights, greater men who would carry on for the baron.

Baron Kensington sighed. "I don't have the strength. We'll have to choose another."

I was about to volunteer when a sweet English accent behind me said, "I will take responsibility."

I spun around and glared at Genevieve. How could she deny my dream, my destiny? I saw the look on her face, the same fire burned in her eyes as the day I met her. I wanted to say something, but held my tongue. My father looked stunned while the baron shook his head, but Grand Master Sinclair smiled at her.

"My daughter will not be driving this machine." The baron slammed his cane upon the ground which echoed through the shop. "I chose my own replacement. Fate has delivered us a warrior. Indihar Singh shall face the Four Iron Horsemen."

Genevieve and I turned to Mr. Singh who simply bowed to the baron, accepting his offer.

"But, father—"

"No, Genevieve. You have the heart of a Kensington, a brave warrior, but you are just a young girl, the only part of your mother I still have. You'll not throw your life away at the hands of Lord Kannard. Indihar is a tried and tested warrior. He has the skills to meet the Knights of the Golden Circle on the battlefield and not survive, but defeat them."

Sinclair nodded. "Your father is right. Mr. Singh is the best and logical choice. You both did a hell of a job rescuing the professor, saving the baron, and bringing Indihar here. You should be damn proud of everything you've accomplished, and I'll make certain her majesty hears of this. You've got my admiration if no one else's." He cast a quick glance at my father.

Genevieve pleaded. "I can help."

"You already have, my dear, but—"

"I'm just a girl, right. I know." Genevieve stormed off toward the main door of the shop.

The baron shook his head and looked to Sinclair who shrugged his shoulders.

I wondered why no one was going after her. They just let her run off into London, upset, and vulnerable to Golden Circle henchmen. I shook my head in disbelief.

Grand Master Sinclair slapped Indihar on the back. "We should get you familiar with the Iron Knight's systems. Tinkerer will you show you how to operate it. Professor, bring that chair over here for the baron."

I started to head after her, when my father called, "Alexander get back over here. You'll help the baron, and fetch any tools these men might need."

I stopped in my tracks, but didn't turn around. My father wanted me as an errand boy, not a knight, but leaving would mean certain punishment. I flinched as the large metal door on the far side of the shop slammed shut. Genevieve wasn't coming back, she was walking home. She'd be exposed for the entire crossing through London, and none of these men would go after her. Even though it meant certain exile from any future plans, I ran for the door. After all, I had already garnered so many punishments due, what was one more? I took off running, but a nagging thought gripped my mind, and stopped me again.

She was betrothed.

To chase her would mean nothing but foolishness to these men. Sinclair caught my eye and winked, with a slight motion, he pointed toward the shop doors. I continued, as my father yelled, "Get back over here."

"No." Again, the power of those words overwhelmed me and I darted out the door in search of Genevieve.

A small scrap yard surrounding the building was littered with old parts waiting for the Tinkerer. I realized I was in the industrial section of London as the towering smokestacks around me belched choking black smoke into the sky.

I searched for any sign of Genevieve. No one stood or moved within my sight, except for the blades of a scrap-piece windmill the Tinkerer must have put together. I noticed the gate of the outer fence swinging in the breeze. She'd made it to the street. I ran after her, and realized there was only one way to go, only one road led back to her home. I jogged after her, knowing I had to find her before a Knight of the Golden Circle did.

CHAPTER 35

THE MACHINE

I spotted Genevieve's halo of hair and ran to catch up with her. She moved through a crowd of Londoners, and I lost her twice as I darted over the cobblestones. I knocked into a woman carrying a parasol. "I'm sorry," I said but paid little attention and continued to scan the crowd. After a deserved smack to the head, I ran off and left the woman with another apology.

I looked up, dark storm clouds settled over London and a glint of bronze zipped over the river. "Rodin!"

I followed the soaring dragon as it flew above the crowd.

Rodin dipped below the retaining wall that lined the river and popped back up to land in the crowd. I rushed forward and found Genevieve leaning against the railing watching the boats cross under London Bridge. Rodin sat on her shoulder getting his head rubbed as he tucked his wings in and wrapped his tail around her.

I slid up alongside Genevieve, and rested on the railing. She turned, surprised to see me. I smiled and shrugged my shoulders.

I saw the puffiness of her eyes. "They were wrong."

"The older I get, the more my father wants me to become a proper lady, but why teach me to use the sword if he's never going to allow me to use it."

"Yeah, all my father cares about is that I don't upset Eton."

"Parents."

I smiled. "That's why running around Europe was so much fun."

"Back to reality, I suppose."

"Yeah," I turned back to the river, kicking the railing with the toe of my boot. "Reality."

Genevieve turned. "It was fun while it lasted, right?"

"It was. Remember Gibraltar and the pomegranate we shared?"

"Remember the monkeys?" we said in unison.

Genevieve smiled and looked out over the dark water. "I almost wish we were back in Paris. I could have stayed a few more days."

I tried not to show my excitement. I felt the same way. "Sorry you didn't get to keep the dress."

Genevieve laughed and covered her face with her hands. "I can't believe we stole that! You're such a ruffian."

"We didn't steal it; we just didn't pay for it right away. It was a nice dress, sorry it became a sail."

"It was a very pretty sail." Genevieve's head lowered and her shoulders drooped so much that Rodin began to shift and stir. "Alexander, Finn told you, didn't he?"

"You're betrothed to the duke's son."

"It was arranged when I was five years old."

"When you were five?" I took a step back. "Are you serious?"

"It's an old tradition of our family, of most noble families. The marriage is a union of our land and holdings, our status within the royal family. It's complicated."

I huffed. "Is he a troll or something?

A smile came to Genevieve's face as she bit her lip and shook her head. "No, he's not."

"I bet he's older. Thirty, forty, something. With a fat gut, a bald head, and bad breath."

"He's eighteen."

"Figures," I groaned. "Have you even met him before?

"Our families are friends."

"Indihar told me that his parents didn't even see each other until the wedding day."

"You talked to Indihar?"

"No, he mentioned it on the Sparrowhawk."

"It's not like that, but I have to confess I haven't seen him in months, he's been traveling in Africa."

Why did he have to sound so perfect? "Of course, he's an aristocratic adventurer." Now I was certain I didn't stand a chance.

She averted her eyes. "Now that we're back, I have duties, responsibilities."

"I understand, even though I'm not nobility." I released her hands.

"Alexander, you're nobler than anyone I know. You gave so much of yourself on this quest. You deserve—" She took my hand.

"Please, you were the amazing one. You defied the whole world to save your father."

Genevieve blushed and looked down at the churning waters of the Thames.

"You're the most amazing girl I've ever met. You wear pants!"

Genevieve giggled and hugged me. I didn't release her, and she never pulled away, but some ladies walking by gasped and we finally separated.

I started to make a snide comment under my breath, but London wasn't like America, their proper nature made them keep everything bottled up behind those high collars. Sometimes it made me want to shake these people out of their tailored wool armor.

"I'm sorry I didn't tell you about being betrothed."
I mumbled. "It's okay … I understand. I don't care."

"You don't?"

I snapped my head up. *Did she not like that I didn't care?*
"What?"

Genevieve shuddered and turned away. "Nothing."

A moment of silence hung in the air, waiting for me to
fill it, but every word I wanted to say got stuck. Finally, I
blurted out one question, the one I'd come to ask.

"May I walk you home?"

"I would like that," Genevieve wiped tears from her
cheek, and I wished I had a handkerchief to give her. A
gentleman would have had one.

We strolled along the cobblestones, through the narrow
shadowed streets with towering brick buildings on either
side. We passed a large house under construction and
strange noises filled the air, drowning out our conversation.

The nagging ache in the pit of my gut almost doubled
me over. Just like at Eustache's house.

Genevieve stopped, her expression changed, and she
began to look around for trouble. We turned toward the
house. A large wall built of wooden planks surrounded the
perimeter and towered high above the street.

I gritted my teeth against the pain and leaned in to
Genevieve. "Not even the carriage drivers can see over this
wall. Let's check it out. Shall we do some lurking?"

Genevieve smiled. "After you, Master Lurker."

Pounding metal and the shrill whirring of steam-drills
echoed out from behind the wall. We crept along the
perimeter trying to peer in between the slats.

Genevieve motioned me over. "I found a plank with a
loose knot."

I pulled my knife out and Genevieve drew closer.

"Captain Baldarich always said to be prepared." I pressed
the blade against the edge of the knot and worked it free.

I peered through and saw workmen in tattered clothes modifying the inside of the house with huge copper coils and other strange contraptions. Every worker seemed to be African, Asian, or Indian.

A large white man with a scraggly beard and a disgusted expression walked around the terrified workmen. An emaciated man dropped a small copper coil as he tried to maneuver around some crates. The foreman rushed over, unfurled his whip, and struck the man three times in his back.

I pulled back from the hole in disbelief. Genevieve and I looked at each other with horrified expressions. Of course I'd read the newspaper accounts of atrocities committed during the American Civil War, but seeing it made my blood boil.

I dared to look again, driven to learn what was happening inside. A strange sound drew my attention upward. The domed roof of the observatory atop the house rotated around and a large, narrow door slid to the side.

I locked eyes with Genevieve. "Why would they be opening the doors for the telescope? It's still daylight, and it's cloudy."

"I don't know."

As I stared up at the observatory, Genevieve peered through the fence and Rodin, sitting on her shoulder, tried to see, too. Her gasp drew my attention. "What is it?"

Genevieve pulled back. "It's Lord Kannard."

I looked through the hole and saw the nobleman standing on one of the balconies. His long white robe billowed in the rising winds as he stared out over the Thames with eager anticipation. Col. Hendrix came up behind him and bowed. The bronze plated Confederate appeared to give him an update and the news must have been good because it brought a large smile to Lord Kannard.

Fuming, I yanked myself from the fence. I wanted to

scale this wooden barrier and challenge them both, but even though I'd done a lot of foolish things lately, I knew that was too foolish. Genevieve spied through the hole as I paced behind her.

She whispered. "I can see into the house. Some sort of machine rises from the basement up to the observatory. What is it, and what could the large coils of wire be for?"

"Maybe it has something to do with the stolen Tesla papers. He works with electricity, maybe it's a giant lightning cannon."

I looked up at the storm that formed overhead, and through a break in the clouds I saw the comet. It was daytime, and the sun, dimmed by the clouds, sat just to the east of the long-tailed star. I turned back to the house, and noticed the observatory's door was aimed directly at the comet. What were they going to do to the comet? *What could electricity do?*

My head snapped up. "An electromagnet, that's it! If the comet has a core of metal, they could drag it down and it would strike the heart of London."

Genevieve eyebrows rose. "Are you sure?"

"We made one in my science class. Wrap a copper coil around an iron nail, charge it with electricity, and it becomes a powerful magnet. They've built one the size of a house and aimed it at the comet. That's why they wanted Plato's papers back on Gibraltar."

Genevieve gasped. "We have to tell Indihar and the others. He has no idea what he's about to face."

"Looks like that walk home will have to wait."

We slipped off from the fence being careful not to be seen by Lord Kannard and ran back to the Tinkerer's shop with Rodin soaring just above us.

When we arrived, I slid the large door to the side and rushed in. I looked for my father, the baron, anyone, but only the Tinkerer sat at one of the tables working on some contraption. I looked for Mr. Singh and the Iron Knight, but they were gone. The Tinkerer looked up and his magnified pupils grew into a stunned expression.

"What are you two doing back here? Everyone thought you went home."

"Tinkerer, they've already left?" I asked.

"Aye, the baron went back to his house with the professor, and Sinclair went to coordinate her majesties armies."

I threw up my arms. "Now what?"

Genevieve charged forward. "We found Lord Kannard's lair."

His eyes widened and he pulled off his goggles.

I stepped closer. "They're building a giant electromagnet. We think they may pull the comet down to strike London."

The Tinkerer jumped up. "Not to mention what it will do to the Iron Templar."

"We have to help Indihar." A worried expression crossed Genevieve's face. "Tinkerer, you must have some other contraptions we can use. If Indihar's already left, there's no way to warn him."

The Tinkerer nodded. "Over here, but your father is going to kill me."

"We'll all be dead if we don't do something," I said.

Genevieve, Rodin, and I followed the Tinkerer to the back of his shop, where no light shone. He walked up grabbed two tarps and whipped them off in a single pull. I strained to see the outline of two more Iron Knights tucked away in the darkness. I saw the glint of bronze from one contraption but the other was too dark to see.

Genevieve stared into the corner. "What are they?"

The Tinkerer flipped on an electric light, tilted the tin shade toward the dark corner, and illuminated the two machines. One, made of dark iron, looked black in color. The second was mostly iron, but the shoulder guards, shield, and other accents were bronze.

I stared in awe. "I thought there was only one."

"The Iron Templar was number two. The Black Knight was the prototype; I worked all the kinks out on that one, and the Bronze Knight, well... I'm not certain why I made it. I had a lot of parts sitting around and couldn't sleep one week."

Genevieve turned and asked, "Do they work?"

"Oh yeah, they just need a few things, ammunition, fuel, and the black one needs a new hose. It burst during testing. They don't have all the goodies the Iron Templar has, but they've got everything that counts."

Genevieve toyed with the locket around her neck. "You did all of this in the last few weeks?"

"The second two. The prototype I've been working on for a year. Ever since Sinclair told me about the horsemen."

"Tinkerer, I know that the baron and the Grand Master, even my father said no, but will you help us get these working so that we can help Mr. Singh fight the horsemen?"

The Tinkerer's greasy hands ran through his tussled hair as he paced in front of the two Iron Knights. He paused, and I leaned forward, but the Tinkerer continued to pace.

The Tinkerer stopped, smiled, and in his thick Scottish drawl said, "It's Archibald's own words. You *want* to be a knight. Knowing the Grand Master the way I do, that means you *are* a knight."

Time slowed as the Tinkerer spoke the words. I repeated them in his head. Could I be a knight? Did someone find me worthy of the title?

Genevieve smiled. "Thank you. You may have just saved London."

"We haven't won yet. Here, let me show you how to operate them. We'll start with the Black Knight."

The Tinkerer opened the iron chest plate. I climbed in and sat on the seat. My legs slipped down into the iron appendages, as I stood on the machine's knees with my feet locked into the pedals. I fit my arms through the holes and felt the controls.

It was like sitting inside an iron box. The walls of the chest seemed far away; maybe if I were bigger, I'd fill in the armor. I was tall enough to fit into the helmet, though. The whole contraption moved like an extension of my body. I felt like I *was* the Black Knight.

The Tinkerer looked at us. "The steam engine on the back powers the knight."

The Scotsman rushed around getting the Iron Knights ready, Genevieve and I helped out, loading the weapons, filling the water tank, and getting the fire hot enough to power the machines. The Tinkerer made the last few adjustments and brought out two thick steel blades that resembled swords. Swords used by giants.

Once everything had been loaded and the Iron Knights were fully powered, Genevieve and I each climbed inside. The Tinkerer closed the chest doors and locked them in. I was surprised by the ease of movement. I stepped on the pedal and the Black Knight rolled forward on its large tank tread feet.

I flipped down the visor from inside with my hand and said, "Open the door, we're ready to roll."

"Remember—they're just machines. Steam and oil may be the blood flowing through their veins, but it's the driver's soul that is their heart. That's their real strength. As Archibald might say, *think like a knight and you will be a knight.*"

Genevieve rolled by and raised the bronze covered arm in salute. "Thank you, we won't let you down."

CHAPTER 36

IRON KNIGHTS VS. IRON HORSEMEN

The rough metal handles bit into my palms as I gripped the Black Knight's controls. I needed a lighter touch or my hands would be bleeding before the battle started. My heart pounded as I rolled down the cobblestone streets, searching for the house Genevieve and I had seen earlier.

I couldn't see her, my armor had no slits behind me, but I heard the Bronze Knight's engine and the treads rolling over cobblestones.

Dark clouds above kept the sun at bay and threatened rain.

I stepped on the pedal and the Black Knight roared. I caught a glimpse of my reflection in a passing window. Dual smoke stacks angled downward sent twin black columns arcing behind me like the wake of a boat. I smiled, I liked being as tall as the second story.

Cannon fire and clashing metal echoed along the narrow street. I signaled Genevieve, and rounded the corner.

Mr. Singh's Iron Templar stood before the four Iron Horsemen. Demons covered in bronze plates and tattered, colored shrouds whipped up by the wind. The ground crumbled beneath their hooves. A deep inner fire shone through their hauntingly absent eyes and through every joint. Tendrils of black smoke spilled out from their nostrils.

The horses were similar to the one we'd seen on Malta, but bigger and meaner looking. The bronze plates, spaced further apart, exposed more of the iron underneath. Two cannons stuck out of thir chests. On the back, the riders sat not on a saddle but within one. Who were the other riders? I was still to far away to see, but I wanted to know their names before I fought them.

My smile faded, as the throbbing in my temples matched the beat of the engine.

This was not about proving I was not a child, this was about doing what was right. Doing what was needed. I couldn't cower or hide as I'd done at Eaton. All London depended on us. *I would think like a knight. I would be a knight.* I thrust the controls forward hoping this surge of confidence would carry me through the battle. Well, at least the charge.

The four Iron Horsemen surrounded the Iron Templar, but Mr. Singh raised his shield, blocked a striking hoof, and locked swords with Hendrix.

As we drew closer, I could see that upon the red-shrouded steed of war, the Colonel carried a huge broadsword sword and screamed a ferocious battle cry. His iron horse not only held cannons within its chest but also a multi-barreled Gatling gun.

Lord Kannard rode the white-shrouded horse; his white robes and cape whipped about in the quickening wind. A golden crown sat atop his head and he held the reins tightly in one hand.

Captain Zerelda rode the black-shrouded horse with a wild gaze in her eyes. Her raven hair and clothes, the color of night, merged with the iron beast whose tail split in two like a tuning fork.

Tobias, Zerelda's first mate, rode the pale-shrouded steed. He wore a gas mask with canvas and brass coiled hoses that stretched into the metallic beast. Two large tanks sat on the hind flanks. Would that have been my steed if I'd accepted the Colonel's offer?

The four of them sent shivers up my spine. My hand flexed repeatedly as I tried to release the tension building within.

No matter what the outcome, I wouldn't let Mr. Singh face it alone. I raised the Black Knight's arm and yelled, "We should announce ourselves. Isn't that what knights do?"

Genevieve stopped. "Let our cannons herald us."

We raised our left arms, aiming at different horsemen. I eyed Col. Hendrix, but hesitated. The weight of this machine nagged at my doubts. Could I really fire? This wasn't a game. Genevieve hadn't fired yet either, I wondered if she felt as I did.

Col. Hendrix slammed his sword against Mr. Singh's shield.

I gasped. "I am the Black Knight!"

Genevieve and I fired simultaneously. The long cannon tucked behind my shield belched smoke. My round smacked into the side of the red steed's head. The explosion ripped past Col. Hendrix and knocked off his hat, but as the smoke cleared, the steed and rider appeared unaffected by the blast.

Genevieve's round impacted Captain Zerelda, but her steed reared up and it exploded harmlessly against the chest plates. The iron horse slammed to the ground. Everything shook and my iron knight wobbled. Fear engulfed me like the cloud of kicked-up dust. I pushed the forced, unnatural, feelings aside as if this fear emanated from the Iron Horsemen and not from within.

Lord Kannard rotated his steed and opened fire. Genevieve and I dodged the shots by weaving down the street as explosions blew cobblestones into the air.

Pebbles rained against the iron skin of my machine, and a feeling of invincibility overtook me. Sitting on the back of their steeds the horsemen looked vulnerable, but encased in iron, I knew no one could touch me.

The horsemen pulled back from Mr. Singh and formed a line across the street.

The Iron Templar bore the order's cross on the shield and chest plate. It was the most complete, the most heavily armored and impressive looking of the three machines. Its crest, made of real horse hair, blazed like a red streak, unlike the Black Knight which had no ornamentation or the Bronze Knight which had bronze plates rising out of the helmet.

Genevieve and I rolled around Mr. Singh and stopped. Rodin jumped off the bronze knight's shoulder and soared over to the Iron Templar. I held up my shield to defend us while Rodin delivered the message around his neck. Genevieve wrote it, and it detailed our plan.

All four Iron Horsemen opened fire. Three rounds slammed into my shield. I struggled to keep my arm in place, but I gritted my teeth and forced my arm to hold. The fourth round impacted Genevieve's shield, but she appeared unaffected.

I cheered. "These knights are amazing!"

As I rolled forward Mr. Singh yelled, "Wait," but the sound of the engine and the whirring tracks drowned the rest of his words. Col. Hendrix's red steed opened fire with the Gatling gun which sprayed my shield with bullets.

Lord Kannard cried out as the three Iron Knights charged. "You cannot defeat the Horsemen, the time has come. The heavens herald our victory!"

I drew the huge blade from the Black Knight's side and it rang like a church bell when I struck Col. Hendrix's sword.

Hendrix locked his eye on mine. "The professor's brat!

Should've taken my offer, boy. You can't stand against my power. When I level this world, I'll make all of you my slaves."

Close enough to smell the mix of sulfur, sweat, and metal, I wanted to say something profound, but all I spit through my gritted teeth was, "Never!"

Soldiers of the Royal Army appeared at the end of the block and opened fire with their rifles.

I shouted. "It's soldiers of the crown!"

The colonel's iron horse leapt backward. Kannard laughed with a dismissive tone and pulled a flare-gun from his belt. He fired and the burning red ember drifted in the wind.

I looked up; dozens of balloons dotted the sky with bombs suspended underneath. A loud whistling sound ended in three explosions, dirt and chunks of cobblestones rained down on my armor. *Balloon bombs?* I couldn't believe it.

Soldiers ran for cover. I heard another whistling sound and seized up as it impacted Mr. Singh's machine. The smoke cleared to reveal the Iron Templar's dented shoulder.

Mr. Singh's armor still moved. I exhaled my held breath and hoped he was okay.

Genevieve fought both Zerelda's Black Horseman and Tobias' Pale Horseman. She swung the Bronze Knight's sword in a large arc, keeping both at bay, then turned her left arm toward Tobias and fired point blank into his steed's chest. The rounds bent and mangled his cannons. Zerelda fired at Genevieve's chest plate.

I only saw a dent, but my heart jumped into my throat and stayed there, choking me. I wanted to roll over and save her. I grabbed the slits of my visor, pulled myself forward, and saw Genevieve still fighting the scythe wielding pale steed.

She was still standing, still okay. Lord Kannard rode past, and I fired my cannon. The round hit the side of the shroud tearing it to shreds.

My heart raced and my temples throbbed. I remembered Captain Baldarich's words, and the training I'd received from every member of the Sparrowhawk's crew. When I aimed, I heard Hunter's words. When I swung the sword, I remembered that first day of training, and as we moved through the streets I pictured Baldarich standing on the bridge before the armada.

We held the Iron Horsemen along the banks of the Thames, but we weren't making any progress attacking the giant electromagnet. *Maybe that was Kannard's plan?*

Zerelda smacked her steed's tuning fork tail against the ground. A swarm of insects burst out of the joints of the horse and engulfed me. They poured through my visor and clung to every surface of the Black Knight. I pulled my arms out of the machine's limbs to swat them, and spit them from my mouth. Their painful bites pinched, the buzzing drove me mad, the thousands of little legs crawling over me sent terror through every nerve in my body.

An orange flickering glow burned through the swarm as Rodin landed on the Black Knight's helmet. Two more columns of fire cleared enough of the bugs to allow Rodin to crawl in beside me.

"Am I glad to see you."

The little dragon gorged himself on insects, as he climbed down me and then back up onto my shoulder. His flailing tail, flapping wings, and snapping jaws forced the bugs out of the armor.

An explosion shook the Black Knight. One round and then another. I saw Kannard and Zerelda. I raised my shield and ignored the irritating bugs. Rodin clung to the visor and shot a small column of flame through the swarm.

"Rodin, let's share with Lord Kannard." I pressed the pedal all the way down and hooked the Black Knight's arms around the white shrouded steed's neck. The insects attacked Kannard. He screamed until choked by the bugs. I laughed, still wrestling with the steed. If I had to endure these pests, so would he.

"Zerelda, recall your swarm and get this brat off of me."

I heard the tuning fork sound and the bugs retreated.

Kannard blasted the Black Knight's chest plate with his cannons, and the force pushed the armor back on its treads and rattled me around inside. I saw the plate dent inward and panic seized me.

I turned to Rodin. "I think it's time to get out of here, what do you say?"

Rodin nodded, or at least something that looked like a nod, and I let go of the steed. I rolled back and slammed my sword down but Lord Kannard and the rest of horsemen had disappeared in a cloud of smoke.

I checked on Genevieve. Her Bronze Knight pointed to the sky. The last balloon bomb floated away, but behind it, German zeppelins cut through the clouds.

"Can things get any worse?" I shook my head as water dripped down the visor and thunder rumbled overhead. "I need to start keeping my mouth shut."

CHAPTER 37

COMET SLINGING

Charred bug guts rolled off the iron visor as the rain poured down in sheets. Water fell in streams from each open slit. Streaming down the inner walls, it pooled around my shoes.

"I wonder if the joints will rust or will I drown first?" I wiped my face. "Did the Tinkerer even think of weather when drawing these machines?"

Lightning lit up the darkened sky.

I followed Mr. Singh and Genevieve down a couple of blocks, and cautiously peered around corners trying to find the demonic horsemen.

I heard an odd sound and my stomach tightened. Whipping around I saw a grappling line secured to one of the nearby buildings. Above me several German soldiers in their single-studded helmets slid down the zip line like fruit on the vine.

I raised the Black Knight's sword, cut the wire, and the German soldiers tumbled into the Thames River. More zeppelins anchored to whatever would hold. They dropped on either side of the Thames and fanned out. The landing, unlike anything I had ever seen or read about, made me marvel at the legendary German innovation.

But they had to be stopped.

Calling to Genevieve, I raised my sword and charged the thick tethers. "Cut the lines, they're landing on the Thames."

"Big Bend and Parliament are nearby and *on* the river."

I charged through the German's fortified landing zones as pings of rifle fire rattled my iron hide. A large shadow passed over me. I looked up as two soldiers secured a box to the zip line. Stenciled black lettering below the double-headed eagle read 'explosives' in German.

I lined up my arm cannon and pulled the trigger. Gray smoke trailed to the box and a gigantic fireball incinerated the Zeppelin. The concussive blast shattered the windows around me, as the flaming remnants crashed into the Thames.

"Woah, I didn't think that would happen."

I started to cheer, but thinking of the airship's crew wrenched my insides. War wasn't fun; it didn't have the excitement I'd always thought it would. War was required, not desired.

Mr. Singh rolled by and cut two more tethers. I shook my mind back into the battle and raised my cannon to salute.

Soldiers from Her Royal Highness's Army formed lines at the end of the block. I pulled back to their line and kept my shield up to block the German gunfire.

Shade came from a large tree, the same one I'd seen by Kannard's. I stood only a few blocks from the house where Genevieve and I had found the electromagnet. I rolled over, coming face to face with her Bronze Knight.

She threw open her visor, and I laughed. Grease smudged her porcelain skin.

I liked it, and watched her lip curl even higher ... *no, Alexander, focus on Kannard, not Genevieve!* I flipped open my knight's own visor and pointed, "Lord Kannard's house isn't far away. I bet they've headed for the machine."

Genevieve nodded. "I noticed that as well. Sinclair and the duke can coordinate the defense of the Thames. We should focus on the Iron Horsemen."

"Agreed. Want Rodin back? Thanks for the loan."

Genevieve patted her chest. "Come here, Rodin."

The little dragon flew out and landed on her knight. His color matched perfectly with the bronze accents. Rodin climbed inside and snuggled around her shoulders.

"Thanks Rodin." I bowed my head and flipped my visor down. "But the celebrations will have to wait. We have to kick Lord Kannard, the Knights of the Golden Circle, and the Germans back across the Channel."

Lightning flashed across the sky accompanied by rumbling thunder and the explosions of cannon fire. Rain blanketed the streets and the wind whipped it into a misty spray. The city around Genevieve and I darkened. As the shelling lulled for reloading, I heard a transmission line spark in the rain.

"It has to be the generators powering the electromagnet" I said as I stepped on the pedal. The Black Knight roared to life and sped down the street with Genevieve rolling alongside.

Three blocks from the house, I heard cackling laughter reverberate down the street with a demonic resonance. I turned, and saw the four Iron Horsemen lined up a block away.

Kannard's white-shrouded steed smashed its hooves upon the ground. The cobblestones broke free in a shower of rock. The street split in two. I rolled around, but as Genevieve continued the ground heaved up in front of her and blocked her way.

Col. Hendrix's red-shrouded steed stepped closer and spewed fire from its mouth and nostrils. I raised my shield. Flames licked the edges and danced across my chest plate. My courage faltered as a spot of orange light burned a hole through the shield that grew to the size of an apple.

Doubt threatened to overtake me, creeping in from the dark recesses of my mind. Pushing the fear back down, the Black Knight powered forward. I swung my left arm to the side, flinging fire off the end of the shield. I fired at the Colonel. The steed intercepted the shot with one of its bronze plates, swatting the round as if it were nothing more than an insect. Then the plate slid back into place. I lowered the shield, raised my sword arm and charged through the next blast of fire.

Lord Kannard shook his head. "Pathetic, do you really think your pitifully built contraptions can kill us. Soon those piles of scrap will be destroyed along with London and the rest of your industrialized world. Out of the ashes … the great rebirth … New Rome shall rise again, and I'll make certain you all have a special place as my house slaves."

I couldn't listen any longer. "Quiet your tongue!"

Kannard's face contorted with rage as his dark locks whipped wildly in the wind.

A flare soared into the sky, and he cackled with a sickening smile. "It is done. Soon the comet will smash this world out of the Industrial Age and back to the Age of Men. Real men. Not boys and girls playing at adventures."

"Not if I have anything to say about it!" I stepped on the pedal but continued to slow down. The Black Knight's engine chugged faster than ever, but I couldn't reach Lord Kannard. Everything still moved so I hadn't rusted. I twisted to see if I was stuck on something. The sign on the building beside me stretched out horizontally, but my armor was clear.

A few British soldiers ran into the street. Their rifles wobbled until ripped from their hands. The guns skidded down the street, and the soldiers tumbled after them. The electromagnet had been fully charged, drawing everything metal toward it. Including me.

I rolled down a side street. The buildings blocked the effect of the magnet, but I couldn't hide here forever. I had to stop them. The Iron Templar pulled in the other end. I turned the Black Knight toward Mr. Singh. "I'll attack the house and destroy the electromagnet. You cover me."

Mr. Singh flipped open the visor of the Iron Templar. "I should be the one to face the ultimate danger, not you."

I popped my visor. "You have to stop Kannard or none of us will reach the magnet." I reached out. "Be careful, the closer you get the stronger the magnet pulls."

Mr. Singh nodded and flipped the visor down.

Zerelda's black-shrouded steed and Col. Hendrix's red-shrouded steed, whipped around the corner and blocked the end of the street. Mr. Singh rolled off to intercept them. He slammed his sword down, but the colonel and Zerelda's narrowly avoided his slashes.

Backing up I spun around. I heard fighting behind me, but entering the main street meant being pulled toward the house.

A shell slammed into the Black Knight's left shoulder, and the whole armor shook. The German zeppelins had gotten creative with their cannon fire. The magnet curved the rounds and set the fuses, making them explode wherever they wanted. Another round slammed into the building beside me. Their aim was improving.

Zerelda's black-shrouded horse rode around me. Her beast moved without restriction, and didn't appear affected by the magnetism at all. Her tuning-fork tail rose to strike the ground and I tensed.

My arm struggled to move against the pull of the magnet. I'd never reach her in time, but Genevieve raced around me, snatched Zerelda's tail and cut it off.

I raised my armor's arms and cheered. Then yelled over the engine noise, "You're moving more easily than me or Mr. Singh."

Genevieve yelled. "It must be the bronze plating."

Bronze isn't affected by magnets. "I should have realized that!"

"I'll deal with the Horsemen." Genevieve rolled forward and attacked. Her quick-hitting style confused the Horsemen as she wove between them.

Debris swirling in the sky allowed me to see the electromagnet beams heading toward the comet. The constant wave of energy flowed into the heavens as arcing bands drew in everything for miles.

Had we lost? I thought I'd have time to stop the electromagnet before the comet crashed to earth, but in truth I didn't know. What if it was pulled so far it couldn't resume its normal course? How long until there was nothing we could do to stop it?

The Iron Horsemen stood between me and the machine. Unaffected by the magnet, they had weapons I couldn't match, and now the aim of the German zeppelins had improved to the point that almost every shot landed beside me.

Rain pelted the battlefield; the streets of London had been gnarled and torn, much like those who fought upon them. Several screaming British soldiers tumbled past as the electromagnet dragged them closer. I wondered if this was it, had we given as much as we could give. Did I have more to sacrifice? Could I save this city, its people, maybe even the world from the destruction wrought by the four Iron Horsemen? The surreal painting that formed outside my visor both horrified me and yet was beautiful. The haze of fire, smoke, and refracted light painted the world in windblown brushstrokes and hues of blended colors.

I watched the bleak painting before me and understood why my father and the baron didn't want me or Genevieve to fight. Our side might lose this battle. But someone had to fight and right now that someone was me.

CHAPTER 38

THE MOMENT

I heard Genevieve's battle cry, spun around, and found her locked in combat with both the pale and black steeds. Her Bronze Knight moved in mechanized grace. Its cannon roared at Zerelda. Genevieve missed and her second shot was deflected by the iron beast. I wanted to help, but it didn't look like she needed me.

Tobias's pale-shrouded steed spewed forth a cloud of toxic gas that smelled like rotten eggs and burned my throat. I tried not to breathe, but in the cloud I caught the outline of the Bronze Knight pushing through the thickest part of the mist.

Mr. Singh raced out of the gas coughing like a choking engine.

I worried for Genevieve and Rodin. I wanted to charge through the mist and grab her, but let the foolish thought slip away.

"Genevieve!" I waved the Iron Knight's arms. "Get out of there!"

Kannard smashed through part of building sending bricks across the cobblestones. "Quit wasting your breath, you're little girlfriend is dead. That toxic cloud has a cyanide base. A nasty little something we were able to create from the remnants of the pale-horse's urn."

The mist crept closer, but I pushed Kannard's words from my mind. "Call off your men, and we'll let you live."

"Still entertaining, boy! But I could never be the equal of some poor commoner. The Iron Horsemen are indestructible unlike your little tin soldiers."

I pulled the control lever and raised the Black Knight's sword arm. I swung the thick-heavy blade but the white-shrouded steed leapt backward and fired its cannon. I braced myself behind my shield which dented from the force. I stared at the dimple and wondered how long until it finally gave out.

Kannard spun his steed around and said, "You can't win! Your industrial science can never defeat the magic and myth of the Old World."

I aimed my sword at Lord Kannard. "You're never going to hurt anyone ever again."

Even as I said the words, I didn't know if I could succeed. My bravado was a façade like an actor on the stage.

"Only a fool would fight me!"

"Then I am a fool," I muttered. My attention darted back to the cloud as it crept closer. The white shrouded horseman looked unconcerned, but my throat burned as the mist drifted through the visor.

Lord Kannard's iron steed leapt over some debris and slammed into my Black Knight. I fell backward and tore up the cobblestones as I gouged a trench down the street.

Mr. Singh thundered around the mist and attacked. He fought like a lion, forcing Kannard to dodge or be impaled. He slammed his shield into the steed, and tried to club the horseman with the barrel of his cannon.

Lord Kannard smashed the steed's hooves into Iron Templar's shield and fired. Mr. Singh and the armor tumbled into a nearby building. The mechanized beast leapt forward and pressed down on the shield.

I had to get up and help. Not watch through my visor. I pulled the lever to release the piston and pushed the Black Knight back up.

Mr. Singh lifted the leg of the Iron Templar, revved up the tread, and smashed his foot into the white-shrouded steed. Kannard fell backward. Mr. Singh charged and smashed the Iron Horseman into the building on the other side of the street. The indented bricks collapsed as horse and rider tumbled into the building. Mr. Singh fired a round into the ceiling to bring the debris down on Kannard and his demon steed.

Kannard's white-shrouded steed lunged out of the ruins and reared up, but Mr. Singh slammed the Iron Templar's shoulder under the horseman to keep it from bringing disaster.

Thunder and lightning erupted in the clouds above, as if the Greek god Zeus himself called my attention to the heavens.

A dark shape cut through the storm and emerged into clear skies: the Sparrowhawk opened fire with all its cannons. One of the Zeppelins exploded in a giant fireball and the aero-dirigible soared through the flames. One after another the German zeppelins fell to the swift Sparrowhawk.

"The captain made it!" I jumped and hit my head on the helmet of the Black Knight. *Ouch.*

With Mr. Singh holding Lord Kannard and Genevieve still lost in the cloud, I knew what I had to do. I rolled for the house, letting the magnet pull me faster.

Above, the Sparrowhawk fired their forward cannon destroying chunks of the house and then banked for a broadside. But the ship kept moving forward, dragged sideways toward the magnet.

I smashed through the fence and fired my cannon. The first shot destroyed the outer wall of the house, the second blew apart the interior, and the third arced wildly. With a loud clunk it stuck to the electromagnet rather than blowing it to pieces.

I was out of ammunition but it didn't matter, they were useless. The Black Knight couldn't break free of the powerful magnet either. I shot a grappling line toward the columns on an adjoining house. For the moment I had stopped, but there was nothing I could do to prevent our failure. London, maybe even the whole world would be destroyed, and it would be my fault. At least I wouldn't be around for my father's punishments.

The Sparrowhawk struggled to break free of the magnet, I heard the deep roar of the engines revving at full power. Then the aero-dirigible aimed its bow at the house. The front cannon fired, and the Gatling gun rained lead.

"But they'll never pull out in time with the magnet on." Uncertain what to do, I looked for my companions.

Tobias's pale-shrouded steed, burst through the cloud with the Bronze Knight hooked around its neck. White vapor poured from its mouth and two canisters on its hips. The pale-shrouded steed kicked the Bronze Knight away. Chuckling behind his gas mask, Tobias turned the steed's chest cannons toward Genevieve.

The Bronze Knight stepped forward and plunged its blade deep into the steed's chest which destroyed the cannon and exposed the urn—the heart of the horseman. She reached in with the armor's clawed hand and yanked it free. She held the ceramic and metal urn high above the armor's head.

Stillness overtook the streets, drops of rain suspended in the air and everything slowed down as if the world held its breath.

I saw it, felt it, even smelled it. My father had always told me stories of my namesake, Alexander the Great of Macedonia. The brilliant young tactician would ride atop his faithful steed, Bucephalus, watching the battle for the critical moment. In that one brief second of time Alexander the Great would strike the fatal blow and claim victory. In doing so he had never lost a battle, ever.

This was my moment, and I knew it. That didn't mean I was ready for it.

Blood pounded in my ears until I was deaf from it. I raised the Black Knight's sword and cut the cable anchoring me.

The armor soared through the air as if drawn by a wire. Through the visor, I saw the shattered remains of the fence and knew the house was next. I thrust my sword into the closest generator. The wide, thick blade sank deep into the layered metal, and the armor swung around the handle.

The electromagnet wrenched the armor's clawed hand from the weapon. I raised my shield, tensed my body and closed my eyes. The Black Knight slammed into the coils.

The Sparrowhawk fired again, striking the coils and generator. The explosion ripped the house to pieces and arced bolts of electricity up into the clouds. Smoke billowed up, and a shockwave blasted out the windows and rattled buildings for blocks. The Sparrowhawk pulled up as the explosion singed the wingsails.

Genevieve crushed the urn in the claw of the Bronze Knight and the raindrops fell to the ground.

Tobias' body shuddered and was thrown backward by the force of the shattered urn. He tumbled from the iron steed which fell apart into chunks of scrap metal.

Kannard screamed. "You will pay for this with your lives! Hendrix kill them all, take no prisoners, no quarter or mercy shall be granted!"

Col. Hendrix rode over and slammed into the Bronze Knight's back. He forced her to the ground and raised his large sword.

I saw this through the shattered house, my gut wrenched

and my knees buckled.

Pain racked my leg as if I'd been shot. I was afraid to reach down. Slowly my hand examined my pant leg. I feared the worst, but ran into bent and twisted metal. The armor had crumpled and pinned my leg, but I could still wiggle my toes and press the pedal.

Dust choked the air as bits of mortar fell through the visor. Bricks and wood crashed down upon the armor. I forced the debris off my machine and pulled on a crumbling wall to get out of the rubble.

The soldiers who'd tumbled toward the house had been stopped by the wooden fence. Those who hadn't been able to get out of the gear that pinned them now ran away without issue. I realized the pull of the magnet no longer had power over my armor. The magnet was no longer magnetized! I refocused on Lord Kannard whose haunted eyes gazed at the house.

Hendrix guttural southern drawl reverberated along the cobblestones. "Boy!"

The sound cut through my pain, I saw Genevieve about to die, but also my opening to attack Kannard who was still held by the Iron Templar.

I yelled. "Kannard, your plan failed, because good men stood against you, and sacrificed everything for this world."

Rodin crawled out from beneath the Bronze Knight's visor and attacked Col. Hendrix.

I thrust the controls forward and the Black Knight sped out of the debris. My leg was injured but I ignored the pain and raced for Genevieve.

Lord Kannard slammed down and knocked the Iron Templar into a building that collapsed atop Mr. Singh.

Rodin scratched Hendrix's face and tore out the electric eye underneath the bronze plate, but flew off as I knocked the Colonel's sword aside. My Black Knight grabbed Genevieve's Bronze Knight and we tumbled down the street.

Artillery rounds whizzed overhead and slammed into the horsemen. It wasn't the Sparrowhawk; it had to be the British army. I cheered.

The Black Knight lay atop the Bronze Knight. I flipped my visor up and Genevieve opened hers.

I smiled. "You okay?"

Genevieve nodded. "Bugger, I think so."

"How did you survive the gas?"

"I held my breath silly." Her smile faded. "Your leg?"

"I'm … I'll be fine." At least I hoped the searing pain would pass.

"Where are the Iron Horsemen?"

I squeezed out onto her knight and looked around—they were gone. The pale steed lay in a pile of disjointed scrap and was surrounded by British soldiers. In the sky above, the Sparrowhawk soared alone. I looked at Genevieve. "I think we won."

"Of course we did."

I wedged open the chest plate of the Bronze Knight and helped her out. We sat on the two knights, surveying the devastation around them. Torn up streets, buildings in ruin, carnage everywhere we looked—but London survived.

Genevieve took my hand. "Thank you for saving my life."

"You're more important than Kannard."

She hugged me, and kissed my cheek. "Indihar!"

"What?" I asked as she pulled away.

"Over here." Out of the rubble a blue turban, grayed by dust, appeared in the street.

Behind us, the familiar Scottish drawl of Grand Master Sinclair broke called out. "Look who just pulled off a miracle!"

CHAPTER 39

BACK AT SCHOOL

I tugged at my vest and tightened my tie before hobbling up the stairs to my father's office. I longed for the comfortable clothes of my adventure, but the leather strap I wound around myself would never pass at Eton. The ripple of pain in my leg reminded me of another memory. It had only been three days since the battle in London, and every step reminded me of our sacrifice.

When I reached the top, I stepped toward my father's office door. It had been replaced; a crack no longer split the center. Voices spoke over each other inside, and given recent events, I crept up to the door and slipped my bag from my shoulder. With a tight grip I wrapped the strap around my hand ready to pummel any trouble I might find inside. I grabbed the doorknob with my other hand and slowly turned the handle. I threw open the door and lunged inside.

My father leaned against his desk, Baron Kensington, Grand Master Sinclair and the duke stood around him. Their heads snapped around in unison, and I lowered the bag and nodded to each of them.

Sinclair smiled as he leaned on his sword cane. "Good to see you haven't lost your instincts, lad."

"It's good to see you too, Mr. Sinclair."

The baron nodded. "We were just letting your father know how grateful her majesty is for all that you have done."

"Well that's good. I'm not being excused for all the time I missed here at Eton; I'll be in detention for weeks."

"I'll see if the queen can't intervene on your behalf, it's the least that we can do." The baron turned to Professor Armitage. "I thank you for everything you've done and hope you'll remain at Eton."

"I intend to, thank you, and please extend my gratitude to her majesty."

I set down my leather bag and asked, "Do you know what happened to Kannard or Hendrix?"

Sinclair nodded and the baron said, "They've fled to America for now. The Knights of the Golden Circle are stronger there, but they'll be back. We must be ever vigilant. Worry not, the Templars will keep our eyes upon them."

The duke spoke up. "Zerelda has rejoined the Storm Vulture. The urn was not among the remnants of her steed."

I wondered about the Iron Horsemen, but already knew the answer. They were still out there. The comet had passed, and no longer lingered in the sky, but fragments still trailed behind it. The stories I'd heard crept back into my mind. The disasters they tried to bring would still loom on the horizon until all the horsemen were destroyed.

Sinclair said. "Don't you worry lad, we've got it handled for now. You focus on school."

"Thank you, I will."

"I've got my eye on you."

The professor stepped forward. "There's no need for that, my son needs to focus on his studies."

I glared at my father, then turned to Baron Kensington. "Excuse me, but I was wondering if Genevieve was at home? I wanted to see if she was okay."

The baron smiled. "Actually she's in the carriage. I think

she wanted to make certain you were well."

"Father, may I go?"

"Yes, but be back soon for dinner."

I ran off, taking the stairs three at a time and ignoring the pain in my leg. Out into the courtyard, Finn sat atop the steam carriage. My heart was pounding and my palms were sweaty. I tried to calm myself, but thinking of her almost made me dizzy. I leaned casually against the wheel.

"Hi Finn. Hope you're well."

"Well enough."

I took a deep breath and started to say something else clever, but Finn beat me to it.

"You gonna stand there all day or what?"

I turned and looked into the steam carriage where Genevieve watched me with a smile on her face. She opened the door and stepped out. A long gray dress with a high collar and flowing skirt spilled out behind her. Her locket shimmered on the silver chain curling around her neck. With her hair bound in an elaborate wrap, and makeup coloring her cheeks, she looked so much older than sixteen.

"You look great, but I think I got used to the pants."

Genevieve laughed. "The uniform looks … uncomfortable. But very dapper."

"It is, and thanks."

Genevieve looked to the ground unable to meet my gaze. "Alexander, I wanted to come so I could tell you myself. My father is headed to Egypt to recuperate, and I'm going with him."

"Oh … will you be back?"

"Yes, but not for awhile."

"May I write you?"

"I would like that."

I smiled, and my heart soared, and I wanted to kiss her right here in the street, but a loud voice called from across the courtyard.

"Well, look who's all dressed up. Where're those two bilge rats that crawled out of the river?"

"Captain Baldarich!" I shook his hand, and nodded to Mr. Singh and Ignatius. The three slapped me on the back and bowed and kissed Genevieve's hand. "What are you doing here?"

The captain laughed. "You are looking at Privateers for Her Royal Highness."

"Privateers?"

"Oh yes, we are official pirates of the British Empire. Can you believe it? Now we're just like Captain Morgan. Looks like your little adventure and our help in that final battle will prove profitable after all. Not to mention we got to stick it to the Kaiser one more time."

"Congratulations. So where to now?"

"We go looking for that pirate witch and continue stealing from the rest of the world and all who oppose the Queen."

Genevieve smiled. "I still need to pay you for our passage on the Sparrowhawk."

Baldarich laughed. "Nope, your father took care of that, too." He put his arms around both of us. "I want you two to take care of yourselves, and if you ever need anything you let me know. I like you. In fact, there's room in the crew if you're interested."

Genevieve shook her head.

I chuckled. "I'd love to skip detention and join the crew. Privateering sounds like fun, but there are things I have to do." I looked at Genevieve and thought about how to win her over from the duke's son. I knew it wouldn't be easy, but I had to try. "Keep in touch, who knows in few years, I may need that job."

Baldarich threw back his head and laughed. "I'd have you on my crew anytime."

I extended my hand. "Indihar, I have to thank you for

everything you did."

We shook hands. Genevieve bowed and said, "Most definitely, and thank you for convincing Captain Baldarich not to throw us overboard."

Indihar bowed. "I was only repaying my debt to your father."

"Only!" Baldarich put his arm around Indihar and pulled him closer. "I'll have you know this man was offered a position in the queen's guard and turned her down. He'd rather be a Privateer."

"I have found my path; I know the road that god has laid before me. It is I who should thank the two of you."

Baldarich laughed. "You two stay out of trouble. I'm sure we'll see you around."

The three of them headed off leaving Genevieve and I alone beside the steam carriage.

"Take care of yourself," I said. "I hope Egypt is fun." I peered up at my father's office window. "I should get back, besides your father will be down in a minute."

"Alexander I—"

"No words are needed; just know that I will prove myself worthy."

She shook her head as a tear formed in her eye. "You are worthy, you always...."

I hugged her and felt her arms wrap around my neck. I didn't care how much detention I'd get.

"I may not be a knight yet, but I will be." I smiled and whispered in her ear so Finn couldn't hear. "Don't worry. Our adventures aren't over."

~ Alexander Armitage will return in *Iron Zulu* ~

ACKNOWLEDGEMENTS

First, I have to thank two wonderful authors, my critique partners, Cole Gibsen and T.W. Fendley. They've read too many of my words and I give them credit for all the good ones. Many thanks to my reader Ashley Harrison, she's been a supporter from the start and that's a really long time. Next I have to thank the board members I served with at St. Louis Writers Guild without their help and guidance I wouldn't be where I am. I've met some great writers, authors, editors, agents, and more over the years and they all had a part in making this book better.

Shout out to the Write Pack – David, Jennifer, Jamie, Matt, Melanie, Fedora, and Kathleen.

The one I truly owe is Mrs. Goldman my first creative writing teacher. Each year we made a book, and it was those books that started me down the road to this book.

I've been informed I must thank the one who tirelessly sits by side as I type every word–my cat.

And thanks mom.

To my wife, all my love and thanks for believing in my dreams.

ABOUT THE AUTHOR

Brad R. Cook is an award-winning short story and historical fantasy writer who handles aquistions and author management for Blank Slate Press. He began as a playwright and joined the board of St. Louis Writers Guild in 2008, guiding the organization as president since 2011. He learned to fence at thirteen and never set down his sword, but prefers curling up with his cat and an old classic novel to swashbuckling with evildoers himself. He writes during the witching hour when his muses are most active.

You can find out more at www.bradrcook.com.

CPSIA information can be obtained at www.ICGtesting.com
Printed in the USA
LVOW07s0839071114

412485LV00001B/1/P